# WHAT READERS ARE SAYING

"A beautifully orchestrated combination of dystopian with a faith-based foundation...well-written, gripping, suspenseful, and action-packed. Bravo, Katherine Barger!"

— REGINA FELTY, AUTHOR OF *PIECES OF ME EVERYWHERE*

"I can't possibly say enough good things about this amazing novel by Katherine Barger, and I could barely bring myself to put it down once I started it."

— KIRBY, *PREPPY BOOKISH PRINCESS BLOG*

"Katherine Barger weaves a masterful tale with vivid characters who grip your heart, a sweeping setting, and unexpected twists and turns that keep you turning the page."

— SUZANNE B., AMAZON REVIEWER

# FORTUNE'S FALL

## THE EXILED TRILOGY
### BOOK 1

## KATHERINE BARGER

 FARAMUND PRESS

# AWARDS

**Winner,** First Impressions Contest
*American Christian Fiction Writers*

**Bronze Medal Winner** (YA category)
*Illumination Awards*

# 1

The buzzer's ear-splitting wail pierces the silent auditorium. I lurch back in my chair and bang my knee on the underside of the desk, jolting it enough that my exam tablet slides off the edge. It lands with a *smack* on the tile.

An annoyed groan escapes my lips. This isn't how I envisioned the end of final exams. I'd prefer more triumph. Less total disaster.

Ignoring my throbbing knee, I scoop my tablet from the floor and check that it still works. Satisfied, I toss it onto the desk and rub my gritty eyes until they water. Too much time spent staring at my tablet has made them as dry as the half-dead plant on my dorm room windowsill. At least I answered all the questions before time was up.

I slide down in the cold metal chair and rest my head on its back, glancing around at my classmates as they stretch and smile, or in a few instances, as they wearily prop their foreheads on desktops. All are understandable reactions to the end of this final test of our final year of school.

"The exam period has concluded," says a robot-like voice into my earpiece.

I wrinkle my nose as I pull the device from my ear and set it on the table. "And good riddance to you, Robot Voice Lady," I say under my breath. "My time with you has concluded, too, thank goodness."

The recently silent auditorium now fills with the swell of voices energized by relief and excitement. I continue to survey my classmates as I tighten the band around my frizzy ponytail. You'd never know that, seven years ago, we were a group of scared kids ushered out of our public schools and into the Presidential Education Program. Confidence has been disciplined into us.

"Congratulations, class of 2090," the mentor says from the front of the auditorium. He's new, younger, with wire-rimmed glasses and the same military-style uniform we all wear: blue jacket with matching pants. "Your *final* final exam is over."

A cheer erupts, and I can't help but smile. Seven years in America's most elite school is over. Two weeks of the hardest final exams I've ever taken: done. No more school, period. I shake my head with disbelief. We're not kids anymore. We're seventeen years old and about to graduate.

"I'll collect your testing tools." The mentor raises his voice above the rising murmur of conversation. "Please leave everything on your desks. Your answers have been sent to the Central Collector and will be graded and recorded by Wednesday. We'll see you back here then."

On Wednesday, my friends will scamper like puppies escaping the crate to make their top three career choices. I'll go with them and pretend to make mine, pretend that I don't know what my future holds. But I do know.

My career has already been decided.

I swallow the sudden resentment that burns my throat and kneel to grab my bag from beneath my seat. "You're about to have the best job in the country," I mutter. It shouldn't matter that I can't anticipate choosing a career like everyone else. But somehow, it does.

I tuck a stray hair behind my ear and stand to scan the auditorium for my friends.

"Nyssa!"

My best friend, Greer, motions to me from the front of the auditorium. He's hard to miss: tall, lanky, buzzed blond hair. His lopsided grin is a welcome sight, and I maneuver around the desks to join him.

"Everyone's outside already," he says by way of greeting. "Come on."

Our school is tucked inside the presidential compound, built like a square minus one side. We step from the auditorium, which sits in the center wing, and into the courtyard. The sun is so brilliant it forces my eyes half-closed. The air hums with bees; the breeze carries a sticky foreshadowing of summer.

"I don't have a lot of time." I squint at my watch as I hurry after Greer. "I have to meet Pallas in five minutes."

He stops so abruptly that my head slams into his shoulder blade, and I stumble backward. "Ow!" I massage my forehead. "What's wrong with you?"

He swivels toward me with a frown. "School's over. You don't have to meet with Pallas anymore." He gestures toward our friends, who are clustered beneath the oak that marks the courtyard's midpoint. "We're going downtown to celebrate."

I glance past the tree and toward the city, which sits beyond the security wall that surrounds the presidential compound. Blocks of skyscrapers plastered with animated advertisements create a rainbow of color in a dizzying display. A massive portrait of President Omri is plastered on the building nearest us. Below it, the words *Victores in obsequio* scroll on repeat. Victors in obedience.

I blink and scan the other buildings. I can't see the streets from here, but I know they're a mass of frenetic energy. They're so full of people that personal vehicles are banned. I prefer the compound. There's order inside its walls that doesn't exist beyond the security gate. It's peaceful and quiet. Aware of its importance without blinding us with flashy demonstrations.

"I can't go." I shift my gaze back to Greer. "I'm sorry."

Greer sighs. "Give me one good reason why you still have to see her."

I search my brain for something. Pallas is a school mentor, and I've lied to my friends for seven years about why I have to meet with her every Friday. *She's my tutor*, I've always said. *If it weren't for her, I wouldn't do nearly so well in math.* But what can I say now that school is over?

"I'm sorry," I repeat. "I'll see you when you get back, okay?"

Disappointment flickers in Greer's eyes. "Fine. See ya later."

I watch him walk away. Our new careers will separate us soon, likely forever. That realization almost makes me run after him. Almost.

Instead, I turn toward the east wing and step onto the elevator that will take me to Pallas's office on the fourth floor.

When the doors open, I exit into sunshine. Floor-to-ceiling windows line the left side of the hall, and I glance out as I pass. The field below is an explosion of bluebonnets and purple verbena.

Pallas's door, the fifth on my right, is ajar. I tap on it. "Pallas?" I push it open, step inside far enough to close it behind me, and lean against it.

"Nyssa? Is that you?"

Pallas peeks out of an inner door to my left. Her face lights in a smile, and she tucks a wisp of graying hair into her bun as she steps out and glides to where I stand. The familiar scent of roses reaches me before she does, and I breathe it in. The perfume reminds her of home, she once told me, though she's never said where home is.

"You're early." She squeezes my arms with affection. "Why aren't you with your friends?"

I sigh. "Greer got mad I wouldn't go into the city to celebrate."

"Ah." She pats my cheek. "That boy has loved you since you were children."

"Pallas!" My face burns at her comment. "We're just friends."

"Mm-hmm."

I roll my eyes but can't help the smile that flits across my face. Pallas might be my mentor, but she's more like a mother. My tension melts with her teasing. "I hate lying to him," I say after a moment. "He's my best friend."

Her arms drop to her sides, and she tilts her head. "You don't have to lie much longer."

"Of course I do." My voice rises in frustration. "I'm glad everyone will finally know I've been selected to be a presidential aide, but I still won't be able to tell anyone the real truth. That I'm going to be President Omri's dream interpreter."

"Most prestigious job in the country," Pallas reminds me with a wink.

I snort. Just saying it out loud—*dream interpreter*—sounds ridiculous. "No one would believe me even if they knew."

Pallas chuckles. "All the more reason to keep it secret."

I sigh again. Then, remembering the open inner door behind her, I jerk my head in its direction. "What were you doing in there?"

Pallas's face wrinkles into a frown. "Oh, yes. That." She links her arm through mine and guides me toward the door. "Maybe you can help me sort it out."

When we step into the small room's semidarkness, Pallas releases my arm, and we stand side by side facing a thin black screen mounted on the wall. An old but familiar scene is frozen on it, like someone's paused a movie. But I know better. This is a dream screen, and the scene isn't from a movie. It's President Omri's dream from one year ago. The only dream we're certain warned us about the future.

"Why are you watching this again?" I turn to her, brows furrowed in confusion.

She presses a button without replying, and the scene plays.

It's short. As a river rushes through a steep gorge, birds erupt from crevices in the rocks. They land in clusters atop three boulders spaced evenly through the water. The image fades, only to reappear less than a second later. Over and over.

Last year, we interpreted the dream to mean that people would try to leave the Central Capital, important people with classified information. The moment Pallas told Omri what it meant, he did everything he could to make sure no one escaped. The Regional Movement Policy was created, and the Guard increased its ranks. But Pallas and I haven't talked about the dream since those things were enforced. Why is she rewatching it now?

"I'm lost, Pallas." I turn to her with a frown. "What's going on?"

She pauses the dream and taps her chin. "I was thinking about Omri's advisers. Remember them? The ones who managed to escape after the new policies were implemented."

"They were caught and executed." I study her with narrowed eyes.

"Did you hear about the three scientists who escaped from Ward C last week?" She turns to face me, and the glow from the screen casts an eerie blue light across her face.

"Of course I did." The entire Central Capital knows about the scientists who disappeared from the compound's top-secret lab. "Is that what's wrong? You think the scientists escaped because you missed something in this dream?"

"I do wonder if we missed something. Something that could've warned us more people would try to leave even after we created new laws."

"The Guard will find them. They're good at what they do."

She gives me a watery smile, then turns and opens the door to her office. "I hadn't told you this yet, but others besides the scientists have fled, despite the new laws." She motions for me to follow her out, and we cross the room to two chairs that face each other beneath the window.

"Omri has no idea where they've disappeared to," she says as she sinks into one. "It's not just happening in the Central Capital, either; it's happening across the country. Some have been caught. But even when they're promised a lesser punishment if they confess where they were going, they refuse. They're willing to die to keep it secret."

I collapse into the other chair and stare at her, my brain racing to keep up with everything she says. "Why didn't I know other people have disappeared?"

"Classified higher than your clearance."

I cross my arms. Could she be right? Did we miss something in the dream? My stomach twists with unease. Will Omri blame us for the people who have gone missing?

"They must really believe in where they're going if they'll die to keep it safe," Pallas says before I can voice my concern. She purses her lips. "But you don't need to be worrying about that right now. You should be celebrating. There's still time to join your friends."

"She's right," a voice says.

Greer.

Startled, I turn toward the door, my heart beating an erratic rhythm. How much did he overhear? He leans against the wall, hands clasped in front of him. When my eyes meet his mischievous, familiar ones, I relax. Like me, his face always gives him away, and there's nothing but regret in his apologetic smile.

"Sorry about earlier, Nyss." He shrugs, and I see the plea in his eyes. *I don't want to argue with you anymore*, they seem to say.

I nod. I don't want to fight anymore, either, not when our time together is dwindling. I turn back to Pallas, my eyebrows lifted in question. She winks at me. "Go on. We're all done here."

I shake my head with affectionate exasperation. If Greer wasn't standing so close, Pallas would tell me that she was right, that Greer loves me. "See you Wednesday." I stand and head toward the door.

"I'll look forward to it," she says.

I can hear the smile in her voice.

# 2

"Where are we going?" I follow Greer onto the elevator and turn toward him.

"Told you before. Downtown to celebrate." He casts a side-eyed glance at me as the doors close. "Don't worry—nothing fancy, just hanging out with Genevieve and Tyrone."

When the elevator opens on the first floor, we leave the east wing and step back into the courtyard. I pause so my eyes can adjust to the glare. There are still people hanging around the courtyard, but the group beneath the oak doesn't include Genevieve and Tyrone.

"This way." Greer strides forward, past the oak and toward the security gate. "I told them I'd catch up."

The security gate is an intimidating steel-barred structure. It's wide enough for two semitrucks to pass through, but the only vehicles permitted inside are presidential convoys and supply trucks. Everyone else must enter and exit on foot through two smaller doors inset at the far left.

Guards stand at each entrance, scanning IDs and waving people and trucks through. The trucks take an immediate left onto a road that skirts the perimeter. Most of the pedestrians enter and head right, toward the compound's main entrance. Others who live or work here pass us on their way to the courtyard and the dozens of private doors that require special access codes.

We join a short line that snakes out the exit and have almost reached the front when I hear the honk of the tram, which is the only vehicle permitted downtown.

"Excellent!" Greer stands on tiptoes to peer through the gate. "I think we can make it!"

I roll my eyes but can't hide a smile. Greer's always had a childlike obsession with the tram. When we reach the front, he bursts through the gate, and I hurry behind him to find it's just pulled away from its stop a few yards away.

"We can catch it!" Greer breaks into a run.

"You're crazy!" I say. "Why can't we just walk?"

"Not nearly as fun." He shoots me a grin over his shoulder. "Come on!"

There's no point arguing against his enthusiasm. I begin to run, too, and soon, we catch up with the slow-moving vehicle.

Greer leaps onto its stairs, holds on to the railing with one hand, and reaches out to me with his other. "Come on, Nyssa. This thing's slower than a snail."

I glare at him, burst into a sprint, and grab his hand.

He pulls me up onto the stairs and laughs. "Thatta girl."

"It would've taken us five minutes to get to city center, you know."

He steps inside without replying, and I follow him to the open windows on the opposite side. A young family sits in the front corner, too occupied with a baby to pay us any attention. I'm surprised there aren't more people, but it's early afternoon, that time of day when most are holed up in offices.

"This is way better than walking." Greer props his arms on the sill. "Besides, I told Tyrone and Genevieve we'd meet them at the food trucks, and I'm starving. We'll get there faster this way."

"Now it makes sense. You just want to eat." I laugh and prop my elbows on the sill next to him, then turn my face into the breeze as we wind along the boulevard, which slices downtown in half. Smaller streets split off on either side of us, and straight ahead, in the center of a huge intersection, is the Central Hub, the largest train station in America. It's an oval monstrosity built of glass and Omri's ego. His prize creation. But it stands out from its surroundings like a bruise on pale skin.

The tram stops beside the entrance to a side street, and I glance out at a nondescript brick building squeezed between two sleek, glass-faced skyscrapers. Music pours out of its open doors, and I can see the shadows of people still hunched over tables alongside the open windows. It's lively and cheerful and makes me smile.

"Thanks for coming back for me." I turn to Greer as the tram begins to move again. "Can we not fight anymore, please? It's not worth it."

Greer doesn't respond at first. He rests his arms on the windowsill, gazing out with narrowed eyes. "I shouldn't give you such a hard time about Pallas," he says at last.

I bite my lip. I've wanted to tell him the truth about my meetings with Pallas for as long as we've been friends. But I swore an oath of secrecy. To break it would be treason. "I'm sorry I'm so bad at math that I had to meet with her every week," I try to joke. "Too bad you're almost as bad, or you could've helped me instead."

His lips lift in a half smile, and he turns so that he faces me with one elbow still propped on the sill. "Well, no more math classes. No more school. We're days away from freedom."

"You and I both know that's not true." I stare into his blue eyes. We might be done with school, but the next chapter will be just as grueling, and this time, we won't be going through it together. He's made it perfectly clear he doesn't want to stay in the Central Region after graduation. And I'm not allowed to leave. I can't imagine what life will be like once we say goodbye.

The tram stops in the shadow of the Central Hub. Greer blinks and turns to look out the window. "We're here. Come on." He grabs my hand and pulls me off the tram. I expect him to let go, but he doesn't. My eyes widen in surprise; my fingers stiffen. Does he not realize our hands are still connected? After all, he's been known to lose track of other things when he's hungry. One time at breakfast, he spilled coffee all over the floor when someone walked past him with a plate piled with donuts.

We circle the Central Hub with still-laced fingers, cross the intersection, and follow the street that makes up the main thoroughfare for the Night Market, a Saturday-night, Central Capital tradition. Right now, the streets are bare, but come Saturday, every merchant and food vendor in the city will set up beneath canvas tents, and the streets will fill with people.

I spot Genevieve and Tyrone sitting at a table in front of our favorite food truck, and the moment they look up and see us, Greer releases my hand and shoves his into his pockets. I curl my fingers into a fist and press my other hand against the back of my neck, which has grown warm. My mind is a jumble of thoughts too disjointed to understand.

"Thought you'd never get here," Tyrone says. His mouth is full of cheeseburger.

"Sorry. My fault." I slide onto the bench beside Genevieve and eye her fries. She hands me one without comment. As I pop it into my mouth, I catch Greer's eye.

"What do you want?" he asks. "My treat." His face is blank, his eyes unreadable.

I swallow my fry. "I can get my own food."

He gives me a dismissive wave. "I'll get it. Just tell me what you want."

I frown. We were having such a good time, and now, he seems mad. Why the sudden change?

"Cheeseburger, please," I say.

He nods and turns without another word.

"What's up with you two?" Genevieve asks me.

I shrug as I watch Greer lope away. "Beats me."

"He probably wishes we hadn't seen him holding your hand," Tyrone says, his mouth half-full again.

My cheeks begin to burn. "You saw that?"

"Come on, Nyssa," Genevieve says. "Everyone knows Greer's obsessed with you. He always has been. He just tries to play it off."

"Shut up. We're just friends." But Pallas's words float through my mind. *That boy has loved you since you were children.* I shake my head. What's the point in wondering whether Greer likes me? It doesn't matter now. Besides, we've been friends for seven years. You'd think he would've said something to me if it were true.

I watch Greer stride back to us, food in hand, then shift my gaze to Genevieve's fries and steal another one. "Pretend we were talking about something else, okay?"

Tyrone snorts. "Easy. We've had years of practice."

Greer slides onto the bench beside me and hands me a cheeseburger without looking at me.

"Thanks." I peek at him, but in typical Greer fashion, he's too focused on his food to respond. I roll my eyes and take a bite. Some things never change.

---

By Tuesday, I'm brain dead from overanalyzing everything Greer does. It makes me want to slap Genevieve and Tyrone and even Pallas for making me question everything I've always assumed was true about my friendship with him. Did his finger linger on my cheek when he wiped that cookie crumb away? Did he mean to cross his leg over my ankle at our Saturday-afternoon picnic? I fall into bed Tuesday night exhausted by my own annoying thoughts.

It seems like I've just fallen asleep that night when the small, square tablet on my nightstand beeps. Loud. Steady. A chirruping so obnoxious I knock it into the gap between table and bed in an overzealous attempt to turn it off.

"Oh, come on!" I slide out from beneath my quilt and onto the floor with a frustrated groan, then fumble blindly beneath my bed in the darkness.

Once I manage to find and silence it, I curl beneath my quilt, squint at the top of the screen, and groan again. 4:00 a.m. I consider turning it off, but the message notification blinking at me from its center reminds me I can't. Pallas ordered the tablet so I'm always available if needed. I can remember only one other time she's used it: one year ago when Omri had his first dream.

That memory jars me awake. I rub the sleep from my eyes, then press the center of the screen to read the message.

To Omri's quarters immediately.

I blink, frozen for half a second before it registers. Then, I burst from the bed, shove my feet into slippers, and tiptoe through the suite I share with my roommate, Ethelind. The front door closes behind me with a gentle click, and I sprint past doors behind which my classmates enjoy their last few hours of sleep.

This is going to be my life. I secure my hair with a band and hurry onto the elevator. Daylight. Midnight. It won't matter. When I'm summoned, I have to go.

*Most prestigious job in the country.* Pallas's voice echoes through my mind.

"Right," I say aloud as the elevator doors close.

The moonlight that brightened the hall is replaced by dim

artificial light that radiates from the elevator walls. My stomach twists as I descend from the fifth to the third floor.

Did Omri have another dream?

The doors open, and I step into a foyer patrolled by two guards.

The older of the two glances up. He's paunchy and droopy eyed and stifles a yawn before he holds up his identification scanner. "Look straight ahead, please."

I obey, pressing my hands against my thighs and the warm familiarity of my faded polka-dot pajamas. The scanner's blue light pulsates in front of my eyes.

When it beeps, the guard jerks his head toward Omri's office. "Go on, Ms. Ardelone. They're in there."

I nod and hurry to the door. The room I step into is lit by a single lamp. It sits on a massive desk to my right, which is framed by two windows that overlook the courtyard. I can see the lights of the Central Capital in the distance.

Pallas faces Omri's dream screen mounted on the wall. She wears a robe wrapped around her nightgown, and her hair hangs down her back. A few silver strands reflect the light.

Omri paces in front of her, tall and imposing even in his obvious agitation. His gray-speckled hair is slicked back, and his gaze is trained on the floor, his mouth turned in a frown. Even now, he wears a suit.

"This means something, Pallas," he says. "It isn't like my regular dreams. It's like the other one."

My breath catches. I was right.

"We'll review the dream and determine whether action should be taken." Pallas's voice is calm, measured.

"I expect your best." Omri stops pacing, and when he looks up, he sees me.

"Sorry I'm late, sir." I step forward to stand beside Pallas.

She glances at me and turns back to the president. "You remember Nyssa, sir, my mentee."

Omri nods. "Thank you for joining us, young lady."

"Now that Nyssa has arrived, shall we?" Pallas gestures toward the dream screen, then squeezes my arm, a silent reminder that I may watch but I don't yet have the authority to present my interpretation to the president. That job remains Pallas's alone.

Omri presses a button, and the screen flickers to life. A shiver of anticipation races up my spine when the scene materializes: a valley with long-stalked grass that waves beneath a cloudy sky. Snow-crested mountains stretch across the horizon.

An oak tree appears in the center of the valley, its branches thick with leaves. A single acorn falls in slow motion from a lower limb, and when it hits the ground, it transforms into a lamb.

The lamb opens its mouth, and two green, tightly closed pine cones fall out. They rest on the ground for a moment before bursting into pine trees. As they grow, they lean against the oak, pressing it down into the earth. Branches break, and I wince. I can hear the cracking in my head even though there isn't any sound.

The pine trees spring back up, towering into a now-cloudless sky. The oak tree is gone. A hawk explodes from the top of one of the trees, and the lamb, which stands between the two pines, turns its head skyward to watch. The hawk hovers for a brief moment, its wings pumping.

The scene changes. The hawk soars across the valley toward the snow-covered mountains. Orchards appear. Rich farmland.

The mountains draw closer, and the hawk crests their peaks.

The screen goes black.

"Play it again," Pallas orders.

Omri presses a button, and the valley reappears. As the scene unfolds, a reaction I've not had since Omri's dream last year washes over me, like someone has turned on a faucet and icy water trickles over my head, all the way to my feet. The sensation is at once startling and familiar.

Omri was right—this dream means something.

The oak tree appears. Goose bumps explode down my arms, and I shiver, but I'm not cold. I haven't moved, but the screen seems closer somehow; I can almost touch the ridges I now see on the leaves of the oak. My finger lifts of its own accord and follows the acorn as it falls from the tree.

The lamb appears, and the pine cones drop from its mouth.

The images swarm my brain, dancing around one another, teasing me.

The pine cones burst into trees and lean against the oak.

I gasp with sudden understanding.

Pallas pinches me, and I close my mouth. But my throat is dry; my legs are shaky. The signs are unmistakable, and my head buzzes with alarm.

The hawk erupts into the sky and flies toward the mountains.

It's over.

My goose bumps fade as quickly as they appeared, but my heart thumps loud in my chest.

"Well?" Omri rocks from one foot to the other, his gaze trained on Pallas.

I hold my breath. How will Omri react when he learns that the meaning of this dream is far more serious than the one from last year?

"Congratulations, sir," Pallas says. "At long last, you and the first lady are going to have a baby. Twins, in fact."

My mouth falls open, and I bow my head. I don't want Omri to see the shock on my face.

"Children?" Omri's voice is laced with confusion, maybe even wonder.

"Yes." Pallas is authoritative, confident. She taps my arm. "You may go." There's a warning in her voice. *Leave. Don't speak.*

I hurry from the office, through the foyer, and into the elevator without a backward glance. Confusion dulls my brain. I squeeze my eyes shut and press my fingers against my temples.

The signs were clear, the warning unmistakable. I open my eyes and stare at the cold metallic doors as a question plays on repeat in my mind.

Why did Pallas lie to the president?

# 3

When I return to my room, I try to sleep, but I can't clear my head. Pallas is one of Omri's most trusted advisers. I want to talk to her, to understand why she lied. But I can't do that now because today we'll both be busy—she, submitting each student's top three career selections to the Central Collector, and I, faking my way through the day's excitement.

I sit up in bed and reach for a small framed photograph that sits on my nightstand. Pallas gave it to me when I was a child. It's a picture of my family, who died fifteen years ago from a disease that somehow didn't kill me.

In the photo, my mom and dad stand in front of a tree. A dark-haired little boy—my brother, Jek—stands in front of our dad, who's tall and skinny with equally dark hair. My mom cradles me in her arms. Her hair, a lighter version of ours, is pulled into a bushy ponytail at the nape of her neck.

Now, more than ever, the image makes my breath catch. I wish I remembered them. But I was too young when they died, and our moments evaporated before they had a chance to stick.

I return the photograph to the nightstand and stretch out

on my bed. Will Pallas's deceit be discovered? Will she be taken away from me, too? I stare at the ceiling until my eyes go dry and I'm forced to blink. I roll to my side and close my eyes, but sleep still won't come.

When light begins to peek through my window, I get up and shift the curtain to peer out. Like Omri's office, my room overlooks the courtyard and the Central Capital skyline. Even now, the downtown is alive like it's the middle of the day. Billboards blink. Skyscraper windows are awash with light. I slump against the wall, watching the sky lighten through heavy-lidded eyes. All I want to do is crawl into bed, but my brain still spins with questions.

A rap sounds on my door, and before I can say "Come in," it bursts open.

"Oh, good, you're awake, too." Ethelind shuffles in and joins me at the window. She wears an oversize T-shirt that falls to her knees. Her blond hair frizzes around her shoulders like an exploded halo. "I couldn't sleep anymore. I'm too nervous about today."

I can't empathize, so I don't respond.

"I heard you leave earlier," she says after a moment. She shifts to lean against the wall, her gaze directed at me rather than the dawn.

I don't answer right away. Ethelind and I aren't close. I guess I know her better than most people, but that doesn't mean much. She's never tried to make friends here because her family lives in the Central Capital and she's usually with them on the weekends. I stopped trying to get to know her years ago. There's no friction between us, though—we get along really well—and after seven years of living together, she knows not to push me to explain things I don't want to—or can't—discuss.

"I've been awake for a while," I finally say. "Had a hard time sleeping, too."

She's quiet for a moment, then sighs. "We might as well get dressed."

I nod. "See you in a bit."

---

ETHELIND and I enter the auditorium a few hours later, but when I join Greer and Genevieve in the front, Ethelind opts to sit alone in the back.

"Your roommate's pretty much the friendliest person I've ever met." Greer pats the seat beside him, and I sit. "Really, butterflies and rainbows, that one."

I shrug. "She's not really a people person."

"That's an understatement," he mutters.

I open my mouth to respond, but Genevieve jumps in. "Not that I love agreeing with him, but Greer's right. Why doesn't she ever want to hang out with us?"

"Remember that time she came back early from class and we were watching a movie in your room?" Greer asks. "If she could've shot me with her eyes, I'd be dead. Didn't even speak to me before she stomped into her room and slammed the door. What'd I ever do to her?"

"Maybe you needed a shower." I grin at him. "It's a well-known fact your feet smell like garlic."

Greer narrows his eyes but doesn't reply.

I shrug, and my grin fades. "I know; I know. She's not exactly the friendliest person, but I live with her, so I kind of have to get along with her. Besides, her family lives ten minutes away, remember? Maybe she's more of a homebody than the rest of us."

Omri walks onto the stage, and our conversation is cut short. A hush falls across the room, and we rise to stand at attention. Two of the Guard follow him, and they turn to face us once Omri steps behind the podium.

"*Victores in obsequio!*" he says.

"*Victores in obsequio!*" we repeat.

Omri smiles. "Class of 2090." He casts a sweeping glance around the room. Nothing in his expression hints at the fear I saw frozen on his face mere hours before. "I know you're excited this day is finally here." He pauses, and his smile fades. "For some of you, this truly marks the end of an era. You know who you are. You've grown up here; we've become your family when yours were tragically taken too soon."

I swallow against an unexpected surge of yearning for what I lost long ago. Omri's speaking about my family, among others. After they died, I was brought from the Western Region to the Central Capital and placed in a government-run orphanage inside the presidential compound. When I was ten years old, I scored high enough on the mandated middle grade tests to be placed into the Presidential Education Program alongside other gifted children. It was scary at first, being taken away from what I'd known for so long and thrust into something new. But everyone else was scared, too, and that somehow made it better. There was solidarity in our fear. For the first time since I could remember, I had a family of sorts, even if it wasn't the family I'd always longed to have.

What my classmates will never know about me, however, is that I made perfect scores on the first-year intuition and psychological exams, something never done before. Pallas, who has the same abilities as me, began tutoring me, teaching me the complexities of the human brain and how to decipher symbols within dreams. I immediately connected with her. She became the mom I didn't have. Apart from Greer, she's the person I'm closest to here.

The training I've received from Pallas is important because Omri is cursed with dreams so intense he often can't return to sleep. Eventually, I began helping Pallas sort through and study those dreams each week, which are recorded via electrodes and sent to the dream screen. Until this morning, the dream from one year ago was the only prophetic dream on record.

"For those of you whose families look forward to seeing you again soon," Omri continues, interrupting my daydream, "albeit for a short break before your work begins, you are as much a part of our family here at the compound as those who have been here a little longer."

Omri pauses again, turning his head to glance around at us. "You are part of the elite. You have trained here at the compound because you're the brightest of your generation. You deserved—and received—an education befitting that.

"Today is important not only for you but for our country. When America was attacked some fifty years ago, when terrorists believed they successfully destroyed us, they were wrong. It did nothing other than make us stronger. Now, you are our future leaders. It's your turn to carry us forward."

"Think he might let the future leaders sit down soon?" Greer whispers to me.

I swallow a laugh and elbow him to be quiet, then refocus on the president. Omri's right. America is stronger than it's ever been, and it's our turn to ensure that it stays that way.

Fifty years ago, every capital city in America, including Washington, DC, was bombed. Our leaders were slaughtered along with thousands upon thousands of innocent people. Then, in the midst of the aftermath, it was discovered that the terrorists were American.

Pallas wasn't born until after the attack, but she told me once what her parents told her, about the days of darkness and riots and fear. Of not knowing who was a friend or an enemy. For years, rumors of another civil war weighed on everyone's mind.

It didn't happen, thankfully. The terrorists were caught, and the country recovered piece by piece. But those who put the country back together decided we weren't going to be the same old twenty-first-century America anymore.

Now, the days of cell phones and the internet are long gone. Days, Omri has often reminded us, when our dependence on technology made us forget to depend on one another.

"Some of you will go to the Eastern Region to serve as diplomats or watch over our financial centers," Omri says, motioning for us to sit. "Others will travel west to watch over our food production, a vital segment of our economy. Still others will stay here in our great Central Capital or perhaps venture into other areas of the Central Region to develop our transportation or lead our military.

"No matter where you go, remember this: Our name might once have been the United States of America, but we were still divided. Culture. Politics. Religion. All were kindling ready to burst into flame. When the terrorists wiped out our way of life, they also wiped out our divisive ways of thinking."

His words stir a memory of a long-ago class about life after the terrorist attack. To unify the country, the states were dissolved. Local governments were shut down because they created discord. Religions were labeled as false belief systems and disbanded, their leaders arrested if they refused to obey, their churches and other houses of worship destroyed. It was necessary to maintain order, we learned. *Victores in obsequio.*

"Our great leaders found opportunity within tragedy," Omri continues.

I blink and refocus on his speech.

"An opportunity to reunite our country," he says. "Today, America is truly united. You, class of 2090, are responsible for ensuring it continues to thrive. Use your skills and your intelligence to bring people together. Now, which career will you choose?"

"I choose whichever one means I won't have to work as hard

as I've worked in this blasted compound," Greer whispers. I elbow him again but keep my gaze focused on the president.

"No matter where you go," Omri says, "you will be a leader. Don't be discouraged if you don't get your first choice. It simply means we believe your talents will be of greater use elsewhere." His smile returns. "Your mentors are waiting across the hall to record your selections. You will learn of your official placement at the graduation banquet Friday night." His smile broadens. "Congratulations, students. Now, make America proud."

## 4

The moment Omri disappears through the door, the auditorium erupts in excited chatter.

"I'm choosing Agriculture Administration," Greer says as we merge into the crowd to exit. "I want to pick oranges all day and sleep."

I snort. "Pretty sure they're not going to let you pick oranges all day."

Greer shrugs. "It could happen."

I wave goodbye to Genevieve before she joins the line for her mentor and then follow Greer into Pallas's line. She's his mentor, too.

"Well, Nyss? What are you choosing?"

I sense Greer's gaze boring into the top of my head. Even though my official choice will be entered today as "Central Region: presidential aide," it comes with the secret expectation that one day I'll succeed Pallas in her role of presidential adviser and chief dream interpreter to the president.

Of course, I can't tell him any of that, so I'm silent.

"I know; I know." He nudges me. "You want to make sure you and I stay together, and if we get sent to different regions, we might not ever see each other again..." His voice trails away, and I glance up to find him staring at me with an unreadable expression.

I blink fast, then look at the ground. He's spoken out loud the dismal reality I'd rather not think about. The Regional Movement Policy, developed after Omri's dream last year, allows movement between regions only for "cultural or professional interest" purposes. Not only do citizens have to get presidential permission to travel, but they're also required to return to their own region within a specified amount of time. As graduates of the most prestigious educational program in the country, our chances of ever leaving the region to which we're sent are low—especially during the first two years, which will be filled with specialty training.

"Come pick oranges with me, Nyss," he whispers.

There's an urgency in his voice, and my head jerks up so my gaze meets his. He's joking, right? He has to be joking. But the intensity in his eyes says otherwise, and my stomach clenches. Pallas and Genevieve and Tyrone are probably right. How have I been blind to Greer's feelings when they're obvious to everyone else? I want to kick him. Or do I want to hug him? I stifle a groan. There's not enough time to sort through my own confusing feelings.

"Ms. Ardelone?" Pallas's voice slices through the moment.

"You're up." Greer steps back and shoves his hands into his pockets.

I blink and turn toward the table. I can't think about Greer right now because this is my moment with Pallas. My opportunity at last to ask her why she lied to Omri.

I bend down. "Pallas, I have to talk to you," I whisper.

She glances at me and shakes her head before returning her gaze to the small device in her hand. "As you already know, Nyssa," she says just loud enough for me to hear, "you have been selected to become a presidential aide under my supervision." She taps the screen, and a chart with my name in the center appears. "You've done very well keeping this a secret from the rest of your class, and I expect you will do so until careers are announced at the graduation banquet. Is that clear?" She taps the screen again, and it turns off.

"Pallas!" I frown in confusion. "Did you hear me? I know what the dream meant. You have to tell me—"

"Hush, Nyssa." Pallas looks up at me again, her mouth set in a straight line, her eyes expressionless. "Now is not the time."

We stare at each other. I'm dumbfounded by her behavior and can't think of a single thing to say.

"Please step aside for Mr. Rines." Pallas's voice is quiet but firm.

I stare at her without moving.

"Nyssa." Her voice holds a warning.

I blink once, twice, then nod and walk away in a bewildered daze to wait for Greer by the door. Did I really expect her to tell me here—in front of everyone—why she lied to the president? I lean my head against the wall. It's not so much her refusal to tell me as the way she treated me like a stranger. I'll get it out of her one way or another. I have to know the truth.

"Everything all right?"

I jump, startled by Greer's voice. He stands off to the side, one eyebrow raised. I study his face, but it's impossible to tell whether he's talking about what happened between me and him or whether he heard my conversation with Pallas. Either way, I don't want to talk about it.

"Genevieve's waiting," I say. I dodge around him and head out into the courtyard. Genevieve waves at me from where she sits on a blanket beneath the oak, and I quicken my steps to leave Greer behind.

I'm already settled with my back against the trunk and eyes closed when he sits down. I'm aware of his presence, of his legs stretched out alongside me, his shoulder pressed against mine.

*Come pick oranges with me, Nyss.* I clench and unclench my jaw, swirling each word around, sorting through what he could have meant by the unexpected request.

"It looked like you and Pallas got in a little fight back there," Greer whispers in my ear.

His breath against my skin makes my eyes pop open. I scoot away from him and squint toward the auditorium. Pallas likes to cross the courtyard to get to her office, and if I see her leave, I'll follow her. She might not tell me the truth in front of other people, but she'll have to talk to me if I confront her alone. And I need space from Greer. I can't think straight around him right now. Too many emotions and thoughts and questions cling to me like spiderwebs.

"Well?" Greer nudges my arm. "Am I right?"

"Drop it, okay?" I swat at him.

He throws his hands into the air in surrender and turns to Genevieve. "So, G, what'd you pick as number one?"

"Eastern Region: diplomatic service," she says. "Since I did so well in French, I'm hoping I'll be selected for the European diplomacy program in Capital East. My family doesn't live too far from there." She studies Greer. "And you? Did you ask to pick oranges?"

Greer twists the cap from his ever-present water bottle. "Western Region: food production; Eastern Region: transportation; Central Region: military."

"Military?" Genevieve raises an eyebrow. "You want to join the Guard?"

"Not really." He sips and wipes his mouth with the back of his hand. "But Gideon's in the Guard. Figured since I had to put three choices down, might as well put that. It wouldn't be so bad getting stuck here if I could be with my brother."

His words barely register. The auditorium door has opened, and Pallas glides out onto the terrace, then turns toward the east wing.

I stand. "I just remembered I promised Ethelind I'd find her before lunch. I'll see you later."

"Tell her we don't say hello," Greer calls as I hurry away.

I dash into the east wing and turn in time to see the elevator slide closed. Instead of waiting, I open a door to the right and take the stairs. It's a long climb to the fourth floor, and by the time I reach it, I have a stitch in my side. I take a few deep breaths, open the door, and step into the hall.

As I draw near to Pallas's office, murmured voices drift out because the door isn't properly closed. I pause in front of it, my hand resting on the knob. Something holds me back from barging in like I'd planned. Instead, I lean forward to listen.

"It was an organized attack, Pallas," a man says. "He knew they'd be there. We managed to get them back to Fortune's Fall, but they won't survive much longer without the antidote."

"And what do you propose I do?" Pallas asks.

I ignore the trickle of guilt that ripples down my arms. I'm not proud that I'm eavesdropping, but my curiosity is piqued.

"We have a way to get someone into the compound Friday," the same man says. "Once he gets the antidote, we want you to leave with him."

Pallas laughs, but I know her too well. I hear the ring of curiosity in the sound. "The chances of your man getting out of here alive are small, and if I'm caught, I'll be hanged the moment they arrest me."

"Pallas." The man is urgent. "There's been a new dream. We need you with us."

I frown. As far as I know, our job as dream interpreters is classified. Nobody knows what we do other than the president. Who is this stranger, and how does he know about us?

"If we'd known an interpretation before the group left for Maren," the man continues, "we might have known not to send them. We could have warned them they would be attacked when they got there. You have to help us. You can go home, Pallas."

My eyes widen. It's been a long time since anyone mentioned Maren. And what is this about it being home to Pallas?

"Home." Pallas laughs, but this time, the sound is bitter rather than curious. "Who can go home?"

"They're waiting for you, Pallas." The man's voice is soft now, gentle. "You don't have to stay here."

The silence seems to last forever.

"Where do I meet you?" she asks at last.

I sway, shaking my head in silent protest. Who are these people who think they can take Pallas away from me? And why would she agree to go?

"Meet our man at the West Gate Friday night at ten," the man says. "He'll know where to go from there."

Another pause.

Waiting.

Waiting.

"I'll be there," she says at last.

I gasp and stumble backward, then turn and hurry down the hall toward the stairs, tripping over my feet in my haste. My brain says to move even faster, but my legs can't keep up.

I wrench open the door and stop on the landing, leaning against the wall to wait for my heart to stop racing.

*Maren.*

Maren was my home, the city in the Western Region destroyed by disease. But it was wiped off the map; there's no record of it ever having even existed. I know because I've checked. I wanted to know about my family, about where I came from. But all my searches led to dead ends.

My head begins to throb, and I squeeze my eyes shut. Pallas is from Maren, too? Why has she never told me? I open my eyes and take a breath, then begin to climb the stairs, my gaze downcast. When I get to the fifth floor, I shove open the door.

And walk straight into a person.

"Watch it!" a familiar voice says before I'm shoved to the side.

Ethelind.

My head jerks up, and her eyes narrow.

"What's the matter with you?" she asks.

"You ran into me," I say.

She studies me in stony silence, eyebrows raised. "I think it was the other way around."

I sigh. "Did you need something?"

"I was looking for you and ran into Greer. He seemed to think you were with me." She raises her eyebrows even higher.

I open my mouth to explain, then snap it shut. I can't think of a single lie to cover what I just overheard.

"Our dresses arrived for the graduation banquet," she says at last, and my shoulders sag in relief. I know she won't press me for answers.

"Oh," I say. "That's great."

She nods and heads back down the hall. I shuffle along behind her, my arms wrapped against my chest to fight a chill that's lodged deep inside me.

Pallas is going to leave.

I take a shaky breath.

*Pallas is leaving.*

And she's going to Maren? How is that possible if Maren doesn't exist anymore?

I shake my head, trying to sift through my shock and revisit the facts I overheard. Someone was attacked in Maren and needs an antidote. A man is sneaking into the compound on Friday to steal it.

"Nyssa? Are you listening to me?" Ethelind's voice rings with irritation.

I stop and glance around. We're at the door to our suite. I don't remember getting here.

Ethelind frowns, then turns to open the door. "You're acting really weird."

I ignore her and follow her inside, but we both stop short.

Greer is on the couch.

"Hey, guys." He waves. His boots are on the floor, his socks strewn beside them, and his bare feet are stretched out on our rug.

"What are you doing here?" Ethelind asks.

Greer stares at me a moment too long before turning to Ethelind. "Told you I wanted to see Nyssa's dress."

Ethelind rolls her eyes. "I'll be in my room." Her door slams behind her.

I stand halfway between the door and the couch, not sure what to do.

"I guess you were right." Greer looks down at his toes and wiggles them.

I narrow my eyes. "What?"

"My feet must really stink. That's the fastest Ethelind's ever run into her room."

I laugh before I can stop myself. He looks up, and our gazes meet.

"Sorry I made things weird." His cheeks burn red. "It hit me today that everything's about to change. And I—" He stops and shakes his head. "It doesn't matter."

A tiny thrill shoots through me at the words he might've said, but I force it away. Even if there might be something between us, Greer wants a career in the Western Region, and I have to stay here. Nothing can happen now.

"Can we go back to normal?" Greer's eyes widen in appeal. "Please?" He pats the cushion next to him.

I hesitate for a second before I make my choice. He's my best friend. I want to enjoy what little time we have left together. I shuffle to the couch and collapse beside him. "Okay. Normal."

Greer leans back with a relieved sigh and rests his arm on the back of the couch. His fingers brush my shoulder, and for a moment, I want to lean into him. I resist.

"Want to tell me why you walked in here looking like you stepped straight out of a nightmare?" He hesitates. "And why you told me you were with Ethelind when you obviously weren't?"

My eyes widen. It's on the tip of my tongue to blurt out everything I just heard in Pallas's office, but something stops me. It might lead him to questions about Pallas's real role here in the compound. And I'm forbidden from discussing classified information. No, until I figure out what it means, I'll keep it to myself.

I shrug. "Just a rough morning. No big deal."

"You mean a rough meeting with Pallas? A meeting that you didn't tell me about?"

I hesitate for a second. "Yeah, sorry." I try to ignore the stab of guilt that darts through me. "It was a last-minute thing. She caught me in the hall, and I had to go. But don't worry—no more meetings. We're really done this time."

"Glad to hear it."

He moves his arm from behind me, and I turn to face him at the same moment he turns toward me. His gaze falls to my lips, then darts back to my eyes so quickly I wonder whether I imagined it. Real or not, it makes my cheeks burn. So much for being normal.

"What was so awful about it that you came in here looking so miserable?" Greer asks.

His gaze searches mine, and I open then close my mouth, desperate to say something but at a complete loss for words.

"Forget it," he says after a moment with a pinched smile. "None of my business, or so you've told me before." He pats my leg and scoots away, and the moment returns to familiar territory. "So, about this dress." He crosses his arms. "That fantastic roommate of yours seems to think it's the most beautiful thing she's ever seen."

"Why can't you be nice to her?" I ask.

"Nope. She started it."

I stifle a sigh.

"Her dress *is* beautiful," Ethelind says from somewhere behind us.

Greer raises his eyebrows in amusement before he leans forward to pull on his socks and boots. "I'll leave you ladies to it, then." He stands and walks toward the door.

I twist on the couch to see Ethelind framed in her doorway, eyeing Greer with suspicion.

"I thought you wanted to see Nyssa's dress," she says.

"Changed my mind," Greer says as he opens the door. "I decided I want to be surprised." He gives us a quick salute, but just before he steps into the hall, the screen mounted between my desk and Ethelind's emits three low-pitched chimes. Greer turns, his hand still on the knob. "Uh-oh."

A Central Capital news bulletin.

I scoot to the edge of the couch, and Ethelind perches beside me. Greer remains by the door. The Central Capital news anchor pops into view.

"Good evening. I apologize for the interruption." The anchor clears her throat. "The president has issued Edict 201. All Central Capital citizens will report to the arena at noon on Friday. I repeat—all Central Capital citizens must report to the arena at noon on Friday." Her smile doesn't quite reach her eyes. "Please enjoy the rest of your day."

The screen turns off.

We're silent. We all know what this means. The scientists who escaped from Ward C have been found, and on Friday, we'll watch them die.

## 5

After Greer leaves, Ethelind returns to her room and closes the door. I stare at the screen now gone black, my knees pulled against my chest, my body numb. I don't know how much time passes, but at some point, Ethelind comes out and rummages in the kitchen.

"Want something to eat?" she asks.

"No." My voice sounds strange and far away.

"Are you okay?"

"I'm fine."

She mutters something I can't understand before her door closes again.

I bury my face against my knees. Pallas. Greer. Another looming public execution. Everything is broken, like I've dropped a vase and it's shattered in a circle around me. I don't know which way to step to avoid cutting my foot. Or how to glue the pieces back together to make it into what it used to be.

I stand and go to my room, close the door behind me, and collapse onto my bed. All I want to do is sleep.

I blink awake hours later, surprised by the weak, early-morning light that beckons through my window. I can't believe

I slept through the whole night. My eyes are still heavy, though, and a dull throb beats behind my right temple. I kick my quilt to the bottom of my bed, roll to my back, and close my eyes, willing my mind to stay blank. But it's a lost cause.

I open my eyes and consider what I want to do. I can't hide in my room and obsess over unanswered questions or pretend things haven't changed. I could confront Greer, demand to know what his true feelings are toward me. I mentally cross through that idea. I don't think I have the courage to do that. But I know someone else I'm brave enough to find. I force myself out of bed, then slip the small tablet on my nightstand into my pocket as a last resort.

I'm going to find Pallas.

She's usually one of three places: in her apartment, in her office, or, on sunny days, on the balcony outside our cafeteria, which is just around the corner from my room. I go there first.

The cafeteria is a nondescript room that spans the entire length of one side of the fifth floor. It has to be big, I guess, since everyone who lives, studies, and works in the compound eats there. It's still early when I arrive, though, and there aren't more than a handful of people scattered at the tables. I do a quick scan but don't see Pallas, so I cross the room to the glass doors that open onto the balcony.

It's empty. I stifle a frustrated sigh and head to the elevator, reminding myself there are two more likely places she'd be this early in the morning. When I reach her apartment on the sixth floor, I knock twice.

"Pallas?" I lean my forehead against the door. "It's Nyssa." I knock again and wait, but all is silent.

"Everything okay, Ms. Ardelone?"

I whirl to find my history teacher standing behind me. His hair is slightly rumpled and his glasses are askew. He holds a steaming coffee cup in one hand and a tablet in the other.

"Oh, hi, Mr. Leos. Have you seen Pallas?"

"No, come to think of it, I haven't." He purses his lips. "We usually cross paths around this time, too." He shrugs. "Sorry."

"That's okay. If you see her, could you tell her I'm looking for her?"

"Will do." He nods and continues down the hall to his own apartment three doors down.

I return to the elevator, and when I exit onto the fourth floor, my steps are hurried. At her office door, I knock hard and loud. "Pallas?"

I tap my foot while I wait, certain she's going to open the door. When nothing happens, I frown and press my ear against it. There's a noise like a chair sliding across the tile or a drawer being closed.

I lean away and knock again. "Pallas?"

Still nothing. I press my ear to the door again, but this time, all I hear is silence. I turn and rest the back of my head on her door. Pallas has always been available when I need her. Why can't I find her now? I press the heels of my hands against my eyes to stem sudden, frustrated tears. Is she avoiding me on purpose?

I wipe my nose on the back of my arm and pull the tablet from my pocket. I'm not supposed to use it. It's strictly for Pallas to send emergency messages to me. But if she sees a message from me, she'll know it's important.

PALLAS, WHERE ARE YOU? I NEED TO TALK TO YOU.

I slip it back into my pocket, then head to the elevator. I need to get out of here. To be alone, away from people and noise and walls that suddenly seem to close in on me. When I exit onto the first floor, I break into a jog.

"Nyssa?" Greer's voice comes from somewhere behind me, but he's the last person I want to see. I ignore him and burst through the doors at the end of the hall, cross the sidewalk that borders the building, and race into the knee-high grass of the wildflower-filled field that stretches all the way to the security wall.

At last, when I have a stitch in my side, I collapse into the grass and roll onto my back, eyes narrowed against the blinding sun. My chest heaves, but my eyes are dry. Wispy white clouds dot a cerulean sky, and bluebonnets dance in the breeze. It's silent and still and exactly what I need right now.

"Want to explain why you just ran away from me?"

I prop myself on my elbows and find Greer hovering a few feet away, arms crossed, a scowl on his face. I lie back down. "Go away."

He ignores me, plops down, and stretches out so that he lies alongside me. I sit up and turn toward him. His eyes are closed. His hands are clasped on his stomach. I punch his arm. "I want to be alone."

"Be quiet. I'm resting my eyes."

I stare at him openmouthed, then throw myself back onto the ground. "Fine. But don't talk to me."

"I'm not here."

I roll my eyes, even though I know he can't see.

A bird warbles from somewhere to our left, and the wind rustles the grass. I reach into my pocket to see whether Pallas has responded to my message but then remember I can't check, not with Greer here. Nobody knows I have one of these tablets. I sigh and clasp my hands on my stomach instead.

"Want to talk about it yet?" Greer asks a few minutes later.

I sigh again. Of course I want to talk about it. I want to tell him about Pallas, but I can't. I want to ask him about us, about why it looked like he wanted to kiss me yesterday, but that would be weird, because what if I'm reading into something that isn't there? And besides, I don't even know whether I like the idea of him as more than a friend. I remember his gaze dipping toward my lips, and my cheeks grow warm. I shove the image away.

"No," I say in a small voice. "I don't want to talk about it."

Greer doesn't respond. A cloud drifts across the sun and a shadow falls over us for a second before the sun appears again. I take a deep, shaky breath, despite my attempt to keep it steady.

"Hey." Greer's voice is soft. "What's going on?"

I turn toward him before I realize what I've done. He's so close I can see the faded freckles that dot his nose. I shake my head and turn away.

"Come here." Greer leans up and beckons me to do the same. He stretches his arm on the ground beneath me, and I lie back down so my head rests on his shoulder. His fingers curl around my arm. "I won't ask any more questions, Nyss. Promise."

I close my eyes, but not before a tear sneaks out and trickles down my cheek to land in the grass. I turn my head away so he won't see me cry. Greer and Pallas are everything to me. And they're both going to leave. I can't imagine a future without them in it.

We lie in silence for a while, and Greer stays true to his word. He never asks me again what's wrong.

## 6

"I can't believe Omri scheduled this on the same day as our graduation banquet," Ethelind says the next morning.

We're squashed into one of the compartments of the Central Capital tram with dozens of other people. It glides along its track in the center of the street, surrounded by people walking to the arena, which sits on the eastern edge of the city. Nothing much has changed about the arena over the last hundred years, except it's no longer used for sports. Now, we go there for rallies, an occasional concert, and, of course, executions.

"He definitely didn't waste any time." I gaze out the window at the air that shimmers with heat. "At least we don't have to walk. It's so hot." I knew the springlike weather was unusual, but this sudden leap into summer is jarring.

"Who knows how long it'll take us to get back?" Ethelind complains. "We won't have enough time to get ready."

I don't reply. Pallas never responded to my message, and today is the day she's supposed to leave. It seems almost certain now that she's avoiding me.

Unexpected tears blur my vision. It's a betrayal I never expected—her refusal to explain why she lied to Omri about his dream and now her decision to leave without telling me. I resist the urge to slam my hand against the window. Does she matter more to me than I do to her?

I brush my hand across my eyes. I could report her—I *should* report her—or at least warn the Guard that someone plans to break into the compound. But I can't do it. Even thinking about turning her in makes my stomach twist with shame. And I'm afraid if I warn the Guard about the looming break-in, I might somehow implicate Pallas in the crime. If something happens to her because of me, I'll never forgive myself.

"Nyssa, come on!"

We've arrived at the arena, and Ethelind gestures for me to follow her off the tram.

"Have I mentioned you've been really weird lately?" she asks.

"Once or twice." I scan the crowd for my friends as we join the throng to go inside. Our class is required to sit together, though, so I'll see everyone inside.

"This whole week..." Ethelind shakes her head. "Never mind."

I ignore her and squint up at the flags that line the arena's rim. Each has the same portrait of Omri drawn on them with *Victores in obsequio* written beneath. They flap with a rippling beat, giving him the appearance of being alive.

When we finally step into the dim corridor that encircles the arena, the air I'd hoped would be cooler is thick and pungent with the sweat of thousands of people. Ethelind and I circle to the opposite side before making our way to the bottom level and back out into the heat. A canopy has been erected above our section, and I sit beside Greer, thankful for the shade.

Greer nudges my shoulder, then nods toward Ethelind, who sits on my other side. "She deigns to sit with us?"

"Be nice." I shoot a glance at Ethelind, who's busy peeling strands of sweat-crusted hair from her neck, her nose wrinkled with disgust.

I lean back and squint at the massive stage situated in the center of the field. A podium sits on the left side of the stage, and behind it are two empty chairs. On the right are two thick wooden beams connected by a metal crossbeam from which two ropes hang.

"Medieval, isn't it?" Greer asks.

I grimace. I'll force myself to watch; I believe in justice. But I'll never get used to witnessing it firsthand. An image of Pallas being led onto the stage, hands tied, bursts into my mind, and my stomach tightens. Just because I choose not to report her doesn't mean she won't get caught. And she was right about one thing I overheard: if anyone finds out she lied to the president or that she plans to leave, she'll be hanged. Will I be forced to watch her die, too?

A door at the far left of the arena opens, and nine people file out: two guards followed by Omri; his wife, Laskin; Assemblywoman Dellis, who's the head of our Judicial Council; and, finally, two scientists in blue prison uniforms escorted by two additional guards.

Greer leans toward me. "Gideon said there's a third scientist still missing. Shouldn't be long till they find him."

I frown. "We're going to have to come back and watch this all over again? Why didn't they wait until they arrest him and do it all at once?"

Greer shrugs. "To set an example? I doubt Omri wants to wait and see if any other scientists from Ward C try to run before he executes these."

The group mounts the stage. The two guards in front stand on either side of the podium, behind which Omri stands.

Laskin and Assemblywoman Dellis sit in the chairs. The remaining two guards place each prisoner beneath a noose, then stand on either side of them. The crowd quiets.

"*Victores in obsequio!*" Omri shouts.

"*Victores in obsequio!*" I say along with everyone else.

"Today," Omri says in a measured voice, "we bear witness to the consequences borne by those who believe themselves to be above the law." He pauses, gazing out at the crowd. "These men are skilled and intelligent. Their service to America helped return us to glory. But they betrayed us!" Omri's voice rises. "They betrayed America!"

The arena erupts into a roar of disapproval. Omri smiles and silences us with his hands. My gaze darts around at the people, the field, and the sky but brushes past the scientists. I can't look at them, knowing they'll be dead in minutes.

"No American is above the law!" Omri says. "Our forefathers taught us that loyalty to our country ensures peace. And those who betray us, who break the laws we've created to keep every American safe, must be punished."

The crowd cheers, and Omri turns and nods to those seated behind him. Assemblywoman Dellis steps to his side at the podium. Even though she's tall like me, she's still dwarfed by Omri.

She tucks her short gray hair behind her ears and clears her throat. "Prisoners EFS-14 and EFS-15, to the charge of violating the Regional Movement Policy: guilty. To the charge of attempting to transport state secrets: guilty. By order of Edict 201, you are hereby sentenced to death by hanging." She steps back and nods to the guards who stand with the scientists.

"Here we go," Greer mutters.

Now, I force myself to look. I know the steps by heart. First, the nooses will be placed around their necks.

Then, the guards will step back.

I inhale once the guards have taken their position.

The floor beneath the scientists' feet splits apart, and they fall into a crevice beneath the stage.

The crowd cheers its approval, malicious glee that makes me want to press my hands against my ears. Instead, I inhale sharply through my nose and stare straight ahead into the sunlight until my eyes burn.

When Omri at last raises his hand, signaling we can leave, I hurry out with Greer and Ethelind without a backward glance. But when we get to the front entrance, the tram still hasn't arrived, and the line waiting for it is long.

"Let's walk," Greer says.

Ethelind groans.

"You already smell, Ethelind," he says. "We'll get back faster if we walk—trust me."

It doesn't take much to convince me. The forty-five-minute walk will be a good distraction from what we just witnessed. But when the compound comes into view, it's my turn to groan. The line to get in through the front gate is longer than it was for the tram.

"Come on." Greer ushers Ethelind and me to the left. "We'll go to the West Gate. Everyone forgets about it."

He's right. No one is at the gate, though I suspect it's because everyone else remembers the sun beats down on this side of the compound during the afternoon. Sweat runs down my sides as we wait for the gate guard to let us through. But he's deep in conversation with another man and either doesn't see us or chooses to ignore us.

"What's taking so long?" Ethelind glances at her watch. "The banquet's in three hours." Most of her ponytail has escaped despite her attempts to keep it contained. Ringlets curl around her head; her forehead glistens. I doubt I look much better. Damp curls stick to my cheeks, and I wipe beads of sweat from my lip.

Greer whistles to get the guard's attention. The guard holds up a finger without breaking his conversation.

"That's rude," Ethelind says.

I agree, but all we can do is wait.

At last, the men step away from each other, and the guard waves us in. But just as Greer steps through the gate, the man the guard had been talking with dashes out of it. He and Greer collide.

"Hey!" Greer stumbles backward but manages to keep his balance.

The man ricochets sideways and falls to his hands and knees, his brows shooting up in surprise. Greer holds out his hand, and the man grabs it, then gives a mighty groan as Greer helps him stand.

"Sorry about that," the man says to Greer. He pats his pocket, frowns, and reaches inside it, his fingers making bumps against the fabric. When he pulls out his still-empty hand, he stares at it for a moment, then bends and scours the ground, dancing in ever-widening circles.

"What's the matter with him?" Ethelind whispers to me.

I don't answer because I've spotted why he's so frantic. I bend and pick up a circular gold pendant the size of a quarter. It has a smaller hole at its top as though it was once a necklace, but there's no chain attached. When I see what's etched on it, I blink up at him, my mouth ajar. "A lamb."

He snatches it from my hand. "Thank you."

"Where did you get that?" I study his face, which reminds me of a basset hound I once saw: saggy eyes, flabby cheeks. He's middle aged and heavyset. His navy slacks and white shirt reveal nothing about his identity.

"Family heirloom." His gaze darts away from mine.

I know it's a lie, but he turns and hurries toward the city center before I can question him further. "That was weird," I say. My mind races with things I don't speak out loud. A lamb again? First, it appears in Omri's dream. Now, this.

"Who cares?" Ethelind says. "Let's go."

I turn to Greer. "You coming?"

He dismisses me with a wave, his gaze still turned toward the city center. "I'll see you at the banquet. Have stuff to do."

Ethelind grabs my arm. "Come on."

I let her drag me away, but I glance over my shoulder before I go inside. Greer hasn't moved.

## 7

Ethelind was right—my dress is beautiful. But I don't enjoy dressing up for the graduation banquet as much as I might if the situation were different. If Omri hadn't had a new dream and if Pallas hadn't lied about it. If she didn't plan to leave tonight.

I secure my crescent-shaped gold earrings and smooth the turquoise and green layers of my dress, which shimmer like a mermaid's tail. The hem snags on the clasp of my gold heel, and I bend to untangle it, revealing two parallel blue lines tattooed on the inside of my right ankle, just beside the bone. I trace my finger over them. They're so small no one has ever noticed them, and I usually forget about them, too. I have no idea why I have the tattoo, and when I asked Pallas about it once, all she did was shrug. It's a mystery that I don't think about too often.

I stand and shake my dress so that it covers all but my toes, then turn back and forth, studying the top, which is my favorite. It's rounded beneath my collarbones, and the sleeves end just past my shoulders. I twist to see my hair. It cascades halfway down my back, tamed for once with pins and hair spray. When I turn back to study my face, a sigh escapes my lips. How can I sit through tonight knowing Pallas won't be here tomorrow? I don't want to stay here—to do this job every day—without her. But what can I do to change it now?

"Wow."

I turn, and my breath catches. Greer leans against my open door. He wears the boys' official dress uniform, navy blue like our everyday uniform but with tails and gold buttons. I've never seen him dressed up before, and I can't tear my gaze away. The blue matches his eyes, which sparkle with appreciation as he studies me. My cheeks begin to burn beneath his inspection.

"You look really pretty." His eyes widen the moment he blurts the words, and he clamps his lips together.

My eyes pop in surprise, and I twirl back toward my mirror to hide my pleased smile. One quick, deep breath, then I twist and grab my clutch from my nightstand, breeze past Greer into the living room, and peek into Ethelind's room. She spins in front of her own mirror, oblivious to me. Her curls are pulled into a sleek bun behind her ear, and her strapless blue gown falls to just below her knees.

"Somebody cleans up nice," Greer murmurs into my ear.

I jump, turn, and smack his arm, trying to ignore a twinge of jealousy.

"What'd you do that for?" he asks, rubbing his arm.

"Ready!" Ethelind says, a little breathless as she spins to face us.

"Oh," Greer says with fake innocence, "we're all walking down together?"

Ethelind's smile fades into a scowl, and I smack his arm again.

"Yes, we are." I give Greer a warning glare.

He opens his mouth like he's going to reply, then snaps it shut with a shrug and turns toward the door. "Let's go. We're going to be late."

When we get to the ballroom, I gawk at its transformation. Shimmering gold cloths cover each of ten round tables set in a semicircle around the dance floor. In the center of each is a bowl of floating white gardenias. We walk around, scanning the nameplates at the tables until we find ours. The three of us are seated at a table near the front, along with Genevieve and one of our other classmates.

Greer pulls out my chair, and I sit facing a long rectangular stage at the front of the ballroom. A podium sits in its center, and a band sets up along its left side. The head table, still empty, sits in front of the stage, and behind both, covering almost the entire wall, is the screen that will reveal our futures later in the evening.

"This is spectacular," Genevieve says when she sits a few minutes later. "Nyssa, your dress is beautiful!"

"Yours, too," I say with sincerity. Her flowing dress is lavender, and the single thick strap accentuates her petite frame.

A bell announces the arrival of the president, and we stand as he, the first lady, and several advisers, including Pallas, make their way to the head table. Once they sit, we do, too, and I study Pallas while we wait for dinner to begin. But there's nothing in her demeanor to indicate this is her last meal with us. How can she seem so calm?

The appetizer—tarts full of pear and blue cheese—comes and goes. Now, waiters deliver the main course to the head table.

"I wish they'd announce our selections before we eat," Genevieve says. "I'm too nervous to be hungry."

"We'll find out soon enough, little one," Greer says to Genevieve, peering at the plates as the waiters pass. He misses the face Genevieve makes at him. She hates it when he makes fun of how small she is.

"Chicken." Greer slouches back into his seat. "I have to wear this getup all night"—he tugs at his uniform—"and all I get is chicken. Why not steak?"

At last, our own dinner arrives, and the ballroom falls silent except for the clink of silverware. There's only one course left before the real show begins, and the tension is rising.

Dessert comes: lemon ice cream and chocolate espresso cake drizzled with caramel.

"This is so good," Ethelind says.

I agree. It's divine. So delicious, in fact, that I forget about Pallas for a few minutes and let myself enjoy the moment.

An excited murmur fills the ballroom when the tables are finally cleared. Omri rises and steps to the podium. Silence descends.

"*Victores in obsequio!*" he says.

"*Victores in obsequio!*" we say in response.

"I'll make this short." Omri gives us a quick smile. "In a moment, your photograph will appear on the screen, and beside it, your chosen career. Of course, this will be in alphabetical order. Sorry, Mr. Zendayer."

Low laughter echoes across the ballroom, and I turn along with everyone else to glance at Michael Zendayer, who will be the last to learn his future career. He smiles and shrugs. He's used to his fate by now.

"Let's get started, shall we?" Omri steps to the side and sweeps his hand toward the screen.

I hold my breath. I'll be first, which is good because I won't have to pretend I'm as nervous as everyone else anymore, but it's also bad because I'm worried my reaction will seem fake. My photograph appears with my name beside it. Then, beneath it: Central Region, Presidential Aide. I widen my eyes and let my mouth fall open.

Greer turns to me with raised eyebrows. "Pretty impressive, Nyss."

I shrug and turn my gaze to the tablecloth. "Thank you." If he sees my expression, he'll know something's off.

The presentation continues. Genevieve shrieks with glee when she receives her first choice: Eastern Region, European Diplomacy.

When Ethelind's turn arrives, she leans forward, her gaze riveted on the screen. I never asked her what she requested, but I suspect it was the Central Region since her family lives here.

Her photograph blinks onto the screen. Then, beside it: Ethelind Paul, Eastern Region, Finance.

I sneak a glance at her from the corner of my eye. Her mouth hangs open.

"I wanted to stay in the Central Region." Her lower lip trembles.

Our table is silent, and I reach across to squeeze her hand. "That's a great career, Ethelind. Your parents are going to be so proud."

She turns to me, eyes wide, fingers clenched around the edge of the table. After a moment, she blinks and attempts a smile that's more of a grimace. "You're right. They'll be proud."

I squeeze her hand again, but before I can think of anything else to say, Greer's picture pops onto the screen.

"I'm up," he says. He rubs his hands together. "Pallas said I shouldn't have to worry about getting posted to the Western Region since most everyone asks to stay in the big cities."

His photograph appears next to his name: Greer Rines. Then: Central Region, Presidential Guard.

"What?" Greer slides down in his seat like a popped balloon.

I press my fingers against my lips to hide my surprise. Greer isn't leaving. He's going to stay here with me in the Central Region. I can hardly believe it.

"The mentors must really believe you'll be a good military leader." Genevieve pats Greer's hand, but he jerks it away.

I clear my throat and wipe any hint of expression from my face. "Maybe they didn't want to separate you and Gideon. He's your brother, after all. Besides, the Guard was one of your choices, too."

"My third choice," Greer says. "Nobody's ever gotten their third choice before. Why me?" He clenches his jaw and stares at the table. I know not to say anything else until after he's had time to process the news.

At last, Michael Zendayer's name is called. It's over. The band begins to play, and a buzz of excitement fills the room. Pallas still sits at the head table, talking with the adviser to her left. I watch her for a moment before peeking at Greer's watch: 9:15 p.m.

And then, it happens—that moment when she stands and makes her way toward the doors. I watch her float through the ballroom, smiling at people, saying a few words to others. She gives nothing away. Despair, thick and aching, settles in my chest as she disappears into the hall. She never once glanced my way.

A lump forms in my throat, and I clench my fingers around the napkin in my lap. Am I really going to sit here and let her walk away?

An idea darts through my head like lightning. I don't question it. That would waste too much time. I pull my napkin from my lap and set it next to my plate. I take a deep breath. Am I really going to do this? It's reckless and dangerous and breaks every rule I've ever followed, but I don't care. Pallas can't leave. She can't.

"Be back in a bit." I keep my gaze downcast as I push my chair back. Then, before anyone can ask any questions, I rise and follow her out the door.

I step into the hall just in time to see a flash of Pallas's dress before the elevator closes. I hope what I suspect is true, that she'll collect things to take with her before she goes to the West

Gate. There's no time to consider other possibilities. I kneel and unclasp my shoes, then hook them around my finger and pull my dress up to my knees before I dash down the hall and around the corner. I stop in front of an unremarkable door that masquerades as a supply closet. But it's not a closet. It has a small black panel where the knob should be, and when I press my thumb against it, it unlocks with a click. I push it open and step into a hidden elevator that descends to the Underground.

Most people don't know about the Underground. Entrance requires security clearance, which I have because of the work I do with Pallas. I've ventured down only once before, to observe Pallas last year when she interviewed Omri's arrested advisers before they were hanged. I squeeze my eyes shut for a second, pushing away the memory.

The elevator stops, and the doors slide apart to reveal a circular lobby. In the center is a large unmanned desk, empty because the day of the graduation banquet is a holiday for all compound workers. It's the perfect opportunity for a crime.

Spread out around the lobby are three steel doors, behind which are three hallways that lead to Wards A, B, and C. Ward A is through the door to my left. It houses the offices of those who have top-secret security clearance: Omri's advisers and members of the Judicial Council. Ward B, which is through the center door, is the prison, where those who have committed crimes in the Central Capital wait until their sentences are decided. Some stay there forever. Others until they're executed.

Then, there's Ward C. The door to my right. Rumors float about what happens inside: experiments, torture. It's the only place where an antidote would be kept, and if the antidote's inside, so is the person who plans to steal it.

My plan is to keep the intruder from getting to the West Gate. If Pallas's guide doesn't show up, she can't leave. I scurry around the desk and hesitate in front of the door to Ward C, my thumb poised above the panel as I take quick, calming breaths.

I press it, but instead of the telltale unlocking click, it beeps once. Access denied.

"Aargh!" Ward C must require higher clearance than I have. I step back and stare at the door, my arms hanging at my sides. I don't have a backup plan. This was my one chance, crazy as it might have been, to keep Pallas from leaving. I slam my fist against the steel door, then grind my teeth when pain ricochets up my arm. If I can't get in with my high-level security clearance, how did an intruder?

I spin around and slump against the door. My eyes smart, and I blink away frustrated tears. It's too late to try to find Pallas. There are a million ways to get to the West Gate, and she could easily disappear with the intruder while I'm still searching for her. Besides, even if I did stumble upon her and beg her to stay, she'd probably still leave.

My gaze lands on the massive desk in the center of the lobby, and I straighten, my jaw set, my shoulders squared. "I'm not leaving," I say out loud, glancing over my shoulder at the door to Ward C. "If you're in there, I'm guarding your only way out."

I stride to the desk, slide to the floor on the opposite side, and drop my shoes beside me. My feet ache. I stretch my legs out and wiggle my toes, but the tile is cold against my bare skin, and I pull my knees against my chest and curl my toes. The minutes tick by, and the silence bears down on me. I sit, tense and anxious, my gaze darting around the lobby, skirting the shadows that seem alive. My breath quickens. I have no idea what I'll do if I actually come face to face with an intruder. What if he has a weapon?

I jump to my feet with a sudden, desperate desire to get out of here. "What were you thinking, Nyssa?" I loop my shoes around my finger and scurry toward the elevator.

"Where do you think you're going?"

I stop, whirl around, and drop my shoes with a clatter onto the tile.

A boy a few years older than me stands in the doorway of Ward C, silhouetted in eerie blue light that emanates from the hall behind him. He takes one step forward. Slow. Deliberate. Dark hair the same shade as mine falls across his forehead.

"How did you get in there?" Fear makes my voice quake.

"Are you supposed to be down here?" He flashes me a cocky grin and takes another step toward me.

I slide to the left, keeping the desk between us. "They'll catch you, you know." My voice is a little firmer now.

He raises an eyebrow. "We'll see." He tilts his head and takes another step. "Only one way out and you're walking away from it." He jerks his chin toward the elevator that's now somewhere behind my right shoulder.

I eye the still-open door to Ward C. If it's like Ward B, a silent alarm button is mounted in the hall. If I can make it inside before the door automatically closes, I can sound the alarm. The Guard will be here in seconds.

But I have to get there first.

I circle past the door to Ward A, my gaze darting between the boy and the open door to Ward C. Each time I move, he does the same.

With my next step, he lunges toward me, his steps spring-loaded, his face rigid with determination. I skid on the tile in my panic to escape, my heart racing so fast my chest aches. I dash toward the open door that's begun its automatic slow close, adrenaline pushing me forward even while my feet seem to move in slow motion.

His footsteps echo on the tile behind me. I leap through the door and race down the hall. Windows span the left side, offering a glimpse into the secret Ward C labs. Vials and microscopes sit silhouetted in shadows cast by the blue night-lights.

I search the wall for the familiar black alarm button, see it, and slam my hand against it. The stranger tackles me, and we hit the ground. My breath gushes from my mouth. My elbow smacks against the floor, and pain shoots down my arm.

He rolls to the side and stands, his chest heaving, his hands balled into fists at his sides. He glares down at me, and I up at him.

"That's the silent alarm." I scramble to my feet and stumble backward, away from him. My hair hangs in strands around my face, and I push it away with trembling fingers. "The Guard will be here any second."

He glances at the button and steps toward me. I take another step back, glancing over his shoulder at the now-closed door that seals us in together. Terror shrieks through every tense muscle, and I clench my hands into fists, my breath raspy and shallow.

"You have no idea what you've done." He inhales through gritted teeth and takes another step closer. "They're your family, too, you know. And they're going to die." His voice grows louder. "He's killing them all!"

The door bursts open, and two guards hurry inside. One of them is Greer's brother, Gideon. The boy tries to rush around them, but it's pointless. They trap him, throw his arms behind his back, and click metal links around his wrists.

"Take him to Ward B," Gideon says to the other guard. The man starts to walk away, pushing the boy along in front of him, but he plants his feet against the tile and wrestles against the guard's grip with spasmodic, violent twists.

"He's killing them all!" he says again.

Gideon steps forward and slaps the boy so hard he slumps forward. Blood trickles from his nose and pools on his upper lip like a single teardrop before falling to the floor.

"Get him out of here," Gideon orders. The guard kneels to pull the boy's limp body across his back. Then, he shuffles out the door, carrying the boy's dead weight without a word.

Gideon turns to me, his brow furrowed. "You okay, Nyssa?"

"Fine." But I'm not. I'm cold and my legs shake.

Gideon wraps his fingers around my arm. "Let's get you out of here." He guides me out of Ward C, into the lobby, and to the elevator. "You're going to have to explain to the Captain what happened, you know." He keeps his gaze trained on the doors as they close. "And why you were down there in the first place."

I shoot a surprised glance at him. How could I have been so stupid? Of course, I'll have to explain why I was in the Underground instead of at the banquet. But even as that sinks in, I can't help the relief flowing through me. I did what I hoped to do. Pallas can't leave without her escort.

When the doors open on the first floor, I follow Gideon out.

"Banquet's over. You'd better head to your room." He gives me a quick nod and turns to walk away. "I'll be in touch soon," he calls over his shoulder.

I stare at his back until he turns the corner; then I trudge to the elevator that will take me to my room. Once inside, I lean against the wall and close my eyes. I can come up with an explanation. I'm certain of it. After all, I've spent my life lying to everyone I know.

# 8

I drag my feet all the way to my room, shuffle inside, and toss my heels beside the door. They land with a thump that's louder than I expect. I shoot a glance at Ethelind's closed door, but the only sound is the soft hum of her noise machine from inside. My bed seems too far away, and I drop onto the couch, grab the blanket from its back, and stretch beneath it, my head propped on the small turquoise pillow Ethelind found downtown a few years ago.

I don't know how long it will be until I'm summoned to the Captain of the Guard. Hours? A day? I burrow into the soft cushions and squeeze my eyes closed. How can I explain why I was in Ward C at the exact moment a stranger was there? Whatever I decide to say, I know I can't implicate Pallas.

I search my brain for an idea, but I'm so tired. It's warm beneath the blanket, and my eyes grow heavy. I give in and sink into sleep.

I'm awoken hours later by a loud rap on the door. Sunlight peeks through the window above our kitchenette, bathing the common room in the pink hues of dawn. The knock sounds again, and I sit up as last night comes flooding back.

Ethelind's door flies open so hard it bangs against the wall. I turn and meet her gaze. "Don't worry. I'll get it," she says with a scowl as she marches past me. She's dressed in her normal oversize T-shirt, her face scrubbed clean. But her hair is still pulled into a bun from the graduation banquet.

She wrenches the door open, revealing Gideon in the hall, tall and intimidating in his uniform.

Ethelind steps back, one hand on the door. "Can I help you?" Nerves replace her scowl.

Gideon's gaze slides past her and meets mine. So, this is my summons.

My hands grow damp. Even though my mind is still blank, I'm positive about one thing: I can't betray Pallas.

"Time to go," Gideon says. Do I imagine it, or are his normally expressionless eyes sympathetic?

"Go? Go where?" Ethelind turns to me, one eyebrow raised. "What's he talking about?"

I swallow hard and force my legs to move, my feet to touch the floor. "Can I change first?" I hope Gideon sees the plea in my eyes.

He nods. "Hurry."

Ethelind follows me to my room and stands in the doorway, hands on hips, eyes narrowed.

I roll my eyes and turn away to strip off my dress and rummage through my drawers for jeans and a shirt.

"What's going on?" she asks.

"Don't worry about it." I pull my favorite purple shirt over my head, wriggle into my jeans, and turn back to my closet to find my white sneakers with the gray stars on the heels.

Ethelind snorts. "A guard is standing in our doorway at six in the morning, and you're telling me not to worry about it?"

I pull the shoes onto my feet and stride to the door. "Get out of the way." I nudge her to the side with my hip and go into the common room while attempting to pull my hair into a ponytail.

She follows at my heels. "Nyssa! Tell me what's going on!"

I whirl, and she's forced to stop. "I have to go see the Captain of the Guard, okay? It's no big deal." I push past her before she can respond and follow Gideon into the hall, then slam the door behind me.

"You all right?" Gideon asks.

"Oh, I'm great," I say. "I have to explain to the Captain of the Guard why I happened to be in Ward C at the same time someone else broke in. No problem."

We step onto the elevator, and the doors close.

"Tell him you saw someone at the courtyard entrance from the window in the restroom, that you got suspicious, and you decided to investigate on your own rather than disrupt the banquet."

I turn to him in surprise. He's right. The bathroom window looks down at the courtyard door that opens into a secret stairwell to the Underground. The lie is so easy. I study his profile. I can see Greer in the shape of his jaw and the slight ridge in his nose. "Don't you want to know why I was there?"

"I don't want you to tell me anything you don't want me to know."

I raise an eyebrow. "Why are you helping me?"

"We're here," he says in response.

The doors slide open onto the eighth floor, the top of the presidential compound. We step out and turn left. The hall is long and narrow with windows spaced evenly along the left side. I glance out at the familiar rolling grass dotted with wildflowers. Wispy clouds dot the brightening sky.

Gideon stops at a door marked *Captain of the Guard*. He raps twice. The door opens, and a young guard faces us.

"Sir," he says, nodding at Gideon. "There's been a change." He glances at me, then back at Gideon. "President Omri wants to see her. You're expected in his office immediately."

Gideon steers me down the hall and back onto the elevator.

I'm so nervous I can't stay still. I tap my hands against my legs and my foot against the floor. Why does the president want to see me?

"It'll be fine," Gideon says. "Omri's been briefed about the break-in. Probably wants to hear what happened from the only person who saw it."

"I saw someone go into the Underground through the courtyard door," I say. "I didn't want to disrupt the banquet. I decided to investigate on my own."

"Good girl," Gideon says.

The doors open, and we step into the small foyer patrolled by two guards. Gideon nods at them, his hand on my elbow.

"In there." A guard jerks his head toward Omri's office.

Gideon ushers me forward and opens the door.

The moment I step inside, I'm embraced, my face pressed against a warm, bony shoulder. When I'm released, I'm shocked to see it's the first lady. She clasps my hands and smiles.

"Oh!" I say.

Laskin is even more beautiful close up. She's nearly as tall as Omri with thick auburn hair twisted into a bun on top of her head.

She laughs at my surprise. "Omri will join us in a moment." She turns to Gideon. "You may go."

Once the door closes behind Gideon, Laskin pulls me toward the twin chairs that sit in front of Omri's desk and pats the back of one.

"Sit."

I obey, and she sits in the chair beside me, watching me with a strange, small smile. Before either of us can speak, a door to my right opens, and Omri walks in. I jump to my feet and stand at attention.

Omri sits behind the desk. "Sit down, Nyssa." He leans forward and clasps his hands, studying me with the same half smile plastered on Laskin's face. "First, let me congratulate you on your selection as a presidential aide."

I open my mouth to respond, but he gestures for me to be silent.

"I know; I know. We've known this would become your role for a long time now, but it's nice to make it official, eh?" His smile grows.

"Yes, sir. Thank you." In my mind, I rehearse what I'll say when he asks me why I was in Ward C. It's hard to concentrate, though, while he and Laskin stare at me like this.

"Of course, the second reason you're here," Omri says at last, "is because of last night." He leans back and stretches his fingers along the arms of his chair. "I've been briefed by the Guard. But I'd like to hear directly from you what happened." He studies me. "I'm especially interested in why you were in Ward C rather than at the graduation banquet."

"I was in the restroom." I cough and clear my throat. "The window overlooks the courtyard, and I saw someone go in the secret door to the Underground." I wet my lips, my gaze darting between Omri and Laskin. It's unnerving how they don't blink, like two snakes trying to hypnotize me before they strike.

"I assumed it was nothing." I punctuate this with a shrug. "I thought someone probably forgot their bag or something. But I figured I might as well check it out. Everyone was busy at the banquet, and I didn't want to make a scene, so I went on my own. If I'd known it was a real intruder, I never would've gone by myself." I force myself to keep eye contact with Omri. My hands lie motionless on my lap; my legs are crossed at the ankles. But all I want to do is run.

"You see!" Laskin says. She beams at me. "I told you, Omri, she's already proving her worth as a presidential aide apart from"—she lowers her voice—"apart from interpreting your dreams."

Omri's lips lift in that strange smile again. "That does seem to be true." He leans forward and props his arms on the desk. "I have to say, Nyssa, I'm very impressed with your initiative. You seem to have prevented whatever that boy was trying to do."

"You mean he didn't steal anything?" I ask.

Omri raises an eyebrow. "Why would you ask that?"

My throat goes dry again. "I assumed that's what he wanted to do."

"Hmm." A single crease is etched between Omri's brows.

"Oh, Omri," Laskin says. "She's a hero, if you ask me." She pats my knee. "Don't let him scare you, Nyssa. He thinks he needs to be intimidating."

"Laskin." Omri's voice holds a warning.

Laskin leans away from me and folds her hands in her lap. "I'm done." She flashes him a sugar-sweet smile.

Omri shakes his head in exasperation, then turns to me. "That will be all, Nyssa. We look forward to when you officially join Pallas in your new role."

"Thank you, sir." I stand and, with a quick nod, turn and walk toward the door.

"Oh, Nyssa?" Omri says. "One more thing."

I freeze.

"Yes, sir?" I turn back around, hoping my expression reflects confusion rather than fear.

Omri stands and walks to the dream screen, stops in front of it, and ushers me forward. Laskin remains seated, following me with her gaze as I join him.

"Would you be so kind as to watch this one more time and give me your interpretation?" Omri tosses me a smile, then turns it on.

The dream that Pallas lied about appears on the screen. My breath catches in my throat. I turn to him, confused. "Pallas already gave you the interpretation, sir."

He glances at me before returning his gaze to the dream screen. "Ah, so, she didn't tell you."

"Tell me what?" My gaze shifts from him to the screen just as the acorn falls from the tree and lands on the ground. The lamb appears.

"Your interpretation of this dream is your final test," Omri says. "Pallas purposely gave the wrong interpretation so we could determine whether you're able to give the right one on your own. Without her help." He gestures toward the screen. "Now, tell me what this means."

I stare at him a moment too long. Laskin glides to us and places her hand on my arm. "It's true, Nyssa. This is your final test before you become an official dream interpreter."

What they say makes sense, but a knot of doubt twists in my stomach. I stare at the dream, trying to decide what to say.

Laskin rubs my arm. "Your final test, dear."

I turn back to the screen and watch the pine trees grow. They press the oak down into the ground. If Omri and Laskin are telling the truth and I lie, my future could be over. But if they're lying and I give the correct interpretation, I'm signing Pallas's death sentence.

"Nyssa?"

I turn toward Omri, who watches me with an unreadable expression. My hands grow slick with nervous sweat. I wipe them against my jeans. *Why would they deceive you?* a voice whispers in my head. *They have no reason to believe Pallas would lie about the dream. It's a test. Just a test.*

I lick my lips and make my decision. "Two will cause your downfall," I whisper. "They come from the same place. I don't know if that means from the same family or the same city. But they'll work together to overthrow you."

Silence falls. The dream ends. Laskin's fingers fall away from my arm.

I glance at Omri. He stares at the now-blank screen. A muscle twitches along his jaw. The knot of doubt explodes and races down my spine. Heat rises to my cheeks. This is wrong. This is all wrong. Omri turns to me, and I see rage glittering in his eyes.

"You may go." His voice is low. Dangerous.

I turn and flee.

# 9

I have to get to Pallas. I race up the stairs to her apartment and bang on the door. "Pallas!" My voice breaks. I'm terrified that she'll ignore me like she's done all week. I take a deep breath and knock with both hands this time. "Pallas, please open the door!"

It opens. Pallas stands in the doorway in a bathrobe, her hair in a braid that falls across her shoulder. My whole body sags with relief. Before she can speak, I throw myself against her chest and wrap my arms around her neck.

"Nyssa?" Her voice is muffled against my hair.

I release her and step back.

"What's the matter, love?" She pulls me inside and locks the door before guiding me to the window seat on the opposite side of the room.

We sit. The light is beautiful in her home. It radiates through the window and reflects off the vaulted ceiling, stretches to the fireplace and piano, and bounces off the wall that separates this room from her kitchen. But I don't have time to relax or ask her where she's been. I have to tell her what happened.

Her expression doesn't change while I speak; her gaze doesn't leave mine. When I'm finished, I grab her hands. "Tell me it really was a test." I try to laugh, but the sound rings hollow. "I'm being paranoid, right?"

Pallas's eyes are alert and thoughtful. She shakes her hands free of mine and places them on either side of my face. "There was no final test."

My breath catches. All I can do is stare at her, my mouth gaping, my heart beating like a jackhammer in my ears. What have I done? My mind races with a thousand questions. Can I fix this? Can I tell Omri it was a mistake?

I've just implicated Pallas in a crime of treason. She lied to the president, and now, he knows. I have an unexpected urge to laugh. I thought I was protecting her by stopping the boy who broke into Ward C. But somehow, she's still in trouble, thanks to my big mouth.

"If it wasn't a test, why did you lie about the dream?" My voice cracks, and I take a deep breath. "You knew it didn't mean they were going to have a baby."

Pallas opens her mouth to respond, but a noise from the hall distracts her. She places one finger across her mouth and tilts her head to listen. The sound is unmistakable: the thud of steel-toed boots approaching her door. Pallas and I turn and watch the knob twist. But it's locked. A mumbled conversation is followed by a firm pounding on the door that makes me jump.

"Open up, Pallas!" The voice is strong and commanding. "Omri's orders."

Pallas grabs my hand and stands, jerking me to my feet. "Quick, Nyssa. Come with me."

I'm too frightened to argue. She pulls me down the hall that leads to her bedroom, our feet silent on the thick gray carpet.

When we enter her room, she releases my hand and hurries

to a desk that sits against the far wall. She's just stooped and opened the middle drawer when the front door bursts open.

"Pallas!" I glance over my shoulder, terrified. "They're inside!"

Pallas closes the drawer and runs to me. She grabs my shoulders and pushes me toward her closet. "In here and don't make a sound. If they know you're here, they'll arrest you, too."

"Arrest me, too?" Panic makes my voice shrill. "Oh, Pallas, why did you lie about the dream?"

She clasps my face in her hands. "You'll be all right, Nyssa. Sometimes, things don't turn out the way we expect, but that's not necessarily a bad thing." She presses something into my hand and closes my fingers around it. "Show this to Greer. He'll know what to do." She steps out and closes the door.

I stand in darkness, surrounded by Pallas's rose-scented clothes. There are voices in her room, but I can't make out the words. I inch closer to the door, mindful of the shoes I nearly tripped over when Pallas shoved me inside, and press my ear against the door.

*Arrest.*

*Treason.*

So, it's true. Pallas is being arrested for treason, and I'm to blame. I rest my head against the wall. If only she'd explained to me why she lied about the dream, I could have been better prepared when Omri made me interpret it.

I straighten and rub the object Pallas gave me. It's circular and fits securely in my palm. *Show this to Greer. He'll know what to do.* I feel down a length of chain. A necklace? I have no idea why Greer would know anything about jewelry. I itch to open the door so I can see it in the light.

At last, the voices fade, and when the front door slams, I open the closet door and peer out. The room is empty and quiet. I step out and open my hand.

My mouth falls open.

Pallas gave me a gold pendant with a chain laced through the top and a lamb etched in the center. It's identical to the one dropped by the man at the West Gate.

## 10

"He just left for orientation. Sorry," Tyrone says. He's stretched out on the couch in the suite he shares with Greer.

I stand in the doorway, bouncing from foot to foot. "Orientation for what?"

Tyrone shrugs. "Something about the Guard."

I stifle a frustrated groan. The pendant, which is draped around my neck and hidden beneath my shirt, is heavy against my skin. "When will he be back?"

Tyrone eyes me with growing curiosity. "An hour? Two?"

"Know where his orientation is?"

"Downstairs somewhere." He narrows his eyes. "What's going on?"

I turn and close the door behind me without replying, then hurry to the stairs.

When I step out onto the first floor, I don't know where to look. I wander up and down the halls, peering into darkened classrooms. Nobody is around, so I go to the second floor.

It's dark, too, except for light that radiates from one door halfway down the hall. I speed-walk toward it, and when I get closer, I hear the rumble of voices. A peek through the small glass window reveals Greer, slouched at a desk facing a screen at the front of the room. I step away and pace up and down the hall until the door eventually squeaks open. When Greer steps out, I grab his arm.

He rears back, startled. But one glance at my face and he nods. "Outside." He steers me to the stairs, to the first floor, and out into the courtyard. When I start to jog toward the oak, he pulls me back. "Slow down, or someone's going to think something's wrong."

"Something *is* wrong."

"All the more reason to pretend everything's fine." He frowns. "Act normal. We're just going for a walk, okay?"

I glance at the windows that surround us. Greer's right. With all that glass, someone is bound to see us. I nod and follow him into the shade, but when I stop beside the trunk, he shakes his head.

"Nope. This way." He laces my arm through his and pulls me through the courtyard, around the edge of the building, and toward the field of bluebonnets. At last, when we're surrounded by nothing but wildflowers, he turns to me and folds his arms across his chest. "What's wrong?"

I pull the necklace from beneath my shirt.

He takes one look and steps between me and the compound, blocking it from view. "Hide it," he whispers. He glances over his shoulder, then turns back to me. "Where did you get that?"

"Pallas was arrested this morning," I say. Greer's eyes widen. I tuck the pendant beneath my shirt. "She said to show this to you, that you'd know what to do." I have a sudden urge to cry, and I clench my jaw to keep my chin from trembling. "What is it, Greer? Why did she want me to show this to you?"

Greer wipes all expression from his face. "Pallas was arrested?"

I nod.

He stares at a point past my shoulder, chewing on his bottom lip the way he does when he's trying to figure something out. After a few seconds, he nods. "Come on. We have to find Gideon."

Greer and I don't speak on our way back to the compound. We take the elevator to the eighth floor, but instead of turning left toward the Guard's headquarters, we turn right, toward their private rooms.

Gideon opens the door half-dressed. He ushers us in, then continues buttoning his uniform. "I don't have a lot of time." He moves to a small table, sits, and begins to lace his boots. "Shift starts in thirty minutes."

"Show him," Greer says to me.

Gideon freezes, his hands on his laces, and looks up. "Show me what?"

I pull the necklace from beneath my shirt and unfasten it. Then, I hand it to him without a word. He takes it without looking at it and grips it in his fist, the chain dangling between his fingers.

"Don't you want to see what it is?" I ask.

"I know what it is," he says. "Why do you have it?"

"Pallas was arrested this morning," Greer says. "She gave that to Nyssa and told her to show it to me, that I'd know what to do."

"What was the charge?" Gideon asks.

"Treason," I say.

Gideon sits back in his chair and presses his free hand against his cheek. "Think it has anything to do with Maren?" The question is directed at Greer.

Greer shrugs. "I can't think of another reason."

"What are you talking about?" I ask, stiffening. There it is again, people talking about Maren like it still exists.

Gideon turns to me. "Pallas was going to leave the Central

Capital last night. Without permission, I should say. Omri launched a poisonous gas attack on Maren ten days ago, and she was going to leave with the guy sent here to steal the antidote to the gas." He pauses, considering me. "The guy you got arrested," he adds after a moment.

"You're the reason he got arrested?" Greer asks. "How'd you manage that?"

I scowl at him, then turn back to Gideon. "I know about the attack on Maren. I was in the hall outside Pallas's office when someone told her about it. I heard them ask her to leave with that guy, too." I shake my head. "But I still don't understand how Omri can attack a place that doesn't exist. Maren was destroyed fifteen years ago."

"That's partly true," Gideon says. "But it wasn't wiped out by disease like the government claims. The real truth is that Omri ordered Maren to be destroyed. It still exists, but it's been abandoned for years." He pauses to scratch his nose. "The group attacked there a few weeks ago was an advance party sent to see what needs to be done before people can return for good."

I lean against the wall, my mind reeling. "How do you know all this?" I ask Gideon.

"I was in Pallas's office while you were spying from the hall."

My mouth falls open. "What? But I don't... This doesn't..." I take a deep breath. "Who else was there?"

"Not important." He jerks his head at Greer. "But he knows about the attack on Maren, too, and that Pallas was going to leave."

I turn to Greer, eyes wide with shock. "You knew Pallas was going to leave, and you didn't tell me?" I search his face for any hint of remorse, but I can't find any. My whole body tenses as anger flares to life.

Greer's gaze slides away from me, and he crosses the room without replying, sits in the chair across from Gideon, and props his elbows on his thighs. "If Omri found out about

Pallas's plan to leave, one of the exiles could be reporting to him," he says to Gideon. "That would explain how he knew when to attack the group that was in Maren a few weeks ago, too."

"It's possible," Gideon says. "But if that's true, how do we figure out who it is?"

"That's not why she was arrested!" I can't tear my gaze away from Greer, and when he finally looks my way, I shake my head at him. "Why didn't you tell me about Pallas?"

"Why was Pallas arrested, Nyssa?" Gideon asks me before Greer can respond.

I watch Greer for a second longer, my heart beating bruises against my ribs, then force myself to look at Gideon. "If you were part of the group in Pallas's office that day, you know why she agreed to leave, right?" I take a shaky breath. "Because she can interpret dreams?"

Gideon's eyes widen. "Her arrest has something to do with that?"

I nod. "Pallas lied to Omri about a dream he had Wednesday morning. A dream that prophesied his downfall." My eyes dart to Greer. His head is bowed now, but I get the sense he's listening very closely. I turn back to Gideon. "Omri learned the real meaning today, and Pallas was arrested almost immediately."

"How did he learn the truth?" Gideon asks.

"Because of me." I hang my head. "He tricked me, and I told him the true prophecy." My voice catches, and I swallow hard before I force myself to look at Gideon again. "I know telling you all this is breaking the oath of secrecy, but if it can help Pallas, you have to know."

"Wait a second." Greer's head jerks up. "Omri has prophetic dreams?" He looks from Gideon to me. "I knew Pallas used to interpret dreams before the exile, but—" He turns narrowed eyes on Gideon. "Why have you never told me Omri has prophetic dreams?" He turns to me with the same angry glare. "And how do you know about them?"

I raise my eyebrows with smug satisfaction but don't reply. Greer frowns.

Gideon clears his throat. "Pallas's job as Omri's dream interpreter is classified," he says. "The same is true for Nyssa. It was information I was forbidden from sharing."

"But how did you *know*?" Greer asks me. His voice is icy. "How did you know what the true prophecy was?"

I stare at him for a moment, my skin tingling. Part of me wants to rush to him. To grab his hands and look into his eyes and say all of this is stupid, that we made a deal not to argue or be angry anymore. But he lied to me, too. My feet are frozen to the floor.

"Because I can interpret them, too," I say. "I didn't meet with Pallas every week because I was bad at math. I met with her because we were studying Omri's dreams."

Greer's mouth falls open, and he stares at me without blinking.

"Guess you weren't the only one keeping secrets." I cross my arms, hoping he doesn't see my chin wobble.

"I know this is a lot to take in," Gideon says. He glances at his watch. "And we all probably have more questions than answers—especially you, Nyssa—but I have to go."

He holds out my necklace. I take it and trace my finger over the lamb. "What's so important about this, anyway?" I hold it up, my brows raised.

"Pallas can explain better than me." Gideon stands, pulls his jacket from the back of the chair, and puts it on. "I'm on duty in the Underground tonight. If you guys can sneak down there at 5:30, I can get you in to see her." He turns to me. "If Pallas gave you that necklace, she thinks there's something you can do. I just don't know what that is."

"5:30," I say.

Gideon nods, strides to the door, and opens it. He glances back at Greer, who sits with arms folded tight against his chest, staring with a frown somewhere to the left of the door.

Gideon meets my gaze. "Lock the door when you leave." He grabs his hat from a hook on the wall and sets it on his head. "See you tonight."

The moment the door closes behind Gideon, Greer's gaze slides to me. "You lied to me for seven years."

"Me? What about you?" My voice is louder than I intended. I press my lips together and take a deep breath through my nose. "You knew Pallas was going to leave, and you didn't tell me! You knew Maren still exists!"

I want to stomp my foot, to shake him and remind him of what my life has been like. He knows I've always wondered about where I came from. He knows Pallas is like a mom to me. Why would he keep such monumental secrets?

"We're supposed to be best friends." Greer's eyes spark with anger. "You lied to me for seven years about something that's kind of important, don't you think? Do you know how stupid that makes me feel? You and Gideon knew all this stuff, and I was totally clueless."

"Oh, shut up, Greer." Bitter disappointment makes my shoulders sag and my anger dissipate. He doesn't understand me at all, and I guess he never has. It makes sense. He lost his parents when he was young, too, in an accident he's always refused to talk about. But his aunt and uncle raised him and Gideon, and they're good, kind people. They visit at least once a month, and it's obvious how close they are. Greer has no memory of what it's like to be alone.

I sigh and push away the morbid thoughts. "Everything was classified. For me. For you. That's one thing I guess we can agree about."

We stare at each other in silence. His eyes are stony, still angry. But I don't have the energy to fight with him anymore.

At last, he sighs, a loud exhalation that makes me blink and straighten. "I don't want to fight with you," he says.

"It's a little late for that."

Greer's lips twitch, and I don't know whether to be angry or relieved.

"I care about you, Nyss. More than anyone I know. You have to know that." The anger fades from his eyes, and something else takes its place. Something I can't quite put my finger on, but it makes my insides warm. "Have to admit, I'm kind of impressed. You've been hanging out with Omri and interpreting his dreams, huh?" He shakes his head. "You're a better liar than I ever gave you credit for."

I narrow my eyes and am about to reply that he is, too, when he holds up his hands in apology. "I shouldn't have said that." He tilts his head. "Is that why you were upset the other day when you ran away from me? Something to do with Pallas?"

I nod. "I was trying to find her and couldn't. She wouldn't tell me why she'd lied to Omri, and then, I overheard all that stuff outside her office." I sigh again. "Everything's so messed up." I lean back against the wall and close my eyes.

Greer's chair slides on the floor, and his footsteps cross the room. My eyes fly open at the same moment he pulls me into his arms. His head rests on top of mine, and my nose squashes against his shirt. He smells like mint and spice and home. I blink against his collarbone and slowly bring my arms around his back, then turn so my cheek rests against his chest.

"Remember when we were kids and you slipped on the balcony during that ice storm?" Greer's chin moves against the top of my head as he talks.

A surprised laugh escapes my lips. "I broke my wrist."

"Mm-hmm. And you barely complained."

I wince at the memory. "It hurt like crazy though, and when we got caught, you told Pallas you forced me to go."

"Yep. Got a week's worth of detention out of it, too."

I loosen my arms and lean back to look at him. "I'd say I still got the worst punishment, though, don't you think? I was in a cast for six weeks."

Greer looks down at me, and my stomach flips. "You're the strongest person I know, Nyssa," he says. "No matter how rough things get, you always pull through. I promise no more lies from me. Or keeping secrets. We work better as a team, wouldn't you say?"

I smile and nod. "I don't have any more secrets to share anyway."

His gaze falls to my lips and just as quickly pops back up to my eyes. He releases me, steps back, and clears his throat. "We'd better get back to our side of the compound."

I swallow a surprising lump of disappointment and follow him out the door.

# 11

Greer and I step off the elevator into the Underground at exactly 5:30. Gideon is waiting for us.

"There's been a development." Gideon motions us forward, and we follow him to the door to Ward B. "Pallas is being moved to Burgus at six tonight. You'll have exactly fifteen minutes with her. If you're still anywhere nearby when they come to transfer her, we're all in trouble."

"They're taking her to Burgus?" I ask in a whisper. It's the highest security prison in America. "Why?"

"Omri's not taking any risks with her," Gideon says. "She's too valuable."

I inhale to ward off the guilt that winds like a snake through my belly. I wish I could go back in time and change what I told Omri about the dream.

Gideon presses his thumb against the panel, and the door clicks open. He steps back and ushers us inside. "Fifteen minutes. Not a minute more."

I nod and step into Ward B, then turn to make sure Greer's behind me, but he remains next to Gideon in the lobby.

"I'll wait here," he says. "You should have some time alone with her."

I know what he's not saying: that this is my chance to say goodbye to Pallas. She'll likely be executed soon. "Thank you," I whisper over the lump in my throat. I turn to Gideon. "Where is she?"

"Cell 3C. Down the hall, on the right." He steps forward and hands me a black rectangular object with three bumps on one side that form a triangle. "The master key."

It's easy enough to find Pallas's cell. I press the key against a panel on the windowless door. When it opens, I pause in the doorway and wait for my eyes to adjust to the dim light from a bulb on the wall.

Pallas is a shadowy figure on a cot pushed against the far wall. "Nyssa!" She rises with a smile and comes to me, then embraces me before stepping back. "I hoped to see you."

She grabs my hand and leads me back to the cot before I can speak. We sit, and I study her, our hands still clasped. She's as serene as always, a sharp contrast to her dismal cell.

"I'm so sorry, Pallas," I say. "This is all my fault." I start to cry.

"We don't have time for apologies." She squeezes my hand. "I have things to tell you, things that maybe I ought to have told you a long time ago, but it never seemed right."

I'm struck again by the peace on her face despite her circumstances. How can she be so calm?

I wipe my eyes. "Gideon said you could explain everything. I have so many questions."

She smiles again. "Gideon's a good boy. Greer, too. The necklace I gave you—where is it?"

I pat its form beneath my shirt. "Here."

She nods. "Good. It's your key."

"My key?"

Her expression sobers. "It's what we've always called them.

The exiles, that is. Every exile who wants one has an exile key. Yours was created for you when you were a baby, and I've kept it safe for you these past fifteen years. They're keys to our identity. Reminders of where we came from and that one day we'll return."

"You have less than fifteen minutes to explain that to me." I don't mean to be abrupt, but I'm desperate for answers, and time is running out.

Pallas chuckles. "That's my girl, always ready to learn. Alright, then. Let me try to explain. Maren, your home, wasn't destroyed by disease."

"I know that already," I say. "Gideon told me."

"Ah. Did he tell you Maren was once my home, too?"

So, what I'd suspected was true, but I'm not ready to admit to her that I eavesdropped. "What happened there? Gideon said Omri destroyed the city, but he didn't explain why."

"The short story is that, fifteen years ago, Omri attacked Maren because he believed the city was plotting a rebellion to overthrow him."

"Is that true?" My fingers ache in her grip, but she seems oblivious to how tightly her hands clasp mine.

"It's complicated," she says. "Maybe I'd better start a little bit earlier in time, so you understand the whole picture." She clears her throat. "Even though the Western Region is known for its agriculture, it was also home to the best university in America. That university was in Maren. Students came from all over to study." She gives me a small smile. "I was a psychology professor there." The smile vanishes. "About six months before Omri became president—this was before you were born, of course—people in Maren began to have dreams. The dreams occurred among three brothers—no one ever knew why—but it was evident from the beginning that some of the dreams meant something.

"One of those brothers was a neuroscientist who taught at

the university's medical school, and together with several of our engineering professors, he developed the electrode that recorded dreams while the dreamers were sleeping. They could then be uploaded onto a screen for us to watch."

"The dream screens," I say.

"Yes." She releases my hand at last, and I stretch my fingers. "I happened to be present when one of the dreams was played," Pallas says. "It was as though I had walked into my own destiny. I knew immediately it warned us about the future."

She pauses for a breath. "To keep track of the dreams and what they foretold, we created a top-secret department to study them and keep record of any prophecies we might learn." Her eyes crinkle. "You were born during this time. I met you when you were a chubby little two-year-old. Hair as wild then as it is now. Your mother—"

"You knew my mother?" I sit up straighter. "Why didn't you ever tell me that?"

Pallas presses her hand against my cheek. "Oh, sweetie. There are so many things I wish I could've told you over the years, but I was forbidden to speak of them. Let me finish explaining, okay?"

I nod and take a shaky breath.

She pats my cheek once then clasps her hands in her lap. "Your mother brought you to me because she was concerned about you. You were experiencing some unusual neurological things. She claimed you couldn't sleep, that every time you closed your eyes, all you saw were objects racing across your brain. If I remember correctly, you frequently saw milk bottles dancing with one other.

"Frankly, I found it fascinating. I ran some tests similar to those you took before you were admitted to the Presidential Education Program and realized you had a gift."

She pauses, as though expecting me to speak. I raise one

eyebrow but say nothing. Time is ticking, and I want to know everything.

"You had an innate ability to match emotions to images and explain the meaning behind symbols on a screen," she continues. "My brothers gave permission for you to study their dreams and—"

"Wait a second," I say. "The three brothers who had the dreams—they're *your* brothers?"

Pallas's face lights up. "Did I not mention that? Yes. Asaph, Zeb, and Thaddeus. I haven't seen them in a long time. Thaddeus and Zeb weren't at the university the day we were taken, and Asaph—he was the neuroscientist who created the dream screen—fled just before Omri attacked. He went to a place in the Western Region called Cardiff." She frowns. "In fact, his grandson—my grandnephew—was here in the compound until recently."

"What happened to him?" I ask.

"He was a scientist here, one of the three who escaped from Ward C a few weeks ago. Somehow, he wasn't caught with the others." A worried crease mars her forehead. "I'm so thankful he hasn't been found."

"Where could he be?"

She shrugs. "I hope he's found his way to his grandfather, but I don't know for certain." She closes her eyes a moment, shakes her head, and opens them. "Let me get back to it, shall I?"

I nod.

"I told your parents I wanted to train you to become a dream interpreter. They were hesitant at first. You were so young, and there were rumors about a mole in the dream department, that Omri had learned about us, and that he believed we were plotting a rebellion against him." She pauses and shakes her head again. "I didn't believe the rumors. I'd seen nothing in the dreams to indicate an imminent rebellion or that we might be in any danger."

She sighs. "I realized too late that I'd become too dependent on prophecies and failed to see signs of problems in the real world. Your parents were worried about what they were hearing. They wanted to leave, flee somewhere else like others were doing. I talked them out of it." She bows her head. "I regret it to this day."

She's silent for a moment, and I resist the urge to shake her. We can't have more than a few minutes left.

"Omri attacked Maren not three weeks later," she says, her voice quieter now. "The Guard came and forced everyone at the university to march to the Central Capital. Every professor. Every student. We became exiles in our own country. Forbidden to stay in our home. Forced to begin new lives in an unfamiliar place.

"You were with me that day, and I couldn't safely return you to your parents, so you came with us." She pauses. "We crossed the whole valley and the mountains to get here. Some died along the way."

She grips my hand again. "And now, we get to the part where I explain why I couldn't tell you anything about your past." She gazes at me with steady, unblinking eyes. "I fought for you when we got here. I begged to be able to keep you with me. But I had no proof you belonged to me. You were placed into the orphanage, and I was forced to enter the president's service. I was thankful that you were at least kept here inside the compound so I could keep an eye on you." A sudden smile lights her face. "And then, a true miracle happened! Your middle grade test scores and entry into the Presidential Education Program were the perfect opportunity for me to take you back under my wing. But it was on condition I never revealed anything to you about your past." She releases my hand and sits back, watching me with an expectant look.

"Thank you for telling me all of this." I don't know what else to say. It's hard to comprehend everything all at once. And something else is bothering me, something important that she hasn't mentioned. "What happened to everyone left behind after Omri attacked Maren? After you—the exiles, I mean—were forced to come to the Central Capital?"

Pallas inhales sharply through her nose, and when she exhales, her whole body deflates. "As we were marched away, the Guard burned everything to the ground, so there was no food supply." Her voice is quiet and sad. "They destroyed all transportation in and out of the town and forbade all of the surrounding cities and towns from providing aid to those left behind. They even threatened to shoot on sight anyone who helped refugees who fled to other places." She sighs. "We always assumed everyone starved or the Guard killed them after we were taken."

"But why was Omri so cruel?" I whisper. I try to stop myself from imagining the horrible deaths my family might have faced on Omri's orders.

"Because the rumors were true. We never found out who, but there *was* a mole. Omri learned of a dream my brothers had and was told it meant the city was planning a rebellion."

"But you said you didn't see any dreams that showed a rebellion," I say.

"Omri didn't know that. He believed what he was told." Pallas rubs her temples. "The dream Omri learned about did indicate a rebellion could occur sometime in the future, but I'm absolutely positive no one in Maren posed an immediate threat to him. We had no plans to try to fight him at that time. Of course, that didn't matter. Our entire existence was too risky to him, so he destroyed us."

We're silent for a few seconds. My fifteen minutes are definitely over, but I can't make myself leave.

"Now, however, things are changing," Pallas says. "It's

almost as though Omri's decision to destroy Maren all those years ago was the catalyst that began his downfall."

"That doesn't make sense," I say.

She tilts her head and taps her chin the way she always does when she's trying to decide how to explain something. "When we—the exiles—were forced to leave Maren, we left behind everything we loved. Our families. Our friends. Our homes. And like I said, we assumed the people we left behind died. When we arrived in the Central Capital, we were forbidden from ever talking about our past, from being anything other than who we were told to be."

Pallas stops, and her gaze becomes intense. "That's when the seed of bitterness began to grow. The exiles' hatred toward Omri has exploded during the past fifteen years."

I sit up straighter as the pieces start to fall into place. "So, the rebellion that Omri was afraid of fifteen years ago is actually happening now?" I study Pallas. "I'm right, aren't I? That's why you lied to Omri about his dream the other night. You didn't want him to know the dream warned about his downfall. You *want* him to be overthrown." I stand and look down at her. My whole body tingles.

Pallas lifts her chin. "The dream Omri had is almost identical to the dream my brother Asaph had fifteen years ago, the one Omri used as an excuse to destroy Maren." Pallas hesitates for a moment, then sighs. "When I saw Omri's dream, I knew the time was coming—sooner rather than later—when those of us who have been oppressed for too long will rise up against him."

"But how do you know that? And when will it happen?" I shake my head. "Don't the exiles have a good life here?" I clamp my mouth closed. Pallas is an exile, and she's in prison.

"It would take too long to explain how I know," Pallas says. "But to answer your other question, yes, some of the exiles have accepted our life here—that's true. But most of us long for

Maren. You were too young when it happened. You can't understand what it's like to be forced from your home and denied
your identity.

"Over the past few years, the exiles have learned that some
of those left behind after the attack actually survived. Quite a
few, in fact. You have no idea how overwhelming it was to learn
that. I knew that Asaph was all right, of course. He and I
manage to communicate, though not often. But I learned that
my brother Zeb is alive, too."

"And Thaddeus?" I ask.

"Ah. That brings me to a fascinating point. The exiles and
the survivors have developed a communications network of
sorts. I don't get very involved; it's difficult for me to directly
communicate given my closeness with the president. But I hear
things every now and then, and I learned that the survivors fled
to the mountains after the attack and created a city there that's
completely unplottable. They call it Fortune's Fall—and Omri
has no idea it exists." She smiles, but it quickly fades. "I
recently learned that my brother Thaddeus is there, in
Fortune's Fall. But I also learned the survivors hope to return to
Maren—which also confirms what I suspected after I saw
Omri's dream: there's a plot brewing to bring Omri down."

Pallas pauses for breath, and it's in that moment of silence
that something dawns on me. I take a step backward, my gaze
boring into hers. "You found out people survived the attack
fifteen years ago." I take a shaky breath. "What about my
family? Did they survive, too?"

Pallas doesn't reply at first, then nods. "Yes, I have reason to
believe they're alive. But there's more."

"More?" I clench my hands at my sides. My family is alive.
It's so unexpected I can't make sense of it.

"A few weeks ago, a group from Fortune's Fall traveled to
Maren—likely to see whether a permanent return was possible
—but they were attacked when they arrived." Her gaze is steady

on me. "Your brother, Jek, was sent here to steal the antidote to save those caught in the attack. But he was caught and arrested."

The reality of all she's said hits me, and my stomach lurches. "Jek was the one I got arrested?"

"You?" Her eyes widen.

I nod. "I heard you in your office that day talking about the attack on the group in Maren, about someone coming here for the antidote. You agreed to leave with him. With Jek." A laugh of shock and horror escapes my lips. "I waited for him in the Underground, and I called the Guard. I thought if he couldn't leave, neither could you." I sink to the cold concrete floor, my gaze settling somewhere on the dark wall behind Pallas. Not only am I responsible for Pallas's arrest, but I'm the reason my brother is in prison, too. If they're executed... I pull my knees to my chest and bow my head against them. How do I live with myself if that happens? I'm cold suddenly, and it hurts to breathe. "What have I done?"

"Oh, Nyssa." Pallas's voice is sad. "I'm sorry for so many things. Not telling you about your family in particular." She sighs. "And I'm sorry I wasn't going to tell you goodbye. I'm not very good at them, you know, and I couldn't bear the thought of leaving you behind, but I felt it was my duty to go. There's been a new dream, you see, and I was asked to go and interpret it. It could be critical for our survival, for our ultimate return to Maren."

I sense her hesitation, and when I look up, I find her watching me, lips pursed. "What is it?" I ask.

"You ought to know that your parents were with the group attacked at Maren," she says. "Without the antidote—"

"They'll die," I say. I wrap my arms tighter around my legs. "He warned me. Jek, I mean. Before the Guard arrested him, he screamed at me. He said, 'They're your family, too! They're going to die!'" My breath catches on a gasp, and my chest tightens. "I didn't know he was my brother. I didn't know he was talking about my family." I hide my face in my hands. "I've ruined everything."

"It's not ruined yet," Pallas says, and something in her voice makes me look up at her. She gazes at me with an intensity I've never seen. "Take my place, Nyssa. Get your brother out of here, and get the antidote to the survivors, to your family. Save them, and be the dream interpreter they need."

# 12

I step out of Pallas's cell and close the door, then turn and lean my forehead against the cool steel. This was probably the last time I'll ever see her, and it hits me like I've been rammed by a truck.

I slide to the floor and bury my head in my hands. Part of me wants to stay here and let the Guard find me. I deserve to be caught and punished for everything I've done.

But my family is alive, and another part of me wants to try to save them. I lean back and wipe my eyes. "Don't be stupid, Nyssa," I mutter to myself. I can't do what Pallas asked of me. My entire future would be ruined; I could be executed if I'm caught. I *will* be executed if I'm caught, because Omri isn't the merciful type.

"Nyssa!"

I look up to see Greer hurrying down the hall with a worried frown.

I take a deep breath and push to my feet. "I'm coming."

He grabs hold of my arm and jerks me back in the direction he came. "Gideon's freaking out. You were supposed to be back ten minutes ago."

"Ow! Geez, I'm sorry, okay?" I wrench my arm out of his grip and jog beside him. "Are we going to make it?"

He glances at his watch. "It'll be close."

The door to the lobby opens before we reach it to reveal Gideon standing wide legged beyond. He stretches his hand out to me. "Give me the master key before you forget."

I hand it over.

He slips it into his pocket and gestures for us to follow him past the desk to a door a few feet to the right of the elevator. "You'll have to take the stairs up to the courtyard. Elevator's too risky now."

The three of us step through the door into a brightly lit stairwell, and Gideon pulls the door shut behind us. Greer leaps up the first few stairs, and I'm about to follow when Gideon grabs my arm.

"Hang on," he says.

I pause, my foot on the first step, my hand resting on the banister, and peer over my shoulder at him.

"How did it go?" he asks.

A crazed laugh explodes out of me before I can stop it. I swivel so that we're face to face. "Oh, it was great. Let's see—my parents are still alive, so there's that. Pallas wants me to help get that guy who broke into Ward C out of prison and leave the Central Capital with him. Oh, and the best part? That guy is my brother." I laugh again. It's manic and panicky. "So, to sum up: Pallas is in jail. My brother is in jail. Both of them will probably be executed, and it's all my fault. My parents will probably die unless I save them. Any more questions?"

Gideon studies me so intently the back of my neck begins to burn. Does he sense that my heart is screaming at me to do what Pallas asked because going means I'll be reunited with a family I've believed was dead for fifteen years? But does he also sense the warning my brain wails on repeat about the consequences of breaking the law?

Greer descends to where I stand and grabs my hand. When his fingers lace through mine, my gaze darts to his face, but I don't pull away. He's comfort and familiarity in a spinning new reality.

"What did you tell her?" Greer asks. His voice is quiet, but I sense an underlying excitement.

"I told her no!" I say. "It's insane." Greer and Gideon exchange a glance, and I turn my glare to Gideon. "You think I should have said yes?"

They're both silent, and it sends me over the edge. I wrench my hand free of Greer's and throw both of mine into the air. "I can't do this! I have a life here! A plan! She thinks I should throw it all away?" But even as I say the words, my heart grows louder. *Your parents will die if you stay here. You're the reason Pallas is in prison.*

"I can't do this," I repeat, but uncertainty is obvious in my voice.

Greer wraps his arm around my shoulder. "Come on, Nyss. Let's get you back to your room."

I let him guide me up the stairs. I don't look at Gideon again. Every step pulls me farther from Pallas, away from everything she said and asked of me. My legs are heavy, and I have to force myself to climb.

"Why do you and Gideon know so much about everything Pallas told me?" I ask Greer at the top of the stairs.

Greer stares at the wall. A muscle twitches along his jaw. "There's something about me you don't know." He glances at me, then returns his gaze to the wall. "Our aunt and uncle who raised us—" He pauses and clears his throat. "They're not really our aunt and uncle."

My mouth falls open, but I'm too dumbstruck to say anything.

"Gideon and I are from Maren, too." Greer's voice is quiet, and I have to strain to hear him. "Our parents were killed when

Omri attacked Maren. Somehow, Gideon got us out of there, and an incredible family in the Central Region raised us. They're the aunt and uncle you've always believed to be mine. They even forged fake documents claiming we were related. They made us keep our real names, though, even when Gideon thought we should change them. They said we should always remember where we came from, and the Guard would never know so long as we didn't tell them."

"I can't believe it." I press my clammy hands against my cheeks. "Anything else you want to tell me while you're at it?"

He gives me a withering look. "I'm sorry, okay? I know we said no more secrets, but this one—" He shakes his head. "This one isn't about just me. They could still be arrested if the Guard finds out. Besides, we had enough to fight about earlier, don't you think?"

I don't reply.

He sighs. "I don't remember any of the bad stuff that happened before they took us in, but Gideon does. And he made sure every day to remind me of it. Every day that we've been here, forced to live a life we didn't choose, to pledge allegiance to a president who murdered our family." He looks down at me, and I see in his eyes something I've never seen in him before: hatred.

"When Gideon learned about the network between the exiles and the Maren survivors, he started helping the exiles escape to Fortune's Fall." He scowls. "I didn't want anything to do with it at first. I'm like you—I wanted to move on, stay alive. But Gideon kept hearing stories from people through the network. Stories about torture. People arrested all over the country for no reason. Kids taken away from their parents. That's what did it for me, knowing that innocent kids were being ripped away from their parents. So, I've started to get involved when I can."

"But why is this happening?" I ask.

"Because of Maren," Greer says in a flat voice. "Ever since he learned Maren was planning a rebellion, Omri's grown more and more paranoid that people want him gone. So, whenever he hears that someone doesn't like a law or a speech he's made, he has them thrown in prison. That's the way it is now. *Victores in obsequio.*" His voice drips with disdain. "More like *obey or die.*" He gives a derisive snort. "The great country of America."

I consider this. "Why haven't I ever heard about it?" I finally ask.

"Why would you?" He glances at me from the corner of his eye. "We're the elite, remember? Raised with the best, hidden away from regular people. There's nothing here in the compound—or in the Central Capital really—that would make you think things aren't what they seem."

I don't want to hear any more. I want to sink into my bed and lie there until tomorrow. Tomorrow, the sun will shine, and Ward B will be a fuzzy memory.

I chew on my bottom lip. Tomorrow won't change the fact that Pallas is in prison. Or my brother. And my parents—could I really see them again? I sigh. This is all too much to think about. I reach toward the door, but Greer wraps his hand around mine before I can turn the knob. I can feel his gaze on me, but I keep mine focused on the door.

"You have a choice, Nyssa," he says. "You could see your family again and save a whole lot of people. You could help us get back to Maren."

"Why does everyone care so much about Maren?" I ask. "Nobody's lived there for fifteen years."

Greer's grip tightens, and the knob presses into my palm. "Wouldn't you want to go back to your real home if you could?"

"Omri will never let people go back. Not after what happened."

"He might not have a choice in the end."

I close my eyes. "I can't do it. I'm sorry."

Greer is quiet for a moment; then, he steps away from the door. "After you." His voice is sad.

---

MY ROOM IS HOT, and I can't sleep. Ethelind's noise machine hums from across the common room, teasing me with its lullaby. But my brain is too wired, my body too hot. I kick the covers from my legs, then go to the window and watch the lights blink from the billboards downtown. Omri's portrait is lit with an ominous glow from the words that scroll beneath his face. *Victores in obsequio.* The words taunt me, and I force my gaze away, toward the dark plains that stretch beyond the Central Capital. Somewhere out there is a whole network of people from the same place as me. Somewhere out there are my parents. And my brother is here with me in the compound.

I press my forehead against the windowpane, wishing it were cold instead of sticky warm. I have a brother. What would it be like to reunite with my real, blood-related family? "It doesn't matter," I whisper. But it does. To have a mom and a dad. A different life from what's been planned for me. "It's crazy, Nyssa," I say out loud. "Don't think about it anymore."

But I can't help the flutter in my chest. The prickling of my skin. My family is alive. *Alive.* I still can't believe it. Can I stay here knowing they'll die because I refused to try to save them?

*Of course you can't.*

I step back from the window, my skin sticking to the glass like a suction cup before popping loose, and turn to survey my room. Shoes. Clothes. I could have them on and be out the door in a matter of minutes. What are my chances of actually making it to Fortune's Fall? Not high. Then again, according to Pallas, there's a network helping people get there. True, some people have been caught. But what if I'm not?

"Can I really do this?" I say aloud to my empty room. I scan the furniture. The walls. My messy bed. It's all so familiar to me after seven years that I usually overlook the paisley on the quilt and the stain on the rug, where an exhausted Ethelind tripped and dropped an entire pan of accidentally undercooked brownies one night. We ate them anyway. A mud puddle laced with carpet fibers, scooped up with spoons and laughed about later. I blink, and the memory is gone.

"I'm going to do this." I turn toward my closet, grab a shirt, and pull it over my head.

"I have to do this for my family." I zip my jeans.

"For Pallas." I tie my shoes.

I'm a robot. Don't think. Just act.

"I'm going to do this," I repeat.

If I stop talking, if I stop moving, the likelihood of failure will paralyze me. I pull my hair into a ponytail and open the door, tiptoe across the common room and into the hall. The door closes behind me without a sound. It's not that late, maybe 10:00 p.m., but we have a 9:30 p.m. curfew. The hall is empty and silent. I jog around the corner and enter the boys' side.

Greer opens his door after one knock. His gaze meets mine for a second before his drifts down my body and back up. "Going somewhere?"

A nervous laugh explodes from my lips. All I can do is nod.

A smile darts across his face, and he leans against the door-frame like we're chatting about weekend plans. "It won't be easy, you know." He wiggles his eyebrows.

"I figured." I know he's testing me, seeing whether I'm really going to go through with it.

"It's going to be a long trip. No fancy beds. No one around to make you food."

"What's your point?" I hope my eyes show defiance instead of fear.

He shrugs. "No point." He straightens and starts to turn into his room, then stops. "I almost forgot." He pulls a chain from beneath his shirt and holds it out for me to see. "I'm coming with you."

I smile when I see what it is. A pendant just like mine. "I hoped you'd say that," I whisper. "I don't want to do this without you."

His smile returns—only this time, it lingers. "Give me one minute."

## 13

"**G**ideon thought you might change your mind," Greer says as we descend the stairs to the courtyard.

I glance over at him. "What did he do?" My voice is wary.

He opens the door, and we step outside. The humidity blankets us, and I smooth my hair before it can explode into a frizzy mess. As we sidle along the brick facade, I listen to the hum of cicadas that have recently swarmed the oak tree. It's a comfortable summer sound, and an unexpected surge of grief floods through me for what I'm about to leave behind.

Greer stops at the door to the Underground and pats his pocket. "He slipped me a copy of the master key before he rotated over to patrol Ward A."

I sense he's not telling me the whole story, but I can't see his face in the darkness. "Anything else?"

A pause. "He might've drugged the new guard's coffee so he'd be knocked out if you decided to sneak back into the Underground."

"Greer! That guy's going to get in so much trouble! Not to mention Gideon if he gets caught."

"You have a better plan?" He presses the key into the panel beside the door.

I'm silent.

"Didn't think so." Greer pushes the door open, and we hurry inside and down the stairs to the next door. When I move to step inside, Greer holds his hand out to stop me. "Wait. Let me make sure he's nice and unconscious." He peeks inside, then motions me forward. "All clear."

We pass the guard slumped over his desk. Will he be arrested—or worse—when Omri learns he was the one on duty when we broke someone out of prison? I hurry past. I can't think about that.

Greer unlocks Ward B, and we scurry inside. I gaze down the long hallway with its closed doors on either side. Will I be thrown into one of them soon? I swallow hard. It's not too late. I don't have to go through with it. I can go back to my room and pretend none of this happened.

"You're making the right choice," Greer says, reading my mind. He grabs my hand and pulls me forward.

*As long as you're with me*, I silently add. When we come to Pallas's door, I tug on Greer's hand to make him stop.

"She's already been transferred," he says.

"I know." I press my fingertips against her door, wishing I could see her one more time. Wishing she could come with us. But I know we can't linger, and after a moment, I allow Greer to pull me away.

"We're here." Greer stops at a door at the end of the hall with the number six on it. He peers down at me, the key hovering above the panel. "Ready?"

I nod, though my hands have begun to sweat. There's really no turning back now.

The door clicks open, and Greer pushes it wide enough for us to step inside. The air is stale, the light gloomy. I pinch my nose as I survey the tiny space. It's bare except for the boy—Jek

—who's curled in a ball in the corner. Alarmed, I step forward, my hand outstretched to touch him. But just as I move, Greer clears his throat, and Jek jumps to his feet, fists out, eyes alert and wary. I scamper backward, straight into Greer. He puts his hands on my shoulders, and we stand like that, frozen, staring at Jek.

"What are you doing here?" Jek glares at me, nostrils flaring.

My heart drums in my chest, but I'm not afraid. I study him with a new perspective. We have the same dark hair, but his eyes are brown where mine are green. "Are you really Jek?" I ask.

"I really am."

We stare at each other for a moment.

"Did you know I was your sister?"

He continues to stare at me in silence. "I had my suspicions," he says at last. "But there's one way to know for sure."

I raise an eyebrow. "How?"

He leans down, pulls his pant leg up and his sock down. He points to the inside of his ankle. "If we're really brother and sister, you have it, too."

"Two lines," I whisper. I squat, push up my jeans leg, and pull my sock away from my ankle to trace the mysterious tattoo. A glance up shows he's seen it, too. "I never knew what they were for."

"One for me, one for you," he says. "Our mom had them tattooed onto us when we were babies. Even then, before things started happening, she was prepared for the worst. She thought, if we were ever separated, we could know each other by those marks."

Fifteen years have made us strangers, and I don't know what to say. I'm more curious than anything, and I stare at him, trying to picture what our life was like. Did we play together? Did we fight?

"What are you doing here?" he repeats. "It's not like you can have me arrested again."

I frown. "I didn't know you were my brother when I did that!"

"Would knowing have changed what you did?"

I open my mouth to reply, then close it. I'm not going to admit I don't know the answer to his question. But my silence is answer enough.

Greer steps to my side and puts a placating hand on my arm. "We're getting you out," he says to Jek.

Jek's attention shifts to Greer. "You look familiar."

Before Greer can respond, Jek winces and presses his hands to his forehead. He takes deep, shaky breaths while Greer and I watch in silence. After a few seconds, his breathing quiets, and he drops his hands. "Sorry. This place has given me some pretty nasty headaches. They pop up out of nowhere and go away just as fast."

"I can't imagine what it's like in here." Greer holds out his hand. "Greer Rines. I think you know my brother, Gideon."

"Oh, yeah. Good guy, your brother. Is he going to help get me out of here, too?"

"Not exactly," Greer says. "It's just us."

"And we're coming with you," I say.

Jek's eyebrows soar into his hairline. "You had me arrested, and now, you want to break me out and leave with me?" He laughs once, and I wince at its bitter edge. "I find that hard to believe."

"I thought our parents were dead." I lift my hands in apology. "Do you have any idea what it's like to believe that for fifteen years and then be told they're actually alive? Please. I want to see them again."

Jek studies me through narrowed eyes. Finally, he sighs. "Listen. I'm all about 'Stay low and go.' That's my thing. If you think you can move fast, stay under the radar, then fine." He smiles, then shrugs. "I want our parents to see you again, too." He touches his wrist and frowns. "What time is it?"

Greer glances at his watch. "10:15."

"I don't know how much you know." Jek rakes his hand through his hair, making it stand up in different directions. "But I have to get somewhere fast. A lot of people are depending on me, and I need to be on the midnight train to the Western Region."

"That doesn't give us a lot of time," Greer says, "especially if we still have to get into Ward C and get the antidote."

Jek's eyebrows disappear again beneath his hair. "So, you know about that."

Our silence is all the answer he needs. A grin spreads across his face. "I already have it."

"There's no way you had the antidote and kept it hidden from the Guard when they arrested you," I say. "They would've found it when they searched you." I pause, tilting my head to study him. "How'd you actually get into Ward C, by the way?"

"No time to explain the details." He turns to Greer. "How do we get out of here?"

I frown at Jek. "Wait a second. I want to see the antidote before we go anywhere."

"No way," he says.

"We're not leaving until you prove you actually have the reason we're both risking our lives to get you out."

Greer smiles. "Girl has a point." He holds out his hand and wiggles his fingers. "Show us the treasure."

Jek rolls his eyes. "Don't say I didn't warn you."

He lifts his shirt, then peels back a small segment of skin on his stomach like he's opening a container. A burst of cool air hits me in the face. I step back, startled, and swallow hard against the sudden urge to throw up.

Jek grins. "Sorry you asked?" He pulls a vial from the cavity and holds it out for me to see. "There's your antidote." He sets it back inside and presses his skin back together.

"What is that?" Greer asks in fascination.

"Fake skin with a container attached. It wraps around my entire torso. Makes my pants a little tight, but there's no way to know it's not part of my own body unless you're me or the guy who made it." He pats the section that holds the vial. "That little compartment is like a freezer, and it's insulated so I don't feel a thing. Have to keep the antidote at a consistent temperature; otherwise, it's useless."

I turn away from Jek with a grimace. "How are we getting out of here?" I ask Greer.

Greer stares at Jek a moment longer before turning to me. "There's a tunnel from the end of this hall all the way to the arena. It's how they transport prisoners on execution days. We'll hike it back to the city center from there and then to the Central Hub to catch the train."

My mouth falls open. "But that's miles! We'll never make it by midnight."

"Guess we'd better hurry, then, huh?" Jek gives me a wry smile, then nods at Greer. "Lead the way."

Jek and I follow Greer out of the cell and hurry to a windowless door at the end of the hall. I hold my breath as Greer slides the master key against the panel to unlock it. Jek hops from one foot to the other beside me.

The lock clicks, and the door swings inward, revealing absolute darkness. We step inside, and the door closes behind us.

"Give me a second," Greer mutters.

A beam of light appears from a small flashlight he now holds. The tunnel is vast and cavernous. The ceiling is somewhere above us, but all I see is black. Greer shines the light to our left, revealing three open-sided government jeeps parked in a row.

"Nice!" Jek says.

Greer hands the flashlight to Jek, then slides into the driver's seat of the nearest one and pulls the master key from his pocket. "Shine the light on the dashboard," he says to Jek.

Once he can see, Greer presses the key into a center indentation and pushes a circular button next to the steering wheel. The jeep murmurs to life with a gentle hum.

"Ha!" Greer says. "That was almost too easy." He gestures for us to hurry. "Get in!"

Jek jumps into the passenger side, and I climb into the back behind Greer.

We take off, and I lurch to the side, my fingers wrapped around the metal bar that frames the door. The jeep is fast. What would have been at least an hour on foot will take less than ten minutes.

Greer slows to a stop near two steel doors at the end of the tunnel. We hop out, and I walk slowly forward. Will the Guard lead Pallas out of these doors as a prisoner? Will she be forced to listen to the morbid cheers of the crowd that waits to see her die? My knees give way, and I tip forward. But I steady myself before anyone notices and force my attention on Greer.

He places the master key against the now-familiar panel, and the doors move slowly outward. The arena comes into view. It's empty and eerie in the dark.

"This way." Greer begins to run, leading us halfway around the circumference toward the south entrance. The moon is a sliver, but it's bright enough to light our way. He opens the door, and we race inside, across the cool concrete interior, out another door, and into the dusty lot outside.

We've just stepped onto the road that leads downtown when the citywide alarm begins to blare. We stumble to a stop, panting, and stare at one another.

"What's that for?" I ask once I've caught my breath, but I'm pretty sure I know the answer.

"What do you think?" Jek asks. He's doubled over, his hands on his thighs, his face puckered in a grimace.

"Are you alright?" Greer leans down and pats his shoulder.

"My head again. It'll pass." He stands. "How long do you think we have until the Guard's searching for us?"

"They started searching five minutes before that alarm began," Greer says.

"I figured." Jek turns and gestures for us to follow him. "It's too risky to go straight to the Central Hub. Follow me. I know where we can go."

He takes off, and Greer and I follow without a word. My heart pounds, and my legs are tight and tired. I try not to think. Thinking will make me panic, and there's no time for that.

Just before we reach the city center, we veer off the main road and onto an empty side street. The alarm is louder here. It vibrates in the air and sinks into my skull. We follow close on Jek's heels, too scared to ask where we're going. I glance behind me, the hairs on the back of my neck standing on end as I search the darkness for any sign of the Guard.

At last, Jek skids to a stop in front of a restaurant. I survey the brick facade and the scrawled sign—*Talos's Place*—tacked above the door. "I've seen this place before," I say. It's the bustling restaurant I saw from the tram the day Greer and I came into the city. It's strange to see it quiet and empty when my memory of it is full of music and people.

Jek kneels to the left of the door, his back to us, and when he stands, my gaze wanders to where he knelt. Something catches my eye in the moonlight, and I squat to see it better.

"Greer!" I motion for him to bend down. "Look!" A circle is carved into the wood, and inside it is a lamb.

Greer kneels beside me and traces the lamb with his finger. A glance at him shows he's smiling. "It's a safehouse."

"Hurry!" Jek pushes open the door and motions for us to follow him inside. He locks the door behind us, and we stand in darkness. The alarm continues to wail, though from inside it's more a ghostly, muted echo.

The distant rumble of a vehicle grows louder. Since personal cars are prohibited downtown, it must be the Guard. I reach for Greer's hand, find it, and squeeze.

"Where's the kitchen?" Jek mutters. His footsteps move away. Something clatters to the floor, and the noise is deafening in the quiet.

A light pops on through a doorway just beyond where Jek is sprawled on the floor, scowling at a toppled chair. The alarm stops with frightening abruptness, and footsteps patter above us and then down a set of creaky stairs beyond our sight.

"Thank goodness." Jek stands and disappears through the door.

The roar of the Guard's vehicle is close, maybe a few blocks away. The hairs on the back of my neck rise in anticipation of a knock on the door and a command to open up. Greer and I hurry after Jek into a small kitchen as a man descends a staircase in the back corner.

I gasp. It's the man who collided with Greer at the West Gate.

He gestures to us, his arms jiggling in his white shirtsleeves. "Get in here, quickly. They'll be at the door any minute." He turns to the cabinets that line the wall beneath the sink, bends, and opens one. Then, he turns back to us. "In here."

"Is he serious?" I mutter to Greer. "He wants us to hide under the sink?"

At that moment, a knock sounds on the front door, followed by the ominous "Open up!"

"'Stay low and go,' remember?" Jek says with a wink. He falls to his knees, crawls inside, and disappears to the left.

Greer drags me to the cabinet. I follow Jek's lead and, with a deep breath, inch inside and turn to the left, expecting to be squashed beside him. Instead, I find myself in a short—and empty—tunnel. At its end is a gaping hole from which dim light radiates. Curious, I crawl toward the light, with Greer close behind, and into a small, low-ceilinged room.

Jek sits on a broken-down couch against the far wall, a satisfied grin plastered on his face and Greer's flashlight in his hand. The room has a concrete floor, and the scent of onions is almost overpowering, though there's an underlying sweet smell that makes it bearable.

"So, this is a safehouse." Greer stoops and looks around with interest. "Gideon told me about them, but I've never seen one before."

I hunch beside him, one hand pressed against the ceiling, and look around, too.

Jek's grin widens. "Pretty cool, huh? There are only a few in the Central Capital, but there are a bunch more between here and Fortune's Fall."

"How'd you unlock the front door to get inside?" I ask, remembering the carving of the lamb on the door. I shuffle to the couch and sink down beside Jek. Greer sits on my other side.

"With this." Jek pulls a chain up from under his shirt until I see a flash of the gold pendant I'm now very familiar with. "It acts as a safehouse key, among other things."

He puts his finger to his lips, gets to his feet, and goes to the tunnel opening to slide a panel over it, sealing us inside. He presses his ear against the wall. I don't need to do the same to hear voices that carry a hint of warning.

"They're in the kitchen," Jek says.

"Are we safe?" I shoot a terrified glance at him.

"Hope so." His shrug isn't reassuring.

All we can do now is wait.

# 14

The heavy tread of boots thuds through the house, and I hold my breath, my gaze fixed on the panel that covers the door. Jek stands frozen, ear still pressed to the wall.

I scoot to the edge of the couch, every muscle tense. Greer slides forward and wraps his arm around me. When his fingers press into my skin, I know he's as anxious as me.

More muffled voices echo through the wall. A door opens and closes. Silence ensues. It seems to stretch on forever, and just when I start to wonder whether the Guard took the restaurant owner away, the tunnel panel slides open. My heart leaps into my throat, and Greer grips my shoulder so tightly I'm sure it will leave a bruise. A head pops through the opening, and Greer and I both sag back against the couch. It's the man from earlier.

"They're gone," the man says. He heaves himself out of the tunnel and then hunches forward so the top of his head brushes the ceiling. "They've gotten faster at getting from the compound to the streets once the alarm sounds." He wipes beads of sweat from his upper lip as he waddles across the room and sinks onto the couch beside me. It groans beneath his weight. He crosses his ankles and leans forward, his hands resting on his knees, and surveys us. "I suppose you want to be on the midnight train?"

Jek nods. "Will we make it?"

The man frowns and glances at his wrist, but it's bare. "Must've left it in my room."

"11:05," Greer says. "I'm Greer, by the way. You ran into me outside the West Gate a few days ago. I wondered who you were when I saw you."

"Ah, yes." The man jerks his head toward Jek. "I was getting this one inside the compound that day. Did you get what you needed?" he asks Jek.

Jek nods. "And I need to get it to Fortune's Fall fast."

The man purses his lips. "The Central Hub's only four blocks from here, so timewise, you'll be fine getting to the train. It's sneaking around the Guard that'll be the problem."

"Who are you?" I blurt before the conversation can continue.

The man's head pivots toward me, and a slow smile creeps across his face. "Pallas said you were rather forthright. Now I see what she meant. Nyssa, is it?"

I nod. "You know Pallas?"

"Of course." He heaves himself off the couch and goes to a small cabinet mounted on the wall, opens it, and rummages inside. "I'm Talos." His voice is muffled. "I, like you and Pallas, was exiled here after the attack on Maren. I've known her for many years."

He turns to us, holding a small tool in his hand that looks like the one the Guard uses to scan our eyes for identification. "As a safehouse operator, I'm responsible for providing a resting place and supplies for those who wish to make their way to Fortune's Fall. But first, I must make sure the ID coded into your necklaces matches your thumbprints." He taps his finger against the tool. "Safehouse rules."

Talos holds the scanner over the exile key that dangles from Jek's necklace. Once it beeps, Jek presses his thumb against it, and it beeps again. Then, Talos motions for Greer and me to hand over our own necklaces. I hand him mine with an uncertain glance at Jek.

"It's fine," Jek says. "Everybody has to do it."

I hesitate for a split second before pressing my thumb against the scanner. It beeps. Greer does the same, and Talos gives a brisk nod, then replaces the scanner in the cabinet. When he turns back to us, he holds a small box.

"You'll need disguises if you want to make it to Fortune's Fall safely." He opens the box and pulls out three small cases. "These are contacts that will show a fake identity when the Guard scans them. You can wear them day and night. They should last about a month. That's more than enough time for you to get to Fortune's Fall undetected."

"It could take us a month to get there?" I ask.

"Usually a couple of weeks at most," he says. "But it's best to be prepared." He hands one case to each of us. "Your names are on the small paper inside. Read them. Memorize them. Then give them back to me." He returns to the cabinet and pulls out three wigs. "Seems silly, yes? But hair is a memorable characteristic."

I want to argue with him, but he's right, and we can't take any chances. I hold out my hand for a wig. It's brown and long enough to brush my shoulders. I pull my own hair into a tight bun at the nape of my neck and pull the wig over it.

When Greer turns and sees me, he grins. "I prefer the frizz."

"Shut up." I scowl at him before I open my contact case and pull out the paper.

"Neely Flint," I say aloud. I hand the paper to Talos and

then slide the contacts onto my eyes. At first, everything is blurry and distorted, but I blink three times, and all is clear.

Greer stands and adjusts the mousy brown wig that almost reaches his eyes. Apart from his height, he's barely recognizable. Jek sports a wig similar to Greer's, but the color is the same as mine.

Jek bows in my direction. "Jasper Flint, at your service. Apparently, we're related even when it's fake."

Talos claps his hands once. "Listen up. Greer, you'll go first, alone. Nyssa and Jek will follow behind. Keep Greer in your sight, but don't get too close. Understand?"

Jek nods.

"Wait." My gaze meets Greer's before I turn to Talos with growing trepidation. "Can't Greer stay with us?"

Talos shakes his head. "You'll only be separated for a few minutes. It's best this way. Safer."

"Try not to miss me too much," Greer says. I appreciate his effort to ease my worry, but it doesn't help. The stakes are too high.

Talos hands an envelope to Jek and one to Greer. "If anyone stops you," he says to Greer, "this letter is official documentation stating you are permitted to board the midnight train to the Western Region due to your job as an assistant production manager." He turns to Jek. "Yours grants permission to board the train on account of the unexpected death of a relative in the Western Capital. It covers you and Nyssa." He holds out his hands. "Nyssa and Greer, give me your exile keys once more, please."

I glance at Jek.

"Mine's already on," he says by way of explanation.

Clueless but curious, I hand my necklace to Talos. He presses the center of the lamb. It glows for a second before he hands it back to me. He does the same to Greer's.

"The compasses are activated now," Talos says. "They'll

help guide you to the second safehouse. Once you reach it, you'll find instructions for where to go next. Now, listen carefully." He leans forward like we're conspiring, which I guess we are. "The night market is tonight. I suggest you go through there. It's a roundabout route, but you'll be less conspicuous if you follow the crowds. Remember to keep your eyes open at all times."

I nod, and from the corner of my eye, I see the guys do the same.

"There should be help waiting for you at the ivy entrance," Talos says. "It's a somewhat-hidden door on the Hub's western side. Jek, you know where to go, correct?"

Jek nods.

"Good. You'll be instructed where to board when you get there. The journey to the Western Region is about eight hours, but you must get off in the Padres Pass before it pulls into the Western Capital. That's imperative. Jek will know how to disembark."

He looks at each of us in turn to make sure we understand, then clears his throat. "It's a bit of a hike from there to the next safehouse. About five miles to the northwest. Be careful; talk to no one. Understand?"

We nod again.

Talos jerks his head once in a kind of final salute, then turns toward the tunnel and sinks to his knees. "I thought this tunnel was a great idea when I built it." He gives a wry laugh. "Now, I regret it." He maneuvers his bulk through the opening and creeps forward. "Follow me," he says over his shoulder.

———

THE RESTAURANT IS DARK; the street outside is silent. Talos leads us to a back door that opens onto a dark alley.

"The Guard will be a ways away by now," he whispers. "But

there are always a few who hang around the alleys and such. They like to scare people, make them worried they've done something wrong."

"Like us?" I ask.

Talos turns so that I see his profile. His patrician nose is the only handsome thing about him. "You have your letters. You'll be fine."

I don't point out that plenty of people before us haven't been fine. That I've seen their executions. But I figure everyone's thinking it right now. Why point out the obvious?

"I almost forgot!" Talos slaps his forehead, then disappears into the kitchen. When he returns, he carries a book bag, which he hands to Greer. "Some things to eat and drink, money, and a first aid kit." He pats it once it's secure on Greer's back. "Remember, Greer goes first. I'll tell you when to follow."

As Greer steps into the street, Talos grabs his arm. "May He be with you," he says before standing aside and nodding for him to go.

"And with you," Greer says. The exchange startles me, and I make a mental note to ask Greer about it later. But right now, I stand on my tiptoes to watch him over Talos's shoulder, my stomach twisting tighter with each step that takes him farther away.

When he disappears into the darkness, Talos steps away from the door. "Keep Greer in sight, but if you lose him for some reason, Jek, I trust you know the way?"

"Lose him?" I ask, then shrink back at Talos's warning glance.

"We won't lose him," Jek says. "I know the way." His voice is raspy, and I glance at him, alarmed when I see beads of sweat forming on his forehead.

"Are you okay?" I ask.

He scowls. "I wish everyone'd stop asking me that."

Talos touches his shoulder. "Is it your head, son?"

Jek gives a jerky nod, then grimaces. "I'll be fine."

Talos leans into the alley and turns back to us. "It's time." He places his hands on our shoulders. "May He be with you."

"And with you." Jek grabs my arm. "Let's go."

With a final glance at Talos, I follow Jek into the street. Every muscle in my body screams at me to walk faster, but Talos said we shouldn't rush. It could draw attention.

"Keep your eye on Greer," Jek says. "It'll be hard to follow him once we're in the market." His face is set in a frown, and he swings his head back and forth while we walk, looking for an ambush, I guess.

We reach the end of the alley and turn onto a small side street. Greer reappears up ahead, a tall, loping figure that fills me with relief. He turns left and disappears again. We quicken our steps, and when we round the corner, we find ourselves surrounded by people. Some are solo. Others walk in small groups. All are heading toward the lights at the end of the block, which intersects with the night market.

Jek and I aren't more than a few dozen feet from the entrance when a figure steps out of the shadows—a guard. We freeze. Luckily, we're not the only ones he stops, and we wait at the back of a line to show our identification.

"ID," the guard growls to a girl at the front.

She steps forward. I peer past our small assembly and see Greer disappear into the market. Stifling a panicked breath, I turn back to the scene in front of me.

The guard holds the scanner and waits for the beep before he lets each person pass. The group dwindles. Seven. Four. Then, it's our turn. I step forward, lift my chin, and look straight ahead. The scanner blinks blue light in my eyes. It beeps.

The guard glances at me, then back at the screen. He jerks his head in a nod.

Instead of scurrying away like everyone else, I step to the

side. The guard looks at me, brows raised. "I'd like to wait for my brother, please." I point at Jek with a shaky finger.

The guard turns to Jek without a word and places the scanner in front of his eyes. I clench and unclench my fists while I watch. *It's fine*, I remind myself. It worked for me.

It seems like it takes longer for it to beep this time. When it finally does, the guard nods at Jek, then strides past us and down the street.

For a moment, I'm frozen to the sidewalk.

"You all right?" Jek seems unfazed by the scene.

"He didn't ask for our letter."

Jek shrugs. "But we have it if we need it."

I take a deep breath. "We should go. We lost Greer."

The market is blindingly bright compared with the street—and busy, the exact opposite of what it was like the day we came to celebrate the end of exams. Canvas tents are lined up on both sides, so close together that a gust of wind would knock them over like dominoes. People crowd beneath them, searching through produce, crafts, shoes, clothing. The smell is a fusion of spices, leather, and sweat.

"There's Greer." Jek nods toward a tent ahead. Greer stands beneath it, bent over pottery, but his constant glances around means he's searching for us.

He spots us, and Jek nods in his general direction. Greer returns the gesture before he steps into the street and turns left to circle back to the Central Hub. We follow at a safe distance, moving past the Hub's back entrance and around the side. This side of the station is coated with a thick web of broad-leafed ivy so glossy I can see its sheen in the faint moonlight.

Greer waits for us beneath a shadowed archway. A low hum emanates from behind him.

"What's that?" I try to peer around him, but the space is narrow.

"Escalator." Greer steps to the side so I can see it. It rises up the side of the Central Hub, steep and intimidating, at least three stories high. But what's even more alarming is the guard who stands at its base. I grab Greer's arm.

"It's okay, Nyss. She's with us."

"How do you know?"

The guard steps forward and presses something into my hand. I don't need to look down to see what it is.

"Believe him now?" the guard asks with a smile. She takes her exile key back from me and throws it in the air. It catches the light before disappearing in her hand and then into her pocket. "Now, let's get you on that train." She pivots and motions us onto the escalator.

At the top, we step onto a small square platform that connects the escalator to the side of the station. A door sits in the center of the wall.

"This opens into an alcove at the far end of the station," the guard says. "We'll be safe there until it's time for you to go." She leans forward and presses a button where the doorknob should be. It slides open without a sound to reveal a hooded figure standing on the other side. It steps forward and pulls the hood away. Mottled blue bruises mar a previously perfect complexion.

I gasp. "Ethelind?"

## 15

**E**thelind gazes at me through the eye not swollen shut.

"What happened to you?" I step through the door and put my hands on her shoulders, studying her face with horror.

"The Guard." Her gaze slides to the floor. "They came to our room and asked for you. When I told them I didn't know where you were, they hit me."

"How'd you know we were here?" Greer's voice, snide and unsympathetic, comes from behind me.

I turn toward him with a scowl, but he ignores me.

Ethelind raises her chin in defiance. "Gideon told me where you'd be."

"And why would he do that?" Greer crosses his arms and rocks back on his heels.

Ethelind's gaze slides to mine, and I nod encouragement.

"He was with the guard who hit me," Ethelind says. "He came back later and took me to Pallas." She pulls a chain from around her neck and hands it to me. A circular gold exile key hangs from it. "She gave me this and said to tell you to let me come with you."

"Well, that's settled." I return the necklace to her and turn to Greer.

He frowns. "Nothing's settled."

"Please," Ethelind says. "They're never going to believe I don't know where Nyssa's gone. I can't stay here."

"We can't leave her," Jek says. "Look at her—she's a mess. Besides, we don't have time to argue. Let her come, and we'll figure out the details later." He pauses. "Who are you, by the way?"

"This is Ethelind," I say before she can respond. "She's my roommate."

A low hum echoes through the station, and the platform on which we stand starts to vibrate. The train is coming.

Our guard steps to the edge of the alcove and peers out. "There are about two dozen or so people and two guards patrolling." She turns back to us. "Jek and Nyssa go together two cars down. Greer, I want you a few ahead of them." She studies Ethelind. "I'm not letting you through until the train's moving. You don't have a disguise like the others, so keep your head down and hop on as fast as you can. Once the train's good and going, meet in the last car and head to cargo. The Guard won't check it until the final destination. Jek knows how to get inside."

"Are we seriously taking her with us?" Greer frowns at Ethelind, who doesn't seem to hear. She leans against the wall with her eyes closed.

"Greer!" I jab him in the side. "I know you don't like her, but why are you being so mean?"

"Because," he says through gritted teeth. His gaze doesn't leave Ethelind. "We have no way to prove that what she said is true. What if she's lying?"

I roll my eyes. "You think she beat herself up and then developed psychic powers to figure out where we were? Come on."

"I don't like it."

I glance at Ethelind. Could Greer be right? But I can't ignore her bruises and swollen red eyelid. I shake my head. We can't leave her here.

A blur of sleek metal whizzes into the Hub and stops with barely a sound. We all turn toward our guard to await instructions.

"Looks like the Guard's just keeping an eye on everyone as they board, but best to be prepared," she says from her vantage point. She nods at Jek. "Go on then."

"Ready?" Jek asks me.

"Stay low and go," I say.

"Exactly." He grins.

We step out of our hiding place and walk across the platform to the second car from the end. A handful of people already wait beside it, but no one gives us a second glance. The nearest guard is two cars down. He doesn't pay us any attention.

I peer over my shoulder in time to see Greer make his entrance. He saunters past us, hands in his pockets, the book bag bumping against his back. He keeps his gaze straight ahead and joins a few people waiting three cars away.

From the corner of my eye, I see a guard turn his head and watch Greer. Maybe it's his height—he's taller than the others by at least a few inches. Whatever it is, the guard frowns and walks toward him.

"Jek!" I tug on his sleeve and jerk my head toward Greer.

"He'll be fine," Jek says. "Just needs to show his letter."

The guard stops and asks Greer something. Greer turns so that his back is to us. After a moment, he pulls off his book bag and searches through it.

"Get the letter, Greer," Jek whispers.

But he can't seem to find it.

The train door slides open, and Jek grabs my elbow. "Come on, Nyssa. He'll figure it out."

I let him pull me into the car. The other travelers scatter among the closest seats while Jek pulls me into a seat all the way in the back. It's plush and velvety red, but I don't care about any of that. I sit on my knees, gnawing on my thumbnail, as I watch Greer through the window. The platform empties except for him and the guard.

"Don't make it obvious we're watching him." Jek yanks on my arm to make me turn and sit. "Remember, we don't want to draw attention to ourselves."

I scowl. The other passengers are busy putting bags above their heads, leaning chairs back, chatting with their neighbors. I ignore him, push back to my knees, and press my nose to the window in time to see the guard check Greer's ID with his eye scanner.

Greer waits for the scanner to do its job, his fists clenched at his sides. The guard tucks the scanner in his pocket and says something else to Greer, who unclenches his fists and gestures to emphasize a point I wish I could hear.

"Something's wrong," I say to Jek. "Why won't he let Greer on?"

The train starts to move, and I jump up and try to push past Jek.

"Where are you going?" He grips my arm so tight his fingers make indentations in my skin.

"To get Greer." My heart beats fast from fury and fear, and I try to wrestle from his grip, but he holds tight and stands so that we're nose to nose.

"You can't do that."

"Please," I whisper. "We can't leave him behind."

The train picks up speed, and we draw closer to where Greer stands.

Jek darts a glance out the window and releases me. "Stay here. I'll see what I can do."

He hurries to the door, and I return to my seat and sit on my knees, my face pressed to the window. I don't know what to expect. Will Jek jump off the train? Will he yell to distract the guard?

Just as Jek disappears into the alcove where the door is located, Greer turns and sprints toward our car. He catches my gaze through the window and gives me a salute and a wink. But I see the fear in his eyes. My stomach drops.

The guard shouts something and gives chase. Greer glances over his shoulder, pulls the book bag from his back, and tosses it into our car.

My attention turns back to the guard. He stops, plants his feet, and pulls out a weapon I know to be silent. Lethal. I break into a cold sweat and pound on the window to get Greer's attention. But he doesn't hear me.

The guard presses the trigger.

Greer's eyes bulge. He stumbles and falls.

My mouth opens in a silent scream. I beat on the window until my fist aches. "No!" I choke on the word. "Get up, Greer! Get up!"

But he doesn't move. He lies motionless, arms splayed beside him, head turned toward the wall. The guard strides forward and bends over him, blocking him from my view.

I strain against the window. My throat burns; my lungs beg for air. But I can't breathe. The train is fast now, and the scene grows smaller as we move out into the night.

Greer is gone.

## 16

I 'm frozen. Numb. Only my fingers, still pressed against the window, retain any feeling. I stare out as the train climbs a steep track that passes over the streets of the Central Capital, so close to the buildings we could reach out and touch them.

The seat beside me shifts, and I know Jek has joined me. He doesn't speak at first. I don't, either. I'm afraid that if I turn to him, I'll hit him, pound his chest until he's black and blue like Ethelind's face. I know it's not his fault, but I need someone to blame, and he's the closest.

"Nyssa?"

Jek's voice floats around me like someone calling through the ocean.

I don't respond.

"We have to move to the cargo car. The Guard will start at the front and do an ID check through all the cars soon. It's safer if we're not around for it."

He touches my arm, and I flinch but keep my gaze fixed out the window. We've reached the edge of the city. The buildings are smaller, and we glide above them, silent and wraithlike. I can see where the metropolis ends—the track dips toward the ground past where the lights abruptly stop.

"Greer," I whisper.

The moon flickers between clouds that scud across the sky. They're building thicker to the west, their ominous shadows brought to life by an occasional pulse of lightning that makes them glow from within. We're moving straight into a storm.

Greer loves the rain. *Loved.* Greer *loved* the rain.

"Greer," I say again.

A hole opens inside me, deep and hollow. I gasp and slide to the floor, pull my knees to my chest, and press my face against them. Why should I care what happens to us now? I've lost everyone who matters.

*That's not true,* a voice whispers in my head.

I lift my head and see Jek crouched in the aisle, watching me. He's someone who matters. Our parents, too. And we're all the hope they have for survival.

"You have to get up." Jek grabs my arm.

I let him pull me up and into the aisle. I keep my head low, not stopping until I reach the alcove at the end of the car. We pass through two more cars, and at the end of the next, we stop. The exit door is to our left, the bathrooms to the right. Straight ahead is a door with a keypad attached to its face.

"This is how I got to the Central Capital." Jek steps around me and presses in a code that makes the door slide open.

A lump forms in my throat when I see the book bag Talos gave to Greer strapped on Jek's back. I fight a sudden urge to rip it from his shoulders. Greer should have that. He should be waiting here with me to slip into this hiding space, to sit beside me on our way to the Western Region, to do whatever it is we're going to have to do to get to Fortune's Fall.

When the door opens, Jek pushes me inside. The cargo car is dismal. Crates are stacked floor to ceiling with enough space for a small aisle that leads to the back wall, which has a single window in the middle and a keypad attached to the bottom.

"Hurry up!"

I whirl to see Jek standing in the doorway, motioning to someone outside. I gasp on a breath full of hope. In my mind's eye, I see Greer staggering down the aisle, hurt but alive. I shove Jek out of the way and come face to face with Ethelind. My body sags. I'd forgotten about her.

She rushes past me and into the cargo car. Jek presses a button to close the door, and I'm forced to step inside with them. I hug my arms against my chest to drive away a chill that wells up from somewhere deep inside me. It seeps into every limb like someone's dripped ice into my blood.

Before anyone has a chance to speak, I wander down the aisle to the window and press my forehead against it. Clouds blanket the sky now, and lightning flickers all around. I sense the other two behind me, but I ignore them.

"Train'll be to the Western Capital by midmorning, which means we'll get off a little after dawn." Jek slides to the floor beside me and leans against the wall, his legs stretched out in front of him. "Try to get some rest."

I glance down at him. His eyes are closed.

Anger courses through me, quick and unexpected. I pound my palms against the window until they're red and burning, then whirl to face Jek. "How can you act like everything's okay?" My voice rises with each word.

The train lurches, and I fall forward. Ethelind grabs my shoulders to steady me, but we trip over Jek's legs and tumble to the side. My head collides with the side of a crate, and pain ricochets through my skull. Tears leak from my eyes, and I slide to the floor and curl into a ball, my breath coming in raw, aching hiccups. My head throbs with a dull pain. I wrap my arms tighter around myself and squeeze my eyes closed.

I don't know how much time passes. When I eventually sit

up, my whole body groans in protest. I rotate to lean against the wall beside Jek. Ethelind sits on my other side.

"I'm so sorry about Greer." She squeezes my arm.

I resist the urge to say something snarky. *You didn't like him. You're probably glad he's not here.*

Jek takes my hand in his. His grip is strong. Confident. My brother, I remind myself. Here. Beside me. My anger begins to dissolve with this reminder, leaving in its wake a numbness I can't shake.

"Sometimes, I forget how hard it is to lose someone," he says a few minutes later. "It's not the first time, and it won't be the last. But trust me—I *am* sorry about Greer, Nyssa." He releases my hand and pulls something from his back pocket. "Here." He unfolds a thin piece of paper the size of an index card and holds it out to me.

I take it and recognize it as the same photo of our family that sits on my nightstand. "I have this photograph. I know it's us."

Jek smiles. "But I bet you didn't notice anything special about that tree behind us."

I glance at the picture. There's nothing unusual about the tree, and I raise a questioning brow.

"When Omri attacked Maren fifteen years ago, he destroyed every ounce of farmland," Jek says. "Every seed. Every fruit and vegetable. Animals were either destroyed or relocated. And he forbade any outside aid, which he thought was a death sentence to everyone left behind."

"I know that already," I say. "What's your point?"

"My point is Omri *thought* he destroyed everything. But what he didn't know was that a lot of those farmers were scientists, too—our parents included." He leans toward me and taps the tree. "That's an indestructible clone."

"What?" Puzzled, I glance at the tree, then up at Jek.

"It's indestructible. Our parents were part of a project—a

*secret* project—to clone our food production. Almonds. Grapes. Even the animals. They knew a time was coming when we might have to start over. So, they started preparing. Our parents helped keep everyone from starving during that first year after Maren was destroyed. They brought the clones to Fortune's Fall and did exactly what they planned to do: start over."

I bring the photo closer to my eyes, studying every detail of the tree and the landscape behind it. "So, our parents are brilliant?"

"Brilliant and sick," he says with a frown.

I set the photo on my lap. "I know. Pallas told me they were in Maren when Omri attacked it with that poisonous gas."

Jek takes a deep breath. "I showed you that photo to remind you that you made the right choice. Even if Greer isn't here." He stares straight ahead, unblinking. "For some reason, the gas Omri used to attack Maren didn't kill everyone right away. It's just making them sicker and sicker. But as long as they stay alive, we can save them. You can still see our parents again."

I lean my head back and stare up at the boxes stacked to the ceiling. I know he's right. I have to keep going, even if Greer isn't here with me anymore. I can't give up on saving my parents.

Jek pats my arm and slides down onto the floor until he's flat beside me. "Try to sleep," he says, closing his eyes. "We'll be there soon."

———

I WAKE to the soft patter of rain against the roof. The storm left a gloomy drizzle in its wake, and the light that comes through the window above us is weak.

I sit up with a groan and rub my lower back. Ethelind and Jek stir, too. My entire body aches from sleeping on the hard floor, and I stretch my legs, grimacing when my muscles protest.

Jek rises to his feet slowly, one hand pressed to his temple, and peers out the window. "We're nearly there."

Ethelind and I stand and look out, too. We're level with the ground. Massive rolling mountains surround us, their sides sandy and freckled with scrubby trees and scraggly bushes. It's different from anything I've ever seen, but I can't summon any excitement. Everything is dulled by Greer's absence.

"How are we getting off the train?" Ethelind asks Jek. Her face is a little better this morning. It's less puffy, though her bruises are beginning to turn a nasty yellow.

"We'll jump."

Ethelind and I share a wide-eyed glance.

"Are you joking?" I ask, then shake my head. "No way."

"We'll be fine. All you have to do is tuck and roll." Jek bends to the keypad attached to the wall below the window and presses in a code. The wall shrieks as it slides upward.

"Someone's going to hear that," I say to Ethelind.

"Jek doesn't seem too worried about it."

The door clangs into the space above our heads. We stand side by side a few feet from the edge and stare out at the scene. The drizzle is tapering, and the sun appears in an increasing patch of blue. The air is cool. Crisp. I close my eyes for a second and inhale the aroma that's so different from the jumble of smells that stagnate across the Central Capital in summer.

After a few minutes, there's a subtle change in the train's speed.

"That's our cue," Jek says. "See that boulder?" He points at an angular gray rock the size of a small bus as we pass. "Get back there and hide behind it. I'll be right behind you."

The train curves to the right. I clench my fists and take deep, steadying breaths.

"Ready." Jek places a hand on my lower back and pushes me toward the corner of the car until my toes dip over its edge. The ground is a blur as we race across it.

"Can't I wait until—"

"Now!" Jek pushes me, and I pitch forward off the car.

My knees buckle when my feet hit the ground, and I tuck and roll like Jek commanded. When I come to a stop, I take a moment to get my breath, then push to standing and sprint back around the bend toward the boulder. I hear pounding footsteps and glance over my shoulder to see Ethelind running behind me, followed by Jek, who stumbles and falls.

I skid to a stop and wait for him to get up.

"Keep going!" He squints up at me from where he kneels on the ground. "Get to that rock and stay behind it."

Ethelind stops beside me, panting. "We should do what he says." She grabs my arm. "Come on."

Greer's face flashes in my mind, and I jerk out of her grip. "I'm not leaving anyone else behind." I hurry back to Jek, pull the book bag from his back, and throw it onto mine, then lean and drape his arm across my shoulder. "Get up," I say as I struggle to stand.

"It's my head again," he says. "Just leave me alone. It'll pass."

Ethelind appears and pulls Jek's other arm around her shoulder. We stumble forward, our breath coming in spurts. Jek is a dead weight between us. When we reach the small pool of shade behind the boulder, I rip the wig from my head and toss it to the side, grateful for the cool breeze that whispers against my scalp.

The train is gone, and everything's as silent as though it never passed through. How long do we have until it reaches the Western Capital and the Guard sees the open cargo car?

Jek curls into a ball beside Ethelind, and we exchange a worried look.

"Jek?" I touch his arm with one finger.

He doesn't respond.

"Let him rest," I whisper to Ethelind. I pull the wig from his head and toss it on top of mine a few feet away.

"How long do you think we'll have to stay here?" Ethelind leans against the boulder, her eyes closed.

I drag the book bag onto my lap, open it, and pull out one of the two canisters of water. "Doesn't look like we're going anywhere soon." I hand it to her, then grab the other for myself.

Jek is motionless for a long while, and when he stirs at last, I crawl to his side.

"Water?" he asks, sitting up slowly. Purple shadows form crescents beneath his eyes, and his face is streaked with dirt.

I hand him mine.

Once he's drunk his fill, he wipes his mouth and glances at the sky. "We'll stay here until sunset."

"Sunset?" Ethelind moans. "Won't the Guard start searching for us before then?"

Jek shakes his head. "They won't know the cargo car's open until the train arrives in the Western Capital. By the time a search is underway, we'll be at the next safehouse, if not already past it." He pulls his necklace from beneath his shirt and studies the compass. "We'll head northwest, around the edge of the pass." He juts his chin toward the rolling mountains to the right of where the train disappeared. "Not like the Central Capital, is it? Think you can make it?"

I survey the desolate landscape through narrowed eyes. If Greer were here, he'd say something sarcastic. *The only way you'll get up that mountain is if there are French fries at the top.* His voice in my head makes my breath catch.

"I'll manage," I say at last.

## 17

The silence here is strange. A family of quail dart through the brush just past midafternoon, the only reminder we're not alone. I join in the laughter when the cluster of babies sprints after their mother, but my delight is short lived. Greer would've loved it here. The sky. The mountains. I close my eyes and drift into a fitful sleep.

When I wake, the air is chilly, and the sun has sunk beneath the western ridge. The last streaks of sunset are melting into increasing darkness. I sit up, rubbing my arms to warm them. Ethelind and Jek are asleep on either side of me.

"Jek?" I tap his shoulder.

He groans.

"Jek? It's nearly dark."

Ethelind sits up and shivers. "It's getting cold." She pulls her knees to her chest and wraps her arms around them, then peers down at Jek. "He looks terrible."

Jek groans again and slowly sits up. His hair is slicked to his head, and his skin is pasty white. He leans against the boulder and massages his temples. "These headaches are getting old."

I study him for a moment, then, on impulse, I pull my necklace from beneath my shirt and flip it so the compass is on top. "You said we have to go northwest, right?"

Jek nods.

I stand and hoist the book bag over my shoulders. "I'll lead. Let me know if you need to stop." I force a smile and hope it's enough to convince him I can do this. I'm desperate for a distraction, and this will keep my mind from wandering where I don't want it to go.

"Everything here looks exactly the same." Jek frowns at me with obvious doubt. "I can't even navigate to where we're supposed to go without using my compass." He raises his eyebrows. "Have you ever used a compass?"

I consider what to say. No, I've never used a compass. I'd never even seen one until Talos activated mine. But how hard can it be? I catch sight of our dirty wigs piled beside Jek. To avoid his gaze, I bend and grab them, taking more time than necessary to slide the book bag from my shoulders, stuff them inside, and zip it closed. "Let's go." I straighten and look at him at last, hands on hips. "You have enough to deal with. Let me lead."

I turn and march through the growing shadows, relieved to hear the crunch of footsteps behind me. We walk for an hour, sometimes together, sometimes straggling one after the other, as we wind through the mountains. When the moon rises, everything is illuminated, but it doesn't make the hike much easier. The path is steep, and the dirt crumbles beneath our feet. At some point, I flip on the flashlight to better see the ground, but we stumble more than once.

"Remember what state this used to be?" Ethelind asks after a long stretch of silence.

"California." I pause and lean against the scratchy bark of a tree. They grow closer together here, their thick foliage merging into a canopy above us. Starlight blinks between the leaves.

"I'm not impressed." Ethelind stops, hands on hips, and studies our surroundings.

I unzip the book bag, pull out the water, and hand one to Ethelind. One to Jek. We collapse onto the ground for a much-needed break.

"What're those lights?" Jek asks a few minutes later. He points toward a gap in the trees to our right, then stands to see better.

I join him, frowning when I spot the lights that shine like a beacon into the sky.

"Nyssa." Jek spins and glares at me.

"What'd I do?" I shrink away from him.

Jek's response is to jog through the trees, away from us. He disappears from view.

"Should we follow him?" Ethelind asks.

I sigh. "Probably." I take a quick chug from one of the waters, then toss them back into the bag, zip it up, and sling it over my shoulders. It's lighter now, and that worries me. What'll we do if we run out of water?

We follow the soft thud of Jek's footsteps halfway up the nearest mountain. Around to the left, we find him standing on a small ridge, looking down onto the—

"Capital Connector," Jek says without turning. "All eight lanes of it."

The highway runs east to west, connecting the three regional capitals. Government cargo trucks wait in a long line along one westbound lane as they creep toward a cluster of buildings from which the lights beam into the sky.

"That's a weigh station and rest area." Jek turns to me, shaking his head in disbelief. "We were supposed to cross before this part. We're too far west."

How could I have misjudged our direction so badly? I've been careful about checking the compass. Except when we came through the last valley, I remember with dread. We wound around the base of a particularly steep mountain, and we must've veered off course.

"You haven't been checking up on me?" I ask. "I figured you'd at least look at your own compass every now and then to make sure we were going in the right direction." My ears begin to burn, and all my anger and frustration at everything that's happened burst out. "You made it pretty clear you didn't trust me to do a good job."

"I tried to check my compass!" Jek takes a breath and presses his fingers against his temples. "But I can't get my eyes to focus on anything up close. This stupid headache is killing me."

My shoulders sag. He trusted I knew what I was doing, and I failed. "I'm sorry. It was an accident."

"Our best bet is to cross right here." Jek rubs his temples. "All the trucks have to stop at the weigh station, so we have time to cross before they pick up speed again."

Ethelind and I follow Jek down the mountain in uncomfortable silence. Shale and dirt loosen against our shoes and tumble down the embankment, reminding me of the patter of rain against a window.

At last, we reach the bottom, and the trees give way to the highway shoulder. We stop in the shadows, watching trucks leave the station to our left and pick up speed past our hiding place. Jek's right—there's a gap of at least a few minutes between each truck. The lanes going east are mostly empty. We should have time to get to the other side.

"We'll be in plain sight when we cross," Jek says. "Just stay low and—"

"Wave our hands to get everyone's attention?" I say.

He scowls. "Ready?"

Ethelind and I nod.

"It's clear," Jek says. "Move!"

He sprints from behind the trees, across the shoulder, and

onto the highway. We follow across two lanes. Four. A truck moves through the weigh station and picks up speed. We cross the median as headlights blink in the distance on the eastbound side, heading straight for us. Ethelind and I stop and stare.

"Hurry up!" Jek says.

The command spurs us into action, and we run. But the headlights are closer now, too close. In her haste to obey, Ethelind smacks full force into Jek, and they topple to the pavement. Jek's head hits the concrete with a sickening thud.

"Jek!" I rush to his side.

He doesn't move.

I turn to Ethelind, who stands frozen, her gaze darting between Jek and the looming vehicle.

"Ethelind!" I clap once to get her attention. "He's unconscious. Help me drag him to the side."

She blinks, nods, and bends to grab his arm. Together, we drag him from the road, across the shoulder, and throw ourselves into the dirt before a small car hurtles past.

Ethelind and I lie motionless, with Jek sprawled between us. The suddenness of the car's appearance combined with its rapid disappearance is eerie. Will it return? It seems unlikely that whoever was driving didn't spot us.

"It was empty," Ethelind says.

I sit up and look at her. "What?"

"It was empty. It was a solo."

A solo. A driverless car.

"But it should've sensed we were in the road." I push my stringy hair away from my face.

Ethelind sits up and smiles. "Exactly. Something must've been wrong. Its camera probably wasn't working. That's how it knows there's an obstacle it has to navigate around." She peers down at Jek, who's still unconscious. "He's got a pretty big bump on the side of his head, but I don't see any blood."

"His breathing is even," I say. "But we're definitely not going anywhere until he wakes up."

I drag the book bag onto my lap and pull out the half-full water canisters. "We need more water, and he needs ice." I blink at the rest area lights, then stand and look down at Ethelind. "I'll get us more. Stay here with him until I get back."

"Are you crazy?"

I bend and grab Jek's arm. "Grab his other arm, and help me drag him into the trees. No one will see you there."

She hesitates, frowning up at me as though she wants to argue.

"Come on, Ethelind. Unless you have a better plan?"

She sighs, stands, and grabs Jek's other arm. Together, we drag him into the shadows.

"I'll be back as soon as I can, okay?" I hook my thumbs beneath the book bag's straps. "And if I'm not"—I pause, considering the alternative—"you guys go without me."

Ethelind opens her mouth like she's going to argue, then closes it and sighs. "Put on your wig, okay?"

My wig. I can't believe I almost forgot it. I redo my own hair into a bun, wrench the wig from the book bag, and shove it on my head, trying to ignore the musty smell. "How do I look?" I strike a pose. One hand on hip. Lips pouted like a model.

"Like you haven't showered in a month."

I sigh. "That's better than being recognized, I guess." I pat my pocket. "I've got the money Talos gave us. I'll come right back."

Before she can say anything else—and before I can change my mind—I step from the trees, confirm the highway is empty, and dash back across the way we came.

I weave through the trees that line the opposite shoulder, crouching to stay out of the weigh station's bright lights. Between it and the rest area—a large building that appears to be part restaurant, part convenience store—sits a massive parking lot. It's filled with row after row of empty trucks, and I crawl beneath them until I'm as close to the rest area as I can be without being in plain sight.

From behind a tire on the front row, I have an unobstructed view. Two men wearing the green jumpsuits required of all government-employed drivers stomp inside and head left, into the restaurant. To the right is the convenience store. Through the windows, I can see a clerk slouched behind the counter, his chin propped in his hands.

I recite in my head what I plan to say if anyone asks me why I'm here alone. Then, taking a deep breath, I crawl out from beneath the truck, stand, and head to the door.

The clerk acknowledges me with a leer, and I hurry to the back, grab two large waters, and turn to the freezer section. I pull out a bag of frozen peas—we can use it for the bump on Jek's head—and stride to the front.

"How's it going?" the clerk asks. He's around my age, with a goatee and a diamond stud in his left ear. As he checks my items and takes my money, I glance behind him at a small screen on which the news plays.

My eyes widen in horror.

Jek's face. My face. His photograph doesn't have his name attached. But mine is there in big, bold letters, and beneath it is the word *Wanted*.

"Hey, you all right?" The clerk waves his hand in front of my face.

I gather the items without replying and turn from the counter with my head down.

"You forgot this!"

I glance over my shoulder to see him holding out the bag of peas. He can't hide the smirk lurking around his lips. *He knows.*

I swallow hard, scamper back to the counter, and grab it. "Thanks."

"Why don't you stay? Grab some coffee with me next door?"

I hurry toward the door. "Have to go!" I say over my shoulder. "My dad's waiting in the truck. Wants to get back on the road."

"Oh, I doubt that," he says. "From what I hear, Nyssa Ardelone isn't traveling with her dad."

I pause for a terror-stricken second before I turn and race into the parking lot.

And straight into a spotlight.

The sudden brightness forces my eyes closed but not before I see a black van parked beside the store and a figure standing in front of it. Only the Guard drives these vehicles.

Someone grabs my arm from behind, and a water bottle falls from my hand. It lands on the ground with a dull thud.

"Here's your fugitive, sir." The clerk tugs on my real hair, which must have unwound from my bun and hangs loose beneath my wig. He leans forward so that his lips touch my ear. I shudder. "Next time you wear a disguise," he says, "you might want to make sure it's on all the way."

I try to wrench away, but his fingers dig into my arm. The guard standing beside the van steps forward, and the clerk's fingers loosen. I jerk to the right in an attempt to run again, but the guard grabs me before my feet even leave the ground.

"Wouldn't do that if I were you." The guard yanks me to the vehicle and pops open the rear door.

Jek and Ethelind are inside.

## 18

They sit on one of the benches that span the sides of the van. Ethelind's face is contorted in a scowl. Jek's expression shifts between anger and pain.

The guard tosses me inside and slams the door. I collapse on the bench, note the black screen that separates us from the driver, and turn to my friends. "What happened?" I drop the one remaining water and frozen peas on the bench beside me, slide the book bag from my shoulders, then peel the useless wig from my head and toss it on the floor.

"Jek woke up and was totally out of control." Ethelind turns her scowl in his direction. "Said he had to find you before the Guard did and went stumbling down the highway."

I glance at Jek. His arms are crossed, and he stares at the floor.

"I chased after him, but I couldn't catch him. This guy"— Ethelind jerks her head toward the front—"pulled over when he saw us running down the shoulder."

The front door slams, and we all jump. Within seconds, we're speeding down the Connector. I can't believe it. We've been gone less than two days, and we've already been caught. We're not going to make it to Fortune's Fall, the antidote is wasted, and by this time tomorrow, we'll be in prison. I swallow hard against the lump in my throat. I won't ever see my parents again.

"Why'd you leave us there?" Jek taps his foot against the van's floor.

The lump in my throat dissolves into anger. "Why?" I'm caught somewhere between confusion and a growing sense of injustice. "Because you were unconscious—that's why. We needed water. Ice for your head. We couldn't sit on the side of the highway and hope you'd be okay." I pick up the bag of peas and throw it at him. "You're welcome."

"We wouldn't have been on the side of the highway in the first place if you hadn't gotten us lost." He grabs the bag from where it landed beside him and presses it against his head.

My mouth falls open. "Are you serious?" All the anxiety and fear from the last few days explode out of me. "I tried to save your life, and that's how you thank me?" I shake my head. "Some brother you are."

"What was that?" He sits forward, brow furrowed over narrowed eyes.

"I said, 'Some brother you are!' You wave pictures of us in my face, telling me we're doing the right thing, but as soon as you get yourself knocked out, you act like everything's my fault!" I sit back and glare at him.

"Quiet back there!" the guard says.

Jek stares at me a moment longer before turning to gaze out the window. A few minutes later, a smile creeps across his face.

"Why are you smiling?" I snap.

He turns away from the window and sets the bag down. "Have either of you noticed which direction we're driving?"

"East," Ethelind says. "Toward the Central Capital."

Jek's smile grows bigger. "Wrong. We're heading west. Wherever he's taking us, it's not back to the Central Capital."

I sigh. "It doesn't matter where we're going. It's over, Jek."

He's quiet. Eventually, we turn off the highway and bump along a gravel road. I press my face against the glass. "I see something," I say after a while. In the distance, a pinprick of light grows brighter, and a few minutes later, we park in front of a small building. Our driver jumps from the van and slams the door before stomping inside. Another guard rises from a desk in front of the window and greets him.

Jek slides from the seat and rams his body against the door. I hesitate for a split second before I decide to join him, and we push together.

Ethelind taps my back. "You should probably get away—"

The door flies open, and Jek and I fall out onto the hard-packed gravel. It stabs into my cheek, and I grimace.

An arm reaches down and jerks me up. It's the guard from inside the building. He's shorter than me, and I stare down at him, my jaw clenched, but his gaze is focused on the necklace that came loose from beneath my shirt when I fell. It hangs in plain sight.

Before I can react, he rips the chain from my neck. It cuts into my skin before snapping, and I cry out. The guard rubs it between his thumb and finger for a moment, then stuffs it into his front pocket.

"Give that back," I say.

"You're sleeping here tonight." He wrenches me toward the building while our driver follows with Jek and Ethelind.

"Take them straight to the cell, Sander," our driver says. "It's going to be an early morning."

"Yes, sir." Sander leads us inside—bare except for the desk and two cots along the wall—down a hall, past a small kitchen, and into a windowless room in the back.

"Light stays on," Sander says. "Sleep tight." He slams the door.

I survey the cheerless room, one hand pressed to my scratched-up cheek. A mattress fitted with a white sheet and a blanket is tucked into the corner. A door to the right leads to a small bathroom.

"Thank goodness." Ethelind hurries inside.

Jek and I take turns once she's emerged, and then, we stretch out on the bed like crayons in a box. Nobody talks. I'm too wired to sleep but too scared about tomorrow to talk. I suspect they're the same.

"He took my necklace," I say after a while. I touch my neck, naked without the now-familiar weight of the pendant.

"I saw," Jek says. "The other guy took our book bag." He shrugs. "Not much we can do about it."

The mattress shifts as Ethelind turns to her side at the same moment Jek stands.

"We have to get out of here," he says, pacing.

"Doesn't look too promising." I stare at the ceiling. There's no point getting our hopes up now.

An hour goes by. Two. Maybe three. Ethelind and I toss on the mattress, but sleep won't come. Jek sits in the corner near the bathroom, his head resting on his knees.

The lock on the door clicks, and it creaks open. Jek lifts his head, and Ethelind and I sit up.

Sander steps inside. "I'm getting you out of here, but we have to hurry." He tosses our book bag toward Jek.

I stare at him, confused.

Jek leaps up with a grin, grabs the bag, and slings it onto his back. "I knew we'd get out of here!" He gestures for us to get up. "You heard him. Come on!"

"Why should we trust this guy?" I ask Jek without moving.

"Because of this." Sander steps forward and opens his hand. My necklace, broken chain and all, sits in his palm.

Heat spreads across my face and down my neck. I jump up and yank it out of his hand. "That's mine." I stuff it into my pocket with an angry glare.

"You're right." Sander opens his other hand. "But this one is mine."

## 19

We follow Sander down the hall and out a back door. The moon floats low in the west, and the stars are subdued, like they hang behind a translucent curtain.

"We don't have much time; he'll be awake soon." Sander peers over his shoulder at us, his profile outlined in the predawn shadows. "I can take you to the nearest safehouse, but you're on your own after that."

Ethelind and I jog to keep pace with him and Jek. Their already-long strides are quickened by the thrill of escape. Mine are slowed by uncertainty.

"How'd you get that necklace?" I whisper when I'm near enough for Sander to hear me. The cold is bitter against my skin, and I keep my arms wrapped around my chest.

He glances at me, shakes his own jacket from his arms, and tosses it across my shoulders. "Better?"

I nod.

"About two miles this way, and we'll be there." He points straight ahead, up the mountain that towers ahead of us. "This is my regular route when I'm on duty. Have to watch for people like you, you know." I sense the smile in his tone. "The trees thin out at the top. You'll be able to see the safehouse from there."

"What will the other guard do when he realizes we're gone?" Ethelind asks.

Sander shrugs. "Set up a search party. That's why we have to get to the safehouse as quickly as possible."

"But won't you get in trouble?" Ethelind tugs at the jacket on my arms in a silent plea to share. With a sigh, I give it to her, and she tosses me a grateful smile.

"Nah," Sander says. "Just have to tell him you were still inside when I left."

I snort. "You think he'll believe that?"

"The best lies are the simplest ones."

Our shoes are quiet against the dirt, and despite the circumstances, I find myself enjoying the sound of the breeze whistling through the trees. It's the only noise in the all-encompassing silence.

"Are you going to answer my question?" I ask after a while. We've paused to catch our breath and pass around the water canisters that Sander refilled before he rescued us.

Sander takes a long swig and swallows. A bird calls above us, and another one answers a few trees away. As the sky lightens, I can pick out individual leaves in the black umbrella of foliage above us.

"About my exile key?" Sander asks.

I nod. "You're an exile, too?"

"Not exactly." He glances at me, then takes another drink. "Gideon got one for me."

My eyebrows shoot up. "Gideon seems to be involved in everything."

Sander smiles. "We were in orientation together after we were selected for the Guard. You could say I'm a recent convert."

"A recent convert to what?" Ethelind leans against the nearest tree, her face scrunched in a confused pout.

Sander chuckles. "Bit of a long story, and no time to tell it now. Maybe I'll have a chance when we're at the safehouse. Come on. Time to go."

We reach the top, breathless and exhausted, as sunbeams peek from the eastern ridge.

"There it is." Sander points down at a meadow that stretches below us and ends at the edge of a forest. A stone-faced square tower rises from the treetops. "Just through the meadow, and we'll be there. Come on."

We scamper down the mountain like children: arms flailing, grins appearing unbidden on our faces. I allow myself to hope again. Maybe we'll make it after all. We burst into the meadow, a flowing field of knee-high grass. The forest looms before us, dark but friendly, and we run toward it.

Something whistles past my head.

Sander exhales like a popped balloon and tumbles to the ground.

I freeze.

"Get down!" Jek tackles me, and I stumble into Ethelind. We fall facedown into the grass.

Jek army-crawls to Sander and begins to drag him by one arm toward the trees. I scramble forward on my stomach and grab Sander's other arm.

Dirt explodes near my face.

Ethelind screams.

I peer over my shoulder.

"I'm okay," she whispers. "Keep moving."

I grit my teeth and pull Sander's arm with all my might.

"Can't stop until we're at the safehouse," Jek says, panting, when we reach the trees. He pulls up into a crouch and drags Sander's arm across his shoulder. I do the same with his other arm.

Sander groans and moves his head. "I'm all right," he mumbles. He tries to steady himself, but his legs buckle.

Something wet and sticky leaks through my shirt where his arm drapes across my shoulder. Ethelind steps beside me and pulls his arm across her shoulder, too, to help balance the weight. The three of us drag him farther into the trees.

"Well, well. That was easier than I thought it'd be," a familiar voice says from somewhere in the darkness ahead of us.

We freeze, and my mouth goes dry. Four guards materialize out of the shadows with weapons pointed at us. I recognize the one who spoke. It's the guard who took us from the rest area.

"Run when I say," Jek mutters. He moves his hand toward the bottom of his shirt. My eyes narrow in confusion. What does he plan to do?

"What was that?" the guard asks. He takes three steps forward, and his leering face comes into view.

Jek lifts his shirt and reaches into the secret compartment camouflaged like skin. He pulls something out and throws it forward. A small vial hits the ground with a thud. Jek looks at me across Sander's sagging body.

"Run." His voice is eerily calm, as though he's told us dinner is ready and we need to head home.

But I can't move because the vial has begun to make strange hissing sounds. Purple smoke curls into the air, and I can't tear my gaze away.

"What is that?" Ethelind whispers.

All I can do is shake my head. The smoke winds into the air like a snake, and fear like I've never known roots my feet to the ground.

"Go!" Jek jerks to the left so that Sander's arm slips from my shoulders, and his full weight rests on Jek.

The panic in Jek's voice breaks my trance. I grab Ethelind's hand, and we turn and run. When I glance back to make sure he and Sander are following us, I slide to a stop, my feet rooted to the ground all over again. The smoke has divided into five wisps. Four drift forward, almost lazily, toward the faces of the guards, who stand as though in a trance: immobile, eyes wide.

The fifth wisp heads for Jek and Sander.

"Jek!" I scream.

They're close behind, but Jek struggles with each step because Sander can't seem to make his feet move fast.

"Go!" Jek says.

I take one last look at the guards. The smoke has disappeared, and they've collapsed on the ground, their faces crumpled in a mix of horror and pain, their hands clenched against their chests. Has the smoke gone *inside* them?

"Go!" Jek says again.

I see the urgency on his face. The purple wisp follows him like an arrow in slow motion.

I grab Ethelind's hand and run.

## 20

E thelind and I stumble to a stop in front of the safehouse. It's tall and imposing and made of stones cemented together like a misshapen jigsaw puzzle. It looks familiar, but I can't figure out why.

"Nyssa, come on!" Ethelind shoves me forward.

We push open the heavy planked doors and step into a cavernous room that's damp and dismal. Stained-glass windows line the walls to our left and right, but they're dusty and unloved. Small slivers of light stretch through the grime but barely illuminate the gloom.

"It's a church!" I point to the cross that hangs lopsided at the front of the room. In our long-ago class about life after the terrorist attack, we learned that churches were destroyed. Why did this one survive?

"Get to that table."

Jek's voice comes from behind and startles me from my reverie. I'd been so lost in my observations I didn't hear him come inside. I whirl at the same moment he doubles over in a coughing fit. He loses his grip on Sander, who slides to the floor without a sound and lies motionless.

Jek turns and pulls the doors closed, then stumbles down the aisle, past Sander, Ethelind, and me, and to a long wooden table that sits at the front. It's covered in an old, thick crimson cloth that brushes the floor.

He motions for us to come. "Can you two help Sander?"

Ethelind and I grab Sander's arms and drag him down the aisle and to the table. He mumbles something unintelligible before his head lolls to the side. I try to ignore the growing red stain across his chest as we lay him down in front of the table.

"Now what?" I stand and look at Jek.

"Hold this up." He points at the cloth covering the table.

I obey, and he crawls beneath it.

"There's a button on the underside," he says. "Have to press my key against it."

He wiggles out from under the table, and the floor beneath it slides open to reveal a staircase leading down into darkness.

I pull our flashlight from the book bag and shine it down the stairs. "Who's first?"

Jek doubles over in another bout of coughing and can't reply.

Once he quiets, I turn to Ethelind. "Think you and I can get Sander down there on our own?"

She glances between him and Jek with uncertainty. "We don't have much choice."

"Loop your arms under his shoulders, and I'll hold his legs," I say. "We can carry him that way."

Together, we pull him down the stairs and collapse at the bottom. Jek stumbles down behind us and presses his key against a circular button attached to the wall. The door above us slides into place.

I sit on the stone floor for only a second before rolling to my feet and pulling the first aid kit from the book bag. After I've wrapped a bandage round and round Sander's chest, I sit back and study him. Blue circles frame his eyes, and his lips are colorless and slightly parted. His breathing is shallow and raspy. The bandage covers the bloodstain, but something tells me it won't be enough.

A light flicks on behind us, and I turn to survey the room. It's circular and made of stone, which does nothing to alleviate the damp cold. Thick blankets lie folded on a chair, and I toss one each to Jek and Ethelind, wrap another around myself, and cover Sander with the last one. Then, I fix my gaze on Jek.

"What did you throw at the Guard?" I ask.

Jek sinks onto the chair and closes his eyes. He's quiet for so long I begin to doubt whether he'll answer. "It's the gas Omri used to attack Maren," he says at last.

Somehow, his answer doesn't surprise me.

"I thought we'd get out of the way in time, but—" He doubles over coughing.

Ethelind and I exchange a glance.

After a moment, he exhales a shaky breath. "It got to me." A flicker of terror shoots across his face. "It went straight up my nose before I could do anything."

"Why did you have that gas, Jek?" I ask. "You were supposed to have the antidote—that's it."

He stares at me, now wary. "If I didn't have that gas, we'd all be on our way back to the Central Capital right now." He coughs again, and this time, he doesn't recover as well. He leans forward and cradles his head in his hands, his chest heaving with each breath.

"You didn't answer the question." I hear the stubbornness in my voice and the lack of sympathy. This was supposed to be a rescue mission. Why did he have that gas?

"Nyssa?" Ethelind taps my arm.

"What?" I snap. I turn to her, but she's staring at Sander. His breath comes quick, and his eyelids flutter. As we watch, a breath escapes his lips like a sigh. He's still.

"Sander?" Ethelind leans over him, her lips nearly touching his. Her eyes widen, and she sits back. "I think he's dead."

I look down at him, at the smoothed face and half-open eyes, then stand and walk to the wall to press my forehead against the cool stone. How did this happen?

"Tell me why you had it," I say to Jek. I keep my forehead pressed against the wall, my gaze trained on my feet, as I wait for his answer.

When none comes, I whirl to confront him.

He freezes with head tilted back, his closed fist suspended in the air, his expression sharpened by guilt.

"What is that?" My voice rises with each word. I take a step toward him. "Is that the antidote? Give it to me!" I lunge forward, my hand outstretched and trembling.

In one quick motion, Jek opens his fist, pinches a small vial between his fingers, and uses his other hand to twist off the cap. "I'm sorry, Nyssa. I don't have a choice." He puts the vial to his mouth and drinks. When he's done, he twists the cap back onto the vial and places it in his lap.

"Was that the antidote?" I know it was, but I need to hear him say it.

He nods.

"But there's some left, right? You didn't drink it all?"

"It's gone."

A sound somewhere between a groan and a laugh escapes my lips. I sink to the floor, the blanket wrapped around my shoulders. Jek has ended any hope we had of saving our parents. They're going to die. There's nothing to do now. Nowhere we need to be. No way to finish what we started or reclaim the lives we left behind.

I lie on the hard floor and curl onto my side with the blanket wrapped around me. Ethelind has dragged Sander's body to the far wall and pulled the blanket over his face. I can see him from the corner of my eye, and I shift my gaze to a point above the lamp. The glow is hypnotic.

Jek's quiet in the chair. His coughing has stopped, and his breathing is even. It seems the antidote is doing its job. I don't want to check to see whether he's asleep, though. Looking at him will make me angry all over again.

Ethelind lies next to me, curled in her own blanket. "What do we do now?"

## 21

A low hum like the sound of a swarm of bees wakes me from a deep sleep. It grows louder before fading away, then louder again. I rub my bleary eyes as I sit up. My hair is greasy and glued to my cheeks. I peel strands away from my face and turn toward the far wall, hoping, despite everything, that Sander didn't really die. That Jek didn't take the antidote. But there's Sander with the blanket pulled across his body and his nose outlined beneath it. I shudder and take a shaky breath. To be trapped here in this tomb-like place with a dead body is suffocating.

What happens now? The question plays over and over in my head.

"I have some explaining to do."

Jek's voice makes me freeze. I want to be angry. I want to jump up and scream and ask him why he destroyed every chance we had of reuniting with our parents. But it's as though my energy died when he swallowed that antidote. All I want to do is go back to sleep. To curl into a ball and close my eyes and pretend—at least for a moment—that this isn't real.

He slides from the chair and sits on the floor in front of me. Ethelind stirs to my right.

"What's that noise?" she mumbles. Her hair is worse than I've ever seen it, sticking out at every angle. I almost laugh.

"They're looking for us, but we're safe here for now," Jek says. "The door down here is practically invisible. We should rest a little longer."

She doesn't seem to hear him. She yawns and curls into an even-tighter ball on the floor. Her lips part as she falls back to sleep.

"Nyssa." Jek's voice brings me back to reality, and I turn to him.

"Why'd you do it?" I ask. "Tell me."

"I would've died—"

"I'm not talking about the antidote." My reply is sharp, and it energizes me. "I want to know why you stole that gas. Pallas told me you broke into the compound to steal an antidote that will save the people attacked at Maren. She didn't say anything about a poisonous gas."

He doesn't respond, and his face gives nothing away.

I push to my feet and pace with the blanket still tight around my shoulders, making sure to avert my gaze from Sander's body. I stride to the table with the lamp on top, then pivot back toward where Jek sits.

"What's the reason?" My gaze slides to Ethelind. She hasn't moved. I turn back to Jek. "Did you steal that gas because you're a part of the rebellion Pallas suspected? Did you plan to attack the Guard all along? Maybe not here and now but sometime in the future?" I stop and glare at him. "You lied to me! What else did you lie about?"

"It's not like that." Jek's voice is frustrated.

"Some brother you are," I say. "It's not like your plan's going to work now anyway, is it? Look at us." I wave my hand in front of me. "We're trapped. They're hunting us out there, and we have nowhere to go." I gulp down a sudden sob.

"I'm not your brother."

The words are so soft I almost don't hear them, and when they register, my body goes numb. "What?"

"I told you I have some explaining to do." He stares at the floor, refusing to meet my gaze. "Your real brother was actually at Maren when it was attacked. Along with your mom and dad." He glances up at me, then looks back at the floor and clears his throat. "My real name is Duncan. I'm part of a group called the Cord." He stands and paces in front of me, keeping his gaze trained on the floor. "The Cord was created after Omri attacked Maren fifteen years ago. I joined three years ago, as soon as I turned eighteen. That's how old you have to be." He pauses and looks up at me. "Gideon's in the Cord."

"Gideon?" I sink to the floor and take a deep breath. "So, when he knocked you out and arrested you, it was for what? To make sure no one found out he's part of your group?"

"Exactly."

"What about Greer?"

"Not eighteen yet, so not an official member, but he knew about us." He rakes a hand through his hair. "Your brother, Jek, is in the Cord, too. He's one of my best friends, actually. That's how I learned about your matching ankle tattoos.

"Anyway, the Cord's usually responsible for scouting out safehouses across the country for people who want to make it to Fortune's Fall. But after the gas attack on Maren, we were tasked with infiltrating the presidential compound and stealing not only the antidote but the gas, too." He stops and turns wide, pleading eyes toward me. "I don't know what the gas is for. I was following orders. That's the honest truth."

"And Pallas?" I glance at Ethelind. She still hasn't moved. "Did she know you planned to steal the gas, too?"

Jek—Duncan—shakes his head. "I don't think so. It's true

someone had another dream in Fortune's Fall and she was called back to interpret it. Infiltrating the compound was the perfect opportunity to sneak her out." He kneels in front of me, his hands clasped.

"It was Pallas's idea for me to pretend to be your brother. You're the only other person who can interpret the dream in Fortune's Fall, and she thought—if something happened to her —you'd be more likely to go in her place if you believed I was your brother instead of a stranger."

He sighs. "At least, that's what Gideon told me she said. He stole that photo of your family from your room and got it to me. That was Pallas's idea, too. She wanted me to have as much proof as possible that we were related if you asked questions."

"But you were surprised when I came to your cell," I say. "You're telling me it was all an act?"

He smiles. Quick. Gone. "I wasn't sure you'd actually come. When you showed up, I couldn't act like I was expecting you. That would've taken too much time to explain."

I close my eyes and exhale a shaky breath. For a fleeting moment, I had a brother. Here. On this journey with me. But it was a lie, and I'm all alone without Greer, without a plan, without anything, really, except Ethelind and a liar I should be angry with, but I'm too tired to care.

*Let go and listen.* Pallas's voice whispers through my mind as clear as though she's standing beside me.

It's what she always told me before we'd study a dream. She said what set us apart from everyone else was our ability to follow the truth, no matter how strange it might seem.

I inhale. Breathe out and open my eyes. "Duncan." The name sits on my lips like a stranger. I study him, the shape of his nose and the eyes that resemble mine.

"Who's Duncan?" Ethelind sits up and yawns.

"Me. I'm Duncan." He waves at Ethelind, whose mouth falls open in not-fully-awake confusion.

"Duncan pretended to be my brother so I'd leave the Central Capital," I say to Ethelind without looking away from him. "That's about all there is to it, wouldn't you agree?"

Duncan stares at me a moment, then reaches forward and grabs my hands. "Look, Nyssa. I know we probably won't be able to save your family now, and for that, I'm truly sorry. All those people..." He swallows hard. "If only they'd listened to Asaph all those years ago and followed him to the coast. Or stayed in Fortune's Fall. Why couldn't they have done that? Going back to Maren was a stupid idea." He rakes his hand through his hair again. "But maybe I can at least get you to Fortune's Fall in time to say goodbye."

*Let go and listen.*

I close my eyes again as something gnaws at me. My conversation with Pallas after she was arrested.

A town in the Western Region.

Asaph.

Pieces of the conversation swirl around one another, like the objects in the dreams I interpret, and I reach for them, trying to put them into a picture that makes sense.

"You're not really Nyssa's brother?" Ethelind asks.

Before he can respond, a thud reverberates across the ceiling, followed by muted footsteps crossing the floor above us.

"The Guard," Duncan says, glancing at the ceiling.

"Oh no." Ethelind's face turns pale. Her gaze darts from me to Duncan. "I left the jacket up there."

"What?" I ask.

"Sander's jacket. I tossed it on the floor before we dragged him to the stairs." She wrings her hands. "Will they find us?"

"Only way down here is with an exile key, unless they blow the door." Duncan frowns. "But they'll know we're here somewhere if they see Sander's jacket." He stands and turns toward the table. "Time to go."

"How do we get out of here?" Ethelind asks.

"I know what we have to do!" I say before Duncan can respond to Ethelind's question. He whirls toward me, and Ethelind's eyebrows shoot up. "Sorry." I lower my voice, but I can't help the smile that bursts onto my face. The conversation with Pallas has clicked into place. "Please tell me there's another way out," I say to Duncan. I reach for the book bag and pull it onto my back.

Duncan gives me a sly grin. "How'd you know?" The grin disappears, and he raises his brows. "What are you thinking?"

The footsteps echo above us again, and we tilt our heads toward the ceiling. I turn to Duncan, my heart beating loud in my ears. I can't let fear or anger or grief stop me from getting to where we're supposed to go. I'll never know whether my family is dead if we stay here, because staying here means we'll die, too.

"Get us out of here," I say. "I have an idea."

The smile returns to Duncan's face. He turns and taps the base of the lamp three times. The table shifts backward and rotates to the right to reveal a gaping hole.

"Where does this lead?" Ethelind crouches and peers into the blackness.

Duncan crawls inside without replying.

"Are we safe with him?" Ethelind whispers to me. "I don't get why he lied about being your brother."

"It's complicated. But yeah, we're safe."

Something scrapes against the floor above us, loud and heavy.

"They're moving the table." Ethelind stares at the ceiling.

"Duncan?" I peer into the tunnel. "We should probably hurry."

He backs out of the hole with a small, rectangular black device in his hand and sits back on his heels. "I have to notify the Cord about Sander first." He frowns at the device, and the screen glows white when he taps its face.

Sander. How could I have forgotten about him? I still can't bring myself to turn and look at his body. It's easier to pretend he isn't there. "What will happen to him?"

Duncan glances at me, then refocuses on the device. "We'll drag him into the tunnel to be safe. Someone will come get him once the Guard's gone." He speaks without inflection, and I remember his comment about having lost someone before.

Guilt washes over me. It seems so unfair and cruel to leave him here all alone. But there isn't another option.

"How does that work?" Ethelind scoots to Duncan and peers over his shoulder.

"It's an old phone," he says. "The coordinates for the next safehouse are stored in it so people know where to go. We can use it to communicate, too." Just as he presses a button and the screen goes black, something rumbles above our heads.

We glance up.

"Time to move. But first, I have to get rid of this." Duncan pulls up his shirt and peels away the fake skin from around his stomach.

"What are you doing?" Ethelind throws her hands over her eyes.

"It's how he hid the antidote and the gas." I can't tear my gaze away from it, even as nausea wells up into my throat.

The skin separates from his body with a sickening squelching sound, and he tosses it into the tunnel. He yanks his shirt back down and sighs with satisfaction. "That thing weighed a hundred pounds."

Ethelind peeks through her fingers. "That's disgusting."

"Then don't look at it." He jerks his head at me, then at the tunnel behind him. "Help me get Sander in here, Nyssa."

I clench my jaw and force myself to obey. We each grab one of Sander's arms, drag him inside, and lay him against the wall, leaving about a foot of space for us to crawl past.

"You first," Duncan says to me. "Don't forget your flashlight."

I sink to my hands and knees and crawl into the tunnel, pressing against the wall opposite Sander as I move past. Ethelind stays close on my heels. Once past his body, I stop and look over my shoulder. Duncan is behind Ethelind. The table—with the lamp on its top—rotates inward and seals us in darkness. I switch on the flashlight, grip it between my teeth, turn, and begin to crawl forward.

A few minutes later, I stop and swivel the light. The tunnel is made of hard-packed dirt on all sides. "Who made this?" I ask.

"We did," Duncan says. "That is, the Cord did. I didn't actually help. It's an emergency exit. Some safehouses have one, just in case."

"What's the Cord?" Ethelind asks, and I remember she was asleep when Duncan explained it to me.

"A group that helps people get to Fortune's Fall," I say. "Among other things." I inch forward again. "Do you know where to go from here?" I ask Duncan.

"Yep," he says. "The church safehouse was supposed to be one of my stops on the way back to Fortune's Fall, so I had to memorize the emergency alternate route, too."

The hard ground presses into my knees, and the walls close in on me. My breath comes in shallow puffs. Time doesn't exist when you're crawling through the dark, and all I can focus on is putting one hand in front of the other.

At last, I sense a change in the air. It's easier to breathe. I stop and shine the light around. The tunnel is wider, and the ceiling is high enough for us to stand. Two wooden beams that run along the top are attached to evenly spaced posts secured along the walls.

"Good place for a break." Duncan stands and stretches. "We should be out of here soon. The nearest safehouse isn't far, but it's not an easy hike. We'll come out smack in the middle of the mountains."

"Isn't that where we've been the whole time?" I ask.

"Nah. That was nothing compared to this. You'll see." He turns to me, and his eyes glow in the light. "I'm anxious to hear your idea."

I hand out thick slices of bread that Talos provided. It's stale, but we've barely eaten in days, and it tastes like honey. It doesn't take us long to devour it, and when we're done, I smile despite myself.

"Cardiff," I say to Duncan.

"What about it?" He leans against the wall and tosses a canister back and forth, sloshing the water against its sides. Ethelind sits beside him.

I clear my throat. "Pallas's brother Asaph lives in Cardiff."

"We know that already," Duncan says.

"Shut up and listen. Before we left the Central Capital, three scientists escaped. Two were caught, but one got away." I lean forward and clasp my hands. "The one who got away was Pallas's grandnephew. Asaph's grandson. Pallas was convinced he would try to get to Cardiff and find Asaph."

Ethelind sits up. Her eyes remind me of a cat caught in reflected light. "You think he can make a new antidote?"

I grin at Ethelind. "Exactly. Not only do the scientists in Ward C know how to make the gas, but they'll know exactly how to create the antidote, too." I turn to Duncan. "Don't you see? If we can find him and if he can make a new antidote, we can still save everyone!" A new thought occurs to me, and my excitement comes crashing down. "If they're still alive by the time we get there, that is."

"It's an awful lot of *if*s," Duncan says after a few moments, but I can tell he's intrigued. "Even if he can make it, we might not get to Fortune's Fall in time to save everyone. Or what if we get to Cardiff and can't find your guy? Or we *do* find him but he can't make the antidote?" He exhales long and slow. "It might be a wasted trip. And it might mean you don't get to see your family again."

"I know." I hang my head but only for a moment. When I look back at him, my jaw is set. "I think we have to try."

He returns my stare for a moment, then shrugs. "Alright." He stands and brushes the back of his pants. "Want me to carry that for a while?" He points at the book bag.

My eyes narrow with suspicion. "Just like that? You don't want to talk about it anymore?"

"What else is there to talk about? The next safehouse is actually the perfect stop if we want to go to Cardiff." He pulls the book bag onto his back without waiting for my response. "Trust me—I'd much rather try to find this scientist of yours than show up at Fortune's Fall without an antidote."

We walk in single-file silence. The tunnel slants up and down, sometimes so steeply that we have to pause to catch our breath. And then, without warning, it ends.

"Time to get back in the real world." Duncan shines the flashlight to the right, revealing a ladder built into the wall and the outline of a square door in the ceiling. "We'll have to be careful. I don't know how far the Guard's expanded the search."

He hands me the light, and I shine it on the ladder so he can climb to the top. Once there, he lifts and slides the door.

A blast of cold air rushes down into the tunnel. Its bite is so startling I gasp.

Duncan scurries back down the ladder and rubs his hands together. His eyes are lit up like a kid opening a birthday present. "It's snowing."

My mouth falls open. "It's May."

He grins. "I told you. We're in the real mountains now. Anything can happen." He turns to Ethelind. "Want to go first? Coast is clear for now."

Ethelind nods and climbs the ladder. She heaves herself through the opening and disappears.

I climb next without waiting for instructions, taking great gulps of fresh air as I scramble up and out into the open to join Ethelind, who sits with her knees tight against her chest and her arms wrapped around them. Goose bumps erupt across my body, and I quickly mirror Ethelind's position.

"I can't believe it's snowing." She lifts her face to the sky, her mouth open in awe.

We've emerged at dusk—that time of day when the waning light makes everything a little bit blurry—and it takes a second to see the iridescent flakes that drift toward the ground. I turn my face upward, too, and laugh when they tickle my skin.

Duncan collapses on the ground with a thud that startles me. He slides the door back over the hole and covers it with a thick rug made to look like evergreen needles. It's the perfect camouflage, given that we've emerged into a forest of evergreen trees.

He wrestles his necklace from beneath his shirt and checks the compass. "The safehouse is this way." He jerks his head toward the left, then glances up at the sky. "We should hurry. I have a hunch this is going to get worse before it gets better."

## 22

We're no more than a mile into the hike when the wind picks up and the snow falls thick and wet, swirling with increasing abandon. None of us are dressed for a blizzard. I toss a worried glance up at the clouds that hover so low they skim the topmost tree branches, which creak and groan as they're whipped back and forth. Snow stings my cheeks now, a harsh contrast to earlier. I shiver.

"We have to find shelter." Duncan's voice sounds like it's farther away than a few feet.

He breaks into a jog, and we follow with our heads bowed. Soon, it will be dark. What then?

A sharp turn north followed by an exhausting climb finds us at the entrance to a small cave carved into a rocky outcrop. We hurry inside, wet and freezing, my fear only slightly tempered by the unexpected shelter. It might keep us out of the storm, but we're wet and shivering with no way to get dry. Ethelind and I stand together at the entrance—our arms wrapped around ourselves, melting snow glistening in our hair—and watch dusk melt into darkness.

"Blankets are back here," Duncan says from somewhere behind us. "I'll get a fire started."

We spin around, and I grab the blankets Duncan tosses in our direction.

"He knew about this place?" With a trembling arm, Ethelind takes the blanket I offer her. I wrap the remaining blanket around myself while keeping my gaze trained on Duncan, who rummages in the far corner of the cave with his back toward us. When he turns toward us, I break into a smile. He wears a blanket tied around his shoulders like a cape, and his arms are full of firewood.

"The Cord always makes sure there are backup plans in case something goes wrong," he says when he sees my expression. He piles the wood into a small pit to the right of the entrance and lights a match. In minutes, a small fire crackles. Ethelind and I collapse next to it and stretch our fingers toward the heat.

"Isn't this a little risky?" I glance at Duncan. "What if they find the tunnel we used to get here?"

"It's always a little risky. But I doubt the Guard will come this deep into the mountains in a snowstorm." He sits beside me and holds out his hands toward the flames.

We sit in silence, listening to the fire pop and the wind whistle between the groaning trees. Ethelind curls into a ball and falls asleep. I stare into the flames, and my own eyes grow heavy.

"Maybe we should take turns sleeping." I glance at Duncan. "Just in case."

He nods. "Good idea. I'll take first watch."

I don't argue. I curl beside Ethelind and close my eyes.

When I wake, the sky is lighter, and the wind has died. The snow still falls but in a lazy way. Duncan crouches beside me, putting more wood on the fire.

"You should've woken me." I struggle to sit up while keeping the blanket wrapped around me. "Don't you want to sleep?"

"Not tired."

His slumped shoulders and half-closed eyes say otherwise, but I don't comment. My head aches, and I peer around for the book bag. "Any water left?"

Duncan unzips it and pulls out a canister. "The other one's empty."

I take a small sip and glance outside. Snowdrifts frame the entrance, and everything is coated in a thick layer of white. "Are we stuck here for a while?" I frown at the canister, wishing I could drink more but knowing I should share. I twist the cap back on it.

"We need to move as soon as it's light." Duncan glances outside, then turns his attention back to the fire. "If we stay here much longer, we won't be able to get out."

My frown deepens. "How much farther do we have to go?"

"A few miles." He peers outside again, then back at the fire.

When he's repeated this motion four times, I know something's on his mind. "Are you expecting an ambush?" I'm half-joking, even though a sliver of fear darts through my chest.

Duncan shakes his head. "Thought they might've sent help by now."

"Who's coming to help?" Ethelind sits up and shivers. "It's so cold." She wraps the blanket tighter and scoots closer to the fire.

"I sent word from the church that we were on our way to the next safehouse via the emergency route. Figured since we're not there yet, they would've sent help." Duncan sighs. "Doesn't matter. Once it's light, we'll go on our own."

The sky lightens in increments and at last settles on a gloomy gray. I wander to the entrance and lean against the rock, gazing out at an unfamiliar scene. I'm not sure I like the silence of snow. There's something comforting about being able to hear the patter of rain, but this soundless storm is unsettling.

Movement to my right catches my attention. I scan the trees, but nothing moves. Deciding I imagined it, I'm about to go inside when something steps out from behind a tree. I gasp. A mountain lion stares at me, eyes unblinking, muscles sleek and solid beneath her coat. She glides toward me, her gaze never leaving mine, her paws silent on the snow.

"Duncan," I whisper. I move backward into the cave. The mountain lion comes closer. "Duncan!"

"What?" he asks in an overloud voice.

"Shh!" I don't dare look away from the creature, certain one wrong move will have her hurtling through the air to attack.

There's rustling behind me, and Duncan appears at my side. "What's the matter with—"

I point at the mountain lion, and Duncan laughs.

I turn to him. "Shut up!"

"It's Luna!" He falls to his knees and holds his hands out.

The mountain lion pads to us and nuzzles Duncan under the chin like a cat.

"Is he insane?" Ethelind's voice tickles my ear, and I jump.

The mountain lion—Luna—sits on her haunches, nose to nose with Duncan. They gaze at each other as though in silent conversation. After a few moments, Luna stands and walks away, then stops and looks back at us. She does this three times before she returns and sits in front of us.

"We have to follow her," Duncan says. "She'll lead us to the next safehouse."

"Is he insane?" Ethelind whispers again in my ear.

I swat at her. "We can't stay here. Besides, it's obvious they know each other." I turn to Duncan. "Is this the help you expected?"

He nods with enthusiasm. "I figured she'd be the most likely choice in this weather. Easier for a mountain lion to navigate this terrain in a snowstorm than a person."

"A mountain lion." Ethelind stares at the animal with suspicion. "What if it attacks us?"

"Don't be stupid." Duncan bends toward Luna. She licks his cheek, and he laughs. "She's been trained to find people and bring them out of the mountains. She's not going to eat us."

"We have to trust him," I say to Ethelind, though neither of us is happy when Duncan says we have to leave the blankets behind.

We follow Luna through the trees. She makes the hike seem easy as she glides through the mountains. But it's not easy, and my head begins to pulse with pain in sync with each step.

Sometime around midmorning, we take a break beneath a tree whose needles are so thick there's a dry circle around its trunk. I toss the book bag I volunteered to carry onto the ground and blow into my hands to warm them. Luna sits beside us, her tail swishing an indentation in the snow beyond the tree while she scans the area with big, unblinking eyes.

"How much farther?" I ask Duncan.

"Can't be too far." He massages his temples and takes slow, deep breaths. If it weren't so obvious he has another headache, I'd beg him to keep going. The snow has all but stopped, but the air still bites into my skin. My fingers are red and frozen. My hair is damp.

"I thought you knew where we were going!" Ethelind says.

Duncan grimaces and peers up at her, fingers still pressed against the sides of his head. "I do know where we're going, but I don't remember how far it is." He closes his eyes. "Luna knows, though."

"Great," Ethelind mutters. "Our lives depend on a mountain

lion." She slides down to rest against the tree with her knees angled up, then rubs her ankle with a small grimace.

"What's wrong with your ankle?" I bend and try to move her hand so I can see, but she shoves me away.

"Nothing." She wraps her arms around her legs and pulls them tighter against her, then grimaces. "I'm freezing. And it's been forever since I showered. Or slept in a bed. Stop staring at me!" She glares at me.

"Sorry!" I throw my hands into the air. I couldn't help studying the almost-gone bruises on her face or the newly developed blue circles beneath her eyes, a feature I'm certain we share.

"At least the snow stopped," I say after a few moments, hoping to ease the tension. We're all so exhausted I'm surprised it's taken this long for someone to snap. I twirl a strand of hair around my finger and sneak a peek at her. She stares into the distance, a scowl frozen on her face.

Luna stretches and begins to saunter away. Duncan stands and clears his throat. "Time to move."

I pull the book bag over my shoulders and follow him without a word. A glance behind me shows Ethelind shuffling a few feet back, her head down.

We continue west in silence. My shoes have rubbed blisters on both ankles, and my mouth is dry, but I don't want to stop again. I just want to get to the safehouse.

Eventually, the air seems different. It lightens somehow. Without warning, we come into a clearing on top of a hill and are met with drizzling rain that falls from a still-gloomy sky. I ignore it because we also have a perfect view of a line of more hills beyond a valley. And past that—I squint, trying to figure it out.

I turn to Duncan. "Is that—"

"The ocean," he says with a grin.

The gray sky transforms into a murky rolling blue where it

meets the horizon, a shift in color so subtle it's easy to miss. It's a strange sight for someone who's never seen it before.

"So, we're close?" I ask Duncan. Something inside me lifts, and I try not to think about the possibility of food or a warm place to sleep.

He nods and points into the valley. "There's our last safe-house before we go to Cardiff."

I can see the outline of a long rectangular building through the thin mist that drifts along the valley floor. The side closest to us floats in and out of sight. It's deserted and ghostly, but the opposite side is full of movement.

Something wet touches my hand. Luna. She rubs her nose against Ethelind's and Duncan's hands, too, then turns and bounds back the way we came.

"Where's she going?" Ethelind asks, her voice tinged with disappointment.

"She's probably hungry." Duncan clears his throat. "You know, since she decided not to eat us."

Ethelind narrows her eyes, and I bite back a laugh.

"Just admit you liked her, E." I nudge her.

"Never." But her lips twitch.

"We should go," Duncan says. "This mist is good cover."

The memory of our last experience rushing toward a safe-house makes me go with caution, and we descend into the valley without speaking. The building looms ahead of us larger than it appeared from above. As we get closer, I hear raised voices and the whirs and beeps of machinery from the other side of the building. Our side, however, remains deserted. Duncan marches across the paved but empty parking lot to a door inset with a black-tinted window. He knocks three times.

Silence.

He knocks again, harder. The same three raps.

A shadow passes behind the tinted glass.

"Get behind me," Duncan says. "Just to be safe."

We obey as the door opens to reveal...

Nothing.

Duncan leans forward to peer inside. Alarm bells ring in my brain, and every muscle in my body tenses. I grab Ethelind's arm to pull her away with me at the same moment footsteps sound from within. A large person looms in the doorway.

## 23

When the person steps into the light, Duncan exhales in an audible gush of relief. I step out from behind him to find the doorway blocked by a man with a thick gray beard and bright blue eyes that scan each of us in turn, starting with Ethelind. When they land on Duncan, they widen, and the man grins, revealing bright white teeth.

"Wasn't sure ya'd make it." He grabs Duncan in a hug. He wears a green jumpsuit that's tight across his oversize belly, and his hands are red and weatherworn. "That was a mighty snow-storm y'all got caught in."

Duncan nods against the man's chest. "I know." His voice is muffled. The man releases him, and Duncan grins up at him. "Hiya, Sam."

Sam thumps Duncan on the shoulder. "How'd ya get here, kid?"

"Mountain lion," I say.

Sam turns his grin on me. "Good ole Luna found ya, did she?"

"You know her?" Ethelind asks.

Sam nods. "I'm the one who trained her. She's helped many an exile find their way through the mountains. Lucky y'all got out when ya did. Pass is completely snowed in." He chews the inside of his lip and looks past us toward the misty, snow-covered mountains. Then, he turns to Duncan, stretches out his hand, and wiggles his fingers. "Alright, kid. You know the drill."

"Aw, come on, Sam." Duncan runs his hand through his hair. "Let us in already."

Sam shakes his head. "Nope. You know the rules." He wiggles his fingers again. "Hand 'em over."

Sighing, Duncan pulls his necklace from beneath his shirt. Sam pulls a scanner like the one Talos had from his front pocket and holds it in front of Duncan's necklace. Once it beeps, Duncan presses his thumb against it. It beeps again.

After I've completed the process, too, Sam turns to Ethelind. But instead of handing over her necklace, she stares at him, wide eyed, and doesn't move.

"Her necklace won't match her thumbprint." I link arms with Ethelind. "It's a long story, but that necklace was given to her by someone who's trustworthy." My voice catches, and I take a deep breath. "Someone who wasn't able to come with us. But I promise Ethelind's okay."

Sam studies Ethelind with a frown. "I'm under strict orders not to let anyone in who doesn't have their own key. It's about protectin' all these safehouses from Omri, ya see. One wrong person and we're all through." He makes a slicing motion across his neck.

"She's all right, Sam," Duncan says. "I'll vouch for her, too."

Sam chews on his bottom lip for a moment but finally jerks his head in a nod. "Come on, then. In ya go."

We follow him into the hall and turn into a small office. It's warm and inviting. I stand beside Duncan and Ethelind and wait for Sam to close and lock the door.

"Can't be too safe." He turns and gestures to a small couch and a single chair pushed against the wall. "Sit."

Duncan sits in the chair, and Ethelind and I collapse on the couch while Sam rummages in a small fridge beside his desk.

"He's part of the Cord," Duncan whispers to me.

I raise my eyebrows. "Really?"

Duncan nods. "A lot of the safehouse operators are. Not all, but a lot."

"Here y'are."

I turn to find Sam standing in front of me, holding out ham-and-cheese sandwiches and juice. I mumble a quick thanks before ripping off the wrapper. Ethelind and Duncan do the same, and we stuff our mouths full while Sam makes himself comfortable behind his desk.

"Welcome to Warehouse Number One." He leans back in his chair and clasps his hands behind his head. It sounds like the beginning of a speech he's made many times.

"I'm the Lead Inspector here. We're the Western Region's central point for the inspection of goods. Everything foodwise is transferred here before it's transported up and down the region. That's my day job at least." He winks and sits forward. "I'm also one of the closest safehouses to Fortune's Fall. Run a transport directly there, when no one's watchin' of course." He winks again. "I can get y'all there by nightfall."

My throat constricts. For a second, I consider what it would be like to get on that transport, to make Duncan go to Cardiff on his own and find the scientist. I could see my parents tonight.

"Actually," Duncan says, "we need to get to Cardiff. And we need to get there as soon as possible. What do you think about that?"

I blink. Of course, I can't leave Duncan.

Sam raises a single eyebrow. "Cardiff?"

Duncan nods. "It's important."

Sam taps his fingers against his desk and purses his lips. "I don't know about that, kid. The Guard has a checkpoint between here and Cardiff, not to mention the security gate to get into town. It's awful risky." He shakes his head. "We've got a policy to stick to the Fortune's Fall road. No exceptions. Sorry, kid. I don't think I can manage that."

"There was an attack at Maren." I scoot to the edge of the couch and lean forward. "A group left Fortune's Fall to scout out whether returning to Maren was possible, and Omri attacked them, my family included. Everyone will die if we don't get to Cardiff. There's someone there who can help us save them."

Sam stares at me, the silence stretching to an almost-uncomfortable level. "Yeah, I heard about that." He sighs, his gaze not leaving mine. "Can't say I agree with anyone returning to Maren, but I guess that's not the point, eh?" He scratches his chin, his gaze drifting to a point past my right shoulder.

His eyes glaze over, and the only sign he hasn't fallen asleep with his eyes open is the finger that taps his chin. After what seems like ages, he smacks his hands against his desk. "I don't like it. Don't like it at all. But I reckon part of my job means doin' things I don't like for the sake of the survivors. Besides, what Cord member hasn't broken a few rules in his day, eh?" He grins at Duncan, whose face erupts into an identical expression.

Sam's grin disappears, and he scratches the whiskers along his chin, staring into space again and nodding like he's having a silent conversation with someone. "As luck would have it," he says at last, "there's cargo scheduled for Cardiff in the morning. Probably can redo that schedule to get it there faster." He nods as though he's confirming in his head that the plan will work. "Come on, then." He taps his hands twice on the desk and stands. "Let's see what we can do."

Sam disappears beneath his desk and emerges with green

jumpsuits identical to his. He tosses one to each of us and commands us to put them on over our clothes before handing wigs to Ethelind and me. Mine is short and blond; hers is shoulder length and brown. To Duncan, he hands a thick beard the same dark shade as his hair.

"Everyone got their identities?" Sam asks, pointing to his eyes.

Duncan and I nod, but Ethelind raises a timid hand. "I don't."

"Not to worry, young lady." Sam disappears beneath his desk again. He stands and tosses her a small box. "Pop 'em in your eyes. Your name for the rest of this trip is Allison White."

Ethelind obeys without comment. When Sam's satisfied with our disguises, he leads us into the empty hall. The only noise is the soft tap of our shoes on the concrete and the distant hum of machinery through the walls. We stop at a steel door at the end, and Sam peers through a circular window in its middle before turning to us.

"Break bell's in about ten minutes. Once it clears out in there, I'll get you on the truck with the blue top. That's the one scheduled for Cardiff in the morning, so it's already packed and ready to go. Like I said, shouldn't be a problem to get it there earlier than planned. We'll leave within the hour. Should be able to get you there before sunset."

I've just double-checked Ethelind's wig when the bell rings. A minute passes before Sam opens the door and waves us through.

We enter a large hangar filled with crates stacked floor to ceiling. Labels such as *Corn* and *Almonds* are stamped on those closest to us. Parked along the right are cranes, empty now that the workers have disappeared through exits to the left. The far side of the hangar is open, revealing row on row of trucks parked beyond.

We're halfway to the blue-roofed truck when I glance over

my shoulder and see empty space where Duncan should be. I spot him near the door we came through. He's hunched over, his elbows propped on his knees and his eyes squeezed shut.

I jog back to him. "Duncan?" I lay my hand on his arm. "Your head again?"

He nods and exhales as he stands. We shuffle together to the truck.

"You okay, kid?" Sam studies Duncan when we get to him.

Duncan grunts, and Sam's eyes narrow for a split second, but he doesn't comment. Instead, he gestures toward the door behind the driver's seat. "Ladies first."

I clamber up onto a bench in a space so narrow that when I sit, my knees press against the front seat. Ethelind and Duncan slide in beside me, and our arms overlap.

Sam ducks his head inside. "I know you've been in one of these before, Duncan, so I'll let you get everyone settled." He slams the door.

"Move over." Duncan shoves Ethelind up onto my lap. I grunt under her weight.

"Sorry." She twists her head at an awkward angle to keep it from bumping the ceiling.

Duncan reaches beneath the middle seat, and I hear something click. The whole thing slides back, leaving a gap between us and him.

He winks at us before disappearing through it. Ethelind and I follow him into a larger rectangular space lined with a bench along the back wall. He secures the seat back in its position, and we sit and secure our seat belts. The truck rumbles to life.

"And we're off," Duncan says. "A few of Sam's trucks have these hidden compartments. Can't tell they're here from the outside, so they're perfect for Fortune's Fall transports. Clever, huh? From the inside, it looks like part of the cab."

I have to admit, I'm impressed. The road to Fortune's Fall has been well planned out with its safehouses and secret compasses. "How long have people been going to Fortune's Fall?" I ask Duncan.

The truck jerks forward and turns right. After a few seconds, we pick up speed.

"Eight years? Ten?" Duncan turns to me with a shrug. "You sure were sheltered in that presidential compound, huh?" He says *presidential compound* like it's some sort of disease. "The exiles have been heading there for a long time. The Regional Movement Policy definitely cut down on the numbers, but people are still determined to try."

"But why do they go? What's so bad about living in the Central Capital? Or the Western Region? The Eastern Region? I don't understand why people would risk their lives to leave."

Duncan shrugs again. "You thought your home was the Central Capital until you learned your family was somewhere else." He tilts his head. "Real home is a pretty big draw, don't you think? And for the exiles, it's about returning to the life they were forced to leave behind, that they were forbidden to bring with them when Maren was destroyed."

It's exactly what Pallas told me. How the exiles want to live in their own homes with their own families without being forced to pretend they're someone else. Duncan opens his mouth, then closes it again with a slight shake of his head.

"What is it?" I ask.

"Did Pallas talk to you about anything else?"

I frown. "Like what?"

He glances at me from the corner of his eye. "Never mind." He leans back and closes his eyes. "Cardiff's just a few hours away. Won't be long till we're at the checkpoint."

I stifle a frustrated sigh. I want to ask more questions, but the determined set of his jaw tells me he's not going to elaborate.

After a while, the truck begins to slow.

"Are we there already?" I ask Duncan.

He shakes his head. "Checkpoint. Don't talk."

I sit ramrod straight as the truck rolls to a stop. Muffled voices are followed by a long stretch of silence. I press my hands against my thighs, my ears straining for any hint of sound.

"It's taking a long time," Ethelind whispers.

Duncan silences her with a glare.

The front truck door opens, then slams. Raised voices reverberate through our hideaway and move toward the rear. When the cargo door slides open in a shriek of metal on metal, the hairs on my arms tingle.

I glance at Duncan, and his worried frown confirms my fear: something's wrong. Boots thud across the cargo space behind us, coming closer and closer to where we sit. Duncan places one finger against his lips to warn us to stay quiet.

When the footsteps recede and the door grinds closed, I exhale. But it's not over. Whoever was in the cargo space is now outside and walks the length of the truck, stopping beside our secret compartment. Voices grow louder in an argument I can't hear well enough to understand.

The noise stops without warning. The cab door opens and slams. The truck lurches forward. I'm jerked left. Right. Bouncing as we speed around one curve after another.

"Who's driving this thing?" I brace my hands on the fabric-lined ceiling and press my feet against the floor.

"No way to find out until we stop," Duncan says. "Can't open the door from this side."

"We're trapped?" Ethelind's eyes are wide and deerlike.

Duncan grips the seat on either side of himself and doesn't respond.

Just when I'm sure we're going to speed out of control, we slow down, and then, thankfully, we stop. But the sudden stillness keeps me on edge. The front door squeaks open, then closes. Boots crunch on gravel. The side door opens. I squeeze my hands into fists in my lap. Duncan scoots forward, prepared to do who knows what to whoever opens our door.

The middle seat moves backward and to the side. Light floods in with a rush of fresh air that I gulp like water from a bucket.

Sam's head pops through the opening, and I relax my fists. "Be quick about it." He motions for us to get out.

We crawl through the gap, slide across the back seat, and stumble onto the ground. Sam leans against the side of the truck, one hand pressed against his chin.

"What happened back there?" I'm sweaty and shaky but so relieved to see Sam's face I could hug him.

Sam stares straight ahead with narrowed eyes. "Guard said since we weren't scheduled till tomorrow, they were obliged to send someone along with us to Cardiff." He shakes his head. "Didn't like it. Somethin' in my gut said there was more to it than that." He clears his throat. "So, I zapped 'im."

I gasp. Attacking a guard is a serious offense. An image of the arena flashes through my mind. "Why'd you do that? You could be hanged!"

Sam turns to me and blinks as though he's coming back from somewhere far away. "Didn't aim to kill 'im. Got 'im with the stunner. But you're right. Reckon the time's come for me to head to Fortune's Fall." He sighs, and his eyes take on that glazed look again. "Always knew there was a chance I'd have to go, but I sure do like runnin' that safehouse." He points toward the right. "Cardiff's beyond that ridge. This is as far as I can take you, 'specially now that there'll be a warrant out for me. You're on your own."

Duncan strides forward and embraces him. When he steps back, their hands are still clasped. "May He be with you," Duncan says, his voice pitched so low I almost don't catch the words.

"And with you," Sam says.

I'm surprised by the tears that spring into my eyes. I'd forgotten about the phrase, about how I'd wanted to ask Greer what it meant. And now, it's too late. I draw a shaky breath. I've been okay so long as I refuse to think about him, but the moment his face pops into my mind or something happens to remind me of him, I'm overwhelmed with grief all over again.

A single tear drifts down my cheek, but I force myself to wipe it away. I have to focus on what's ahead, not get lost in what I can't change. I just wish it weren't so hard.

I swallow against the lump in my throat and turn to Sam to ask him about the phrase he and Duncan spoke. But he's already stepped up into the truck and closed the door. He veers onto the road and drives away.

## 24

"What's that phrase mean?" I ask Duncan. "The 'May He be with you' thing?"

We stand on top of the ridge that looks down on Cardiff. It's a small town, charming and buzzing with activity. The town center encircles a roundabout full of small cars. Some pull into empty spaces, and people get out to meander through town. Others continue down a road that winds along the ocean cliff toward a small neighborhood.

I loop my fingers through the book bag's straps and inhale the salty air. My gaze wanders back to Duncan, and I study his profile as I wait for an answer.

"Pallas never mentioned it?" His gaze remains focused straight ahead.

"What's she got to do with it?"

Duncan scratches the fake beard glued to his chin and scowls. "I hate this thing." He glances at me, then turns to face the city again. "It's kind of like a prayer of protection."

I'm too confused to respond.

"A prayer to God," he says.

"You're religious?" Ethelind asks before he can say anything more. "But religion hasn't been legal for fifty years!"

"Religion might be outlawed, but that doesn't make it untrue." Duncan's eyes grow hard. "And I hate that word, by the way. *Religious*. It makes me sound so naive. 'Oh, he's *religious*.' Like I have some nasty disease or I'm too stupid or weak to do anything on my own." He snorts. "Do you think Pallas is stupid? Or Gideon and Greer?"

My mouth falls open. "They knew better than to believe that stuff." But doubt wriggles through my brain. I shake it away. "God doesn't exist."

"I'd be careful saying that." His eyes narrow. "Most of the people in Maren kept worshipping God in secret after it was made illegal. When the exiles were brought to the Central Capital, they used that phrase so they could recognize each other, kind of like a secret code. It's a reminder God's watching over us. That He'll keep us safe."

"But Pallas never said anything to me about God," I say. "Neither did Greer."

"I wondered if she'd ever talked to you about it." Duncan shrugs. "Can you blame them for keeping quiet? I know what you were taught in school, and it's obvious what you think about it." He runs his hand through his hair. "I get it, Nyssa. You're smart. You're logical. Believing in something you can't see, that you can't write down or figure out from a formula doesn't make sense. But belief in God is about faith. *Being sure of what we hope for and certain of what we don't see.*" He scratches his beard again. "Is it stupid to trust that Someone is bigger than us, that no matter what happens, He's got us in His hands?"

I chew the insides of my cheeks as I consider what he said, then shake my head. "We don't have time for this."

Duncan studies me for a moment, then nods. "You're right.

But if you want to talk about it later, when we're safe, I'll be here."

"If you talk about it again," Ethelind says, "make sure I'm not around. I'm not interested." She points at the town. "Do we have to go through there to get inside?"

I follow her gaze toward Cardiff's inland border, and everything we've discussed fades to the back of my mind. "We have to go through that?"

A two-lane road winds through the hills and to the city's entrance. A line of cars sits at a security gate that spans the road, waiting for one of the several guards on duty to scan everyone's eyes before each is waved through. To the right of the road is a pedestrian walkway, and this, too, is lined with people waiting their turn with the scanner.

"Yep," Duncan says. "Only residents' cars are allowed inside, so everyone else—tourists mostly—is dropped at the gate and has to walk. We'll join that line."

We shimmy out of our green jumpsuits and hide them in a shallow hole beside a tree before descending the hill. We're back on track, heading toward Cardiff and—hopefully—the missing scientist. It's almost as if the God conversation never happened.

"Why's there a security gate anyway?" Ethelind asks. She stumbles, and pebbles cascade past us.

"It's the closest town to the port of entry for Asian imports, so Omri claims it needs extra security." Duncan pauses to wipe the sweat from his face. "See all those ships docked to the north? A few years ago, someone paid off a captain to fill his crates with people who wanted to leave America. It didn't end well. So now, Omri keeps an eye on everything to make sure Americans stay in America." He smirks. "At least, that's one of the reasons."

"He needs another one?" I shade my eyes with my hand and

squint north. I'd seen the cargo ships, but they're far away, mere blobs against the water, and they hadn't seemed worth more than a passing glance.

"Rumor is that Omri suspects more than one survivor from Maren ended up here," Duncan says. "He stuck the Guard here because he's paranoid about what they might do." His gaze locks on mine. "Speaking of people from Maren, any idea how to actually find Asaph and this missing scientist?"

I don't respond. It's a problem that's bothered me since I had the idea, and I'm still clueless. How do you find someone you've never met in a place you've never been while avoiding the Guard at all costs?

We join the end of the line, making sure to keep a few people between each of us.

"No reason to call attention to ourselves," Duncan whispered before we arrived. "We can meet up on the other side."

The line moves quicker than I expected, and I'm the first of us to reach the gate. Duncan waits his turn a few people back, and Ethelind is even farther down the line.

"Eyes up."

I obey the guard and pass through on trembling legs, resisting the urge to look back at the others as I follow the crowd, stopping only when I reach a storefront window and can pretend to stare at the pastries inside while really watching the reflection of the people coming through the gate.

When Duncan enters, I turn. He spots me and gives a brief nod before wandering in my direction. We stand a few feet apart, and I turn back to the window to watch the reflection for Ethelind.

But she never comes.

"She got pulled aside," Duncan mutters loud enough for me to hear. "They took her into the Guard hut when it was her turn."

I keep my gaze trained on the croissants. "What does that mean?"

"It means we go without her."

"We can't leave her!" I risk a glance at him, then turn back toward the shop window.

"We don't have a choice. Something made them suspicious, and if she gives us away..."

He doesn't need to finish the sentence. If they find out who she really is—if they discover she's traveling with us—we won't stand a chance. A part of me wants to run to the Guard hut and try to save her, but my feet are rooted to the sidewalk because I know I won't do it. Trying to save her isn't logical. It's a risk that will probably lead to our arrest. A guarantee that the group from Maren will never get the antidote and an assurance I'll never see my parents again.

We have to leave her.

My stomach churns with the implications of that choice. I might've been forced to leave Pallas and Greer, but losing them was out of my control. Am I going to willingly walk away from Ethelind?

I stare at my reflection. At the blond hair that makes me unrecognizable. The stretched-out jeans that sag against my hips. I know, deep down, that the wise choice is to leave her, no matter how hard that choice might be. I take a deep breath and turn toward Duncan's reflection. "Where should we go?"

He stares back at my reflection for a moment, as though trying to figure out how serious I am. Then, with a quick nod, he turns toward the cliff road. "Let's head toward the neighborhood. Maybe someone there will know Asaph."

I whisper an apology into the breeze, and we merge into the crowd that ambles toward the cliff. My legs tense with each step that takes us farther from the security gate, and I resist the urge to peek over my shoulder. What's happening to Ethelind right now? Is she hurt? Have they arrested her? What if they let her through after all and she can't find us?

I stop, torn all over again about leaving her. But Duncan keeps moving, and if I don't keep up, I'll end up lost, too. With a deep breath and another whispered apology, I hurry after him across the street that parallels the cliff and onto a sidewalk on its other side. An iron railing separates it from the cliff edge, and I drag my fingers along it, peering at the steep drop to the waves below. The breeze whips the sea-salt air against my face, and I stop and turn my face toward the water. A shoulder brushes mine, and I jump.

"Don't look at me," a quiet voice says.

My eyes widen, but I obey and grip the railing with both hands, my gaze trained straight ahead.

"Listen carefully." His voice is low and so close to my ear I shiver. "I'm going to head south, toward the houses along the cliff. Count to three and then follow me. I'm wearing a green jacket."

A breeze touches my face when the stranger moves past, and then, he's gone.

I turn my head to the left. A brown-haired guy in a green jacket is walking away. I spot Duncan bent over a few feet away with his head propped against the rail, and I step to his side without looking at him. "Another headache?" I stare out at the ocean, my arms propped on the railing. A bird dives into the water, then bursts out with a fish in its beak.

I see Duncan nod from the corner of my eye. "Who was that guy?" he asks.

"You saw?" I glance down the sidewalk. The green jacket is getting farther away.

Duncan stands and braces his hands on either side of his head. "It's like someone's pressing clamps on my brain." He squeezes his eyes shut and exhales through pursed lips.

"He wants us to follow him," I say.

Duncan lowers his arms and wraps his fingers around the railing, then turns to me. A spark of amusement dances in his eyes, and he doesn't have to speak what I know he's thinking. *See? God's watching out for us.*

"What do you think?" he asks.

I take a deep breath. I don't want him to think I agree with him about God, because I definitely don't. But I know what my gut is telling me. "We should do it."

## 25

I lead the way through the crowd, glancing back at Duncan every few steps to make sure he's still there. He stumbles once but waves me away when I stop to help him. Every time I lose sight of the green jacket, a spark of panic ignites, but he always reappears. As we get farther from the city center, the crowd thins, and he's easier to follow.

The shops end abruptly, replaced by a row of houses that line each side of the street. Every house is the same: three stories tall with two windows on each floor. But their colors are different. Blue. Red. Even pink. It's like we've walked into a rainbow.

The stranger continues for several blocks before turning up the stairs of a sky-blue cliffside house. He pauses on the porch and glances around. I stumble to a stop a few feet away and watch him scratch the stubble on his face. He can't be more than a few years older than me—maybe Duncan or Gideon's age—and his brown hair is bushy on top and grown long over his ears. His black-rimmed glasses reflect the light, which keeps his eyes hidden. He motions me forward.

"Nyssa." Duncan joins me, panting a little. He rests his elbows on his thighs and narrows his eyes.

"What?" I bend beside him, alarmed at how pale he is and the droplets of sweat that line his upper lip.

"Is that what I think it is?" He points toward the base of the house's front steps, and I squint to make out what he sees.

"The lamb!" It's small but unmistakable, and I can't help the smile that darts across my face. I grab Duncan's elbow and help him stand. "We're safe. Come on."

I help him up the stairs, and the stranger opens the front door and ushers us inside. I hesitate for a moment before stepping into a foyer that's dim and cool. To our left and right are two closed doors. In front of us, the foyer flows into a bright kitchen. Its back wall is one big window that overlooks sea and sky.

The front door closes with a gentle click, and I turn at the same moment Duncan moans and slides to the floor, his hands gripping his head. I drop the book bag and kneel beside him.

The stranger squats beside me. "Help me get him up. We can lay him down in the library."

We lift Duncan to his feet, shuffle through the door on the left, and lay him on a navy-blue couch next to one of the street-facing windows. I sit on the edge of the couch near Duncan's feet, and the stranger stands beside me, studying Duncan with a frown.

"Stay here." He turns and leaves the room, closing us inside, and I use his absence as an opportunity to examine it.

It's everything a library should be. Built-in shelves line the walls and are filled with books stacked in no discernable order. A blue rug with a geometric pattern sits in the center, its border stopping just short of the couch to reveal mahogany floors.

The stranger returns in less than a minute with water for each of us. I help Duncan sit up and drink while the stranger presses his fingers against Duncan's wrist, frowning as he checks his pulse. Duncan's eyes are squeezed tight against whatever pain rages in his head.

"What happened to him?" The stranger releases Duncan's hand and slides to the floor to sit, looking up at me.

Before I can answer, the door opens, and an old man enters. He's imposing somehow, even though he's hunched over a cane. When he shuffles closer, I see that a white film covers his eyes, and he stares at a point somewhere over my left shoulder. He's blind.

"Cass?" His voice is deep and smooth and completely unexpected.

"I'm here," the stranger says.

"And who's with you?" The old man pauses a few feet from where we sit.

The stranger—Cass—clears his throat and looks at me. "It's Nyssa Ardelone."

My mouth falls open.

"She's with a boy, the same one we saw on the news," Cass says without taking his gaze from me. "Don't know his name, though." He studies my face with such intensity that my cheeks begin to grow warm.

"Nyssa Ardelone?" the old man asks. "Does she have a key?"

I reach into my pocket and pull out my exile key, still attached to its broken chain, and give it to Cass.

He glances at it, then turns and grabs a scanner from the bookshelf. I wait for the now-familiar beep, then press my thumb against it.

"And the boy's?" the old man asks after he hears the beep from my fingerprint.

I turn to grab Duncan's, only to see that he's sound asleep. His face is relaxed. His breathing even. I stand and kneel near his head, pull his necklace from beneath his shirt, and hand it to Cass. Once it beeps, Cass presses Duncan's thumb against it. Duncan never moves.

"There was another girl with them at the gate." Cass stands, walks to the old man, and steers him toward a recliner in the corner. "The Guard wouldn't let her pass."

The old man stops. "Her name?"

"Ethelind," I say.

"Ethelind." The old man turns and taps a path with his cane back to the door. "I'll go and fetch her, then." It's said so calmly, with such assurance, that my mouth falls open again.

"You can do that?"

He smiles. "I think perhaps the Guard can be swayed."

Cass opens the door for him, and I stand and follow them out. The old man descends the front steps, and I step into the doorway beside Cass.

"Who are you?" I say to him. I can't hold back the question I'm dying to ask, and I hold my breath as I wait for his reply.

He turns at the bottom of the steps, his head tilted toward where we stand. "I'm Asaph." He gives us a small wave before turning and walking toward town.

I turn to Cass with a smile I can't contain. "And you—are you the missing scientist?"

A flash of fear crosses Cass's face so quickly that for a moment I think I must have imagined it.

He grabs my arm and pulls me into the foyer, closes the door, and locks it. When he turns to me, his fear has been replaced by anger. "Do you have any idea what might happen if someone heard you?" He takes his glasses off and glares at me while he cleans them on his shirt.

I ignore the stab of guilt and rest my hands on my hips. "Well, are you?"

He stares at me unblinking, and I stare right back. A standoff of sorts. The anger melts away at last, and he puts his glasses back on with a sigh. "Let's go back to the library. I'll explain everything."

We slide to the rug in front of the couch, which is the only furniture other than the recliner in the corner and a small table beside it. He leans back near Duncan's feet, and I settle near Duncan's head, turning so I face Cass with my knees pulled to my chest.

I wait for him to break a silence that's interrupted only by an occasional snore from Duncan. Light streams through the windows behind us, bathing us in sunshine that doesn't quite reach the corners of the room. A single fleck of dust floats through the air, and when it disappears somewhere in Cass's thick hair, he reaches up and scratches the spot where it lands, as though he felt its presence.

"Yes," he says, still scratching his scalp. "I'm the scientist." He turns to face me, his hands clasped in his lap. "But I think you knew that already."

I pull my knees tighter against me. "I wasn't totally sure, but I hoped it was you."

I study him. Black-rimmed glasses over brown eyes. Freckles that dot his nose, and full lips framed by stubble. There's something familiar about him, even though I know we've never met. I'm drawn to him despite myself.

We lock eyes, and I watch, surprised, as his cheeks turn red. I blink and shift my attention to the window. Greer's face flashes uninvited in my mind, and this time, a stab of guilt accompanies the inevitable sadness. I close my eyes, but it only makes the image sharper, the hollowness inside me more intense. I take deep breaths, one after the other until his face dissolves into a murky, melancholy shadow.

"You worked at the compound," I say at last. "But I've never seen you before. I didn't even know Pallas had a nephew." I open my eyes but keep my gaze trained on the window. A blue car moves down the road slowly, like it's searching for the right house. A seagull perches on the roof of the house across the street, head turning back and forth like a robot.

"I'm good at blending in," Cass says. "I saw you every now and then though. And Pallas talked about you, too, of course."

At the mention of Pallas, I turn back to face him. Our gazes meet again, but this time, I refuse to look away.

"I saw you join the line to get into town today," he says. "It was smart to go in separately, although I guess it didn't work out so well for that girl with you." He pauses, and his gaze drifts to Duncan for a moment before returning to me. "Why are you here?"

"To find you."

His brows dip behind the rims of his glasses. "I'm listening."

I clear my throat, trying to sort through how best to explain. "When we left the Central Capital, we were supposed to take an antidote that Duncan"—I jerk my head toward his sleeping form—"stole from Ward C. The plan was to get it to Fortune's Fall and give it to the survivors of the gas attack at Maren." I pause to take a sip of water, swallow, and clear my throat. "You know about the attack?"

He nods.

"The Guard caught up with us. It turned out that Duncan hadn't just stolen the antidote; he'd stolen the gas that was used at Maren, too. He threw it at the Guard so we could escape." I stop as I remember the strange purple smoke that seemed alive, then shudder and close my eyes.

When I open them, Cass's attention hasn't wavered.

"Duncan didn't get away from the gas in time, and it attacked him, too..." My voice drifts into nothing. It sounds ridiculous. *The gas attacked him, too.*

"Keep going," Cass says. Something's changed in his voice. He's wary. Unsettled.

I reach to tighten my ponytail, but my fingers grip the thick strands of the wig I've forgotten I'm wearing. If Cass still recognized me with it on, I should be thankful nobody else did. I peel it away from my hair with a shudder at what might have been and place it in my lap, then run my hands along my greasy, flattened hair.

"Duncan drank the antidote—all of it—to save himself, which meant we had nothing to take to Fortune's Fall. But then, I remembered what Pallas told me about her three brothers and how Asaph came here to Cardiff. She hoped that you'd come here, too, after you fled the Central Capital." I pause. I'm curious why he left. *No, Nyssa. Now's not the time.* "I hoped, if we could find you, that maybe you'd be able to make a new antidote since you were a scientist in Ward C." I study him for a moment. "So, can you?"

Cass's gaze slides away and settles on the wall behind me. He pulls his glasses from his face and twirls them between his fingers. After what seems like ages, he turns back to me. "I know how to make it." He presses his lips into a firm line and slides his glasses back on, pushing them up the bridge of his nose.

"So, you'll help us?" I can't keep the hope from my voice.

Before he can answer, the front door opens with a soft creak. Cass jumps up and jogs to the foyer while I stumble to my feet. I've taken two steps toward the hall when he returns to the library. He's followed by two people.

"Ethelind!" I hurry to the door and wrap her in a tight hug that's not reciprocated. "Are you okay?" I step back to consider her.

She levels a glare at me. "You left me. The Guard was going to send me back." Her lower lip trembles, but her eyes blaze with anger.

"I know. I'm so sorry." I hang my head, at a loss for more words. How do I justify our decision that someone else's life was more valuable than hers?

"You're safe now, young lady." Asaph's cane taps the floor as he makes his way to the recliner. "Those two did what they thought was best. Maybe it was right; maybe it wasn't. But it's all irrelevant now." He lowers himself into the chair and props his cane beside him, keeping his right hand wrapped around its handle.

Ethelind's mouth falls open. "I was already in the transport bound for the Central Capital when you got there!"

I lift my head. "Oh, E, I'm so sorry." I try to grab her hand, but she resists. Her gaze is still locked on Asaph, who stares at her as though he can see her.

I stifle a sigh and turn to Asaph. "How'd you get her out?"

"I was owed a favor," he says without removing his gaze from Ethelind.

Ethelind exhales and glances around the room with wary eyes. "I'm so tired." She slides down onto the floor and leans against the couch near Duncan's feet, her head resting against the arm, her eyes closed.

I'm exhausted, too, and I want to talk to Ethelind alone, to try to make her understand why Duncan and I left her behind and see whether there's any chance she'll forgive me.

"Cass?" Asaph says. His fingers tighten around his cane's handle.

"Here, Grandfather," Cass says from the doorway.

"Bring water and food for everyone, won't you?"

Cass disappears down the hall without another word.

"Now, then." Asaph leans back in his chair. "While we wait on our snacks, why don't you explain to me why you're here?"

## 26

I return to my seat on the floor near Duncan's head. It doesn't take long to repeat to Asaph what I already told Cass. He listens quietly, and when I finish, the silence lingers until Cass returns with a tray filled with food, plates, and water glasses. He sets it on the table beside the recliner.

"Help yourselves." Cass grabs a plate and fills it before sitting beside me on the floor.

Ethelind pads to the table, fills a plate and grabs a glass, and returns to her seat without speaking.

"Pallas told you where to find me, eh?" Asaph asks before I can move toward the food. He flexes his fingers around the cane's handle.

"Yes, sir," I say.

"And why is it that you're here?"

I blink in confusion. "I told you. We need Cass to make a new antidote to take to Fortune's Fall."

Asaph shakes his head. "Taking the antidote to Fortune's Fall is Duncan's responsibility. Why did you—Nyssa Ardelone —leave the Central Capital?"

Cass sets his plate on the floor and goes to refill another

one. When he returns, he hands it to me along with a glass of icy water. "For you." He slides down beside me.

I take it gratefully and sip the drink as I try to figure out how to respond to Asaph's question.

"I knew you before the exile, you know," Asaph says before I can speak. "Of course, you wouldn't remember me; you were too young. But I remember when Pallas took you under her wing. After you were both exiled, she mentioned you now and then through our occasional communication." He pauses. "She's always been fascinated by your skill."

"What's he talking about?" Ethelind asks with mouth full and eyes wide. Curiosity seems to have overridden her anger.

I set the glass down. Pallas shared classified information with her brother? I'm surprised at first, but she must have done it for a good reason. He's her brother, after all. And he knew she could interpret dreams before she worked for Omri.

"Something happened to my sister, didn't it?" Asaph's voice is soft now. Sad. "She sent word she was going to Fortune's Fall. But since the young lady with you"—he tilts his head in Ethelind's direction—"carries an exile key she says Pallas gave her from prison, I have to accept she didn't make it there."

Duncan snores and rolls so that his breath puffs against my neck. I scoot over, aware of Cass's leg now pressed against mine. I sense his and Ethelind's attention on me, but I avert my gaze while I search for how to reply.

I set my plate on the rug. If Asaph knows the truth about Pallas's role—and mine—at the presidential compound, does Cass know, too? That means Ethelind is probably the only one left in the room who doesn't know why I'm here, apart from wanting to see—and save—my family. She slept through the entire conversation about interpreting dreams when we were hiding beneath the church.

Asaph should hear what really happened to Pallas. And it's only fair that Ethelind knows the truth after all she's been through because of me. I take a deep breath and fix my gaze on Asaph.

"Pallas lied to Omri about a dream he had that prophesied his downfall," I say. "I don't know why he got suspicious that she'd lied, but he did, and I was forced to interpret it again." My voice falters, and I take a steadying breath. "I told him the truth. I told him the dream showed he would be overthrown. But I didn't know I was betraying Pallas." The words come out in a rush. "Omri tricked me. He told me it was my final test before I became his aide and that Pallas had lied about its meaning on purpose to see if I could give the correct interpretation." I stop and search Asaph's face, desperate to find any hint of understanding. I need him to know I never wanted to betray her.

But he remains silent; his face gives nothing away.

"She was arrested," I say with a sigh. "I was able to see her, though, and she said she'd been asked to leave with Duncan and go to Fortune's Fall because someone there had a new dream and they needed someone to interpret it." My voice falters again. "She asked me to take her place. She said, if I went, I could see my family again." The last few words come out in a whisper, and I look away. Out the window. At the floor. Anywhere but at Asaph.

"Cass?" Asaph's voice startles me, and I blink toward him.

"Yes, Grandfather?"

"Lower the screen."

Cass casts a side glance at me before he stands and walks to the wall behind Asaph, grabs a small controller, and presses a button. He rejoins me on the floor as a flat black screen descends from the ceiling, stopping midway to the floor to the left of where Asaph sits.

I gasp. "Is that—"

"A dream screen." Asaph smiles.

"What's a dream screen?" Ethelind asks.

"It's a way for us to watch dreams that have been recorded," Asaph says.

"I don't understand." She glances at me. "You interpret dreams? Omri can predict the future?" She turns to Asaph. "I don't understand any of this."

"Hush. Watch." Asaph nods toward the screen.

The screen turns blue for a split second before a hawk appears. It hovers above an orchard-filled valley that stretches to the ocean on one side and to snow-covered mountains on the other. The hawk flies to the ocean, then turns, crosses back over the valley and makes its way to the mountains, where it turns and passes over the valley again on its journey back to the ocean. It does this two more times. Ocean. Valley. Mountains. Repeat. As it heads back toward the ocean on its third flight, a tree appears.

The hawk crashes into it.

I gasp. But it's not over. The hawk disappears on impact, and the tree splits into two trees. From each tree, a pine cone emerges and falls to the valley floor. The ground where they land turns green, and the color spreads all the way to the mountains.

The screen fades to black, and Cass hits a button for it to rise back into the ceiling. Nobody moves. Nobody speaks. A car door slams somewhere nearby.

"Whose dream is this?" I ask.

"Mine," Asaph says, confirming my suspicions. He stares at the wall, tapping one finger against the top of his cane.

I press my fingers against my temples, trying to remember everything Pallas told me about Asaph's dream from fifteen years ago and its connection to Omri's dream foretelling his downfall. But it's no use, and my head begins to ache. I take a deep breath and look up at Asaph. Did Pallas tell him that Omri's latest dream was a version of this one? And more importantly, why would two very different men have such similar dreams?

## 27

"I've had that dream for fifteen years," Asaph says. "That's a long time."

"I don't understand," Ethelind says again. She turns to me. "Nyssa?"

I swallow my own questions. "Sometimes dreams, like this one, predict the future. Omri's had a few, and it was Pallas's job to interpret them."

Ethelind's mouth is half-open like she wants to speak, but then, she shakes her head and closes it.

"It was going to be my job, too," I say. "Pallas and I would watch his dreams on the dream screen, and she would give him its interpretation. I wasn't allowed to interpret them yet because I was still in training."

"That's why you were selected to be a presidential aide," Ethelind says. "You were going to be his dream interpreter?"

I nod.

"Do you know why I showed you this dream?" Asaph asks.

I hesitate again. "Because you know Omri had a similar one?"

He nods. "When Pallas told me he'd had a dream like the

one I've had for so long, we knew things were about to happen."

So, Pallas did tell him about Omri's dream. I lean forward. "Pallas said that, too, after Omri had his dream. That she knew things were about to happen. But she didn't explain it."

"Things were about to happen," Asaph says, "because of the anomalos."

I glance at Cass, and sensing my confusion, he turns to face me. His eyes glow with sudden excitement.

"*Anomalos*," Cass says. "It's a term Grandfather and his colleagues used at the university in Maren to theorize about why the same symbols appeared in different people's dreams. For example, in Grandfather's dream, the hawk flies to the ocean, then to the valley, then to the mountains three times, right?"

I nod, trying to keep up with his train of thought.

"Grandfather wasn't the only one who dreamed that particular scene. Both of his brothers, Thaddeus and Zeb, dreamed the same thing. Fifteen years ago, Pallas interpreted the dreams to mean that each of her three brothers was meant to go to three different places after Omri attacked Maren." He reaches for his glasses as though he'll take them off, thinks better of it, and drops his hand into his lap.

"According to Pallas's interpretation," he says, "Grandfather was meant to come here, to Cardiff—"

"I chose to come here before Maren was attacked," Asaph says. "Though that's a story for another time."

Cass smiles at his grandfather before turning back to me. "Zeb stayed in the valley, near Maren. And Thaddeus went to Fortune's Fall with the survivors."

"This anom—" I stumble over the word. "What does it have to do with everything now? Why does Omri's dream have the same symbols as Asaph's? They don't mean the same thing."

"Anomalos." Cass finishes the word for me. He turns to Asaph. "Grandfather, care to explain your theory?"

"When the anomalos occurs," Asaph says, "that is, when more than one person dreams of the same or similar symbols, we believe it indicates prophecies in our dreams are soon to be fulfilled. When my brothers and I all began having the same dream consistently, we theorized the attack on Maren was imminent and that we would have to go our separate ways soon. And we were right. That's anomalos."

"But even though Omri's dream has the same symbols as yours, it doesn't mean the same thing," I say. "His is a prophecy about his downfall, not where you and your brothers were meant to go."

Asaph smiles. "I'm getting there." He clasps his hands. "Pallas and I believe Omri's dream is an extension of mine. It's a new scene that both overlaps and adds on to a chain of prophesied events."

"Okay," I say. "But why would Omri have the dream at all? I thought the prophetic dreams were limited to you and your brothers."

"Ah," Asaph says. "A question that has plagued my sister and me." He presses his thumb between his brows. "The only theory that seems to make sense is that Omri's dreams serve to warn the exiles of things to come more so than him. It's no accident Pallas serves as his interpreter, and with her there, she's able to see what he's plotting in response to his dreams and then warn the other exiles." He wraps his hand around his cane again. "Now, to answer your earlier question about why anomalos matters in regards to Omri's dream. As I said, I've had this dream consistently for fifteen years, which means I was dreaming it at the same time Omri dreamed it. And remember, even though his doesn't contain the same original prophecy as mine—that my brothers and I would leave Maren—both dreams have the same symbols playing out in scenes that we believe connect to one another. It's still anomalos. And if anomalos means prophecies are soon to be fulfilled, we can assume Omri's downfall is imminent."

Duncan moans, and I turn toward the couch. He rubs his eyes and struggles to sit up. Cass and I scoot apart so he can plant his feet between us.

"How are you feeling, young man?" Asaph asks.

Duncan touches the side of his head and grimaces. "Not much better." He looks at Cass, then Asaph, then Ethelind. His eyebrows shoot up.

"Yeah, it's me," Ethelind says with a sarcastic wave. "No thanks to you and Nyssa."

I stare at her with a frown, but she avoids my gaze. With a sigh, I turn to Duncan. "That's Asaph in the chair. And this is Cass." I tilt my head toward him. "The missing scientist who's going to make our antidote."

Duncan's brows shoot down and his eyes narrow. "How old are you?"

The question is so unexpected, but also exactly what I've wanted to know, that a giggle slips out of my mouth before I can stop it.

Asaph sits back in his chair and chuckles. "He's nineteen. And a bit of a prodigy." He winks in Cass's direction.

Cass rolls his eyes. "I hate that word."

"He was the youngest scientist in Ward C." The pride is obvious in Asaph's voice. "But it's best if you don't remind him of that. As you can see, he gets a little... testy." He winks again.

Cass shoots Asaph an exasperated frown. Duncan's expression is a mixture of envy and respect.

"You never actually said you'd help us," I say to Cass.

"Of course he will," Asaph says before Cass can respond. "Won't you, grandson?"

"I will." Cass gives me a solemn nod, his gaze steady with the same intensity I saw in it earlier. He smiles, and unexpected warmth ripples through my insides. I blink, frown. Stamp it down.

Asaph pushes to his feet and leans on his cane. "Show them to their rooms, Cass." He gestures toward the door with his free hand. "They need rest. We've given them a lot to think about, and you'll all need your energy in the days to come."

Cass directs Duncan into a room on the second floor before leading Ethelind and me to a room on the third floor with two twin beds in front of the street-side window.

"Bathroom's down the hall if you want to shower. Good night," he says before he leaves.

By the time Ethelind and I've taken turns in the shower, the light has faded enough to shroud the corners of the room in shadows. We settle into our beds, and I turn off the lamp that sits on a table between us.

But neither of us, it seems, can sleep. I stare at the ceiling, listening to her toss back and forth. When she's finally still, I roll to my side so I'm facing her. "Why didn't the Guard let you through?"

She doesn't respond, and just when I've decided she either didn't hear me or, more likely, decided to ignore me, she sighs. "Random check."

I frown. "But that doesn't explain why they put you in the transport back to the Central Capital."

"You think I know the answer to that? You think the Guard had a little chat with me to explain why they wouldn't let me through?" She rolls to her side, facing the wall. "I'm going to sleep."

I listen to her breathing become even. I'd hoped her anger was gone for good, but I guess I was wrong. I sigh and roll to my back. The darkness amplifies sound, and I listen to the hum of an occasional car on the street below. Clanking echoes through the walls from downstairs, like someone is rearranging pots in the kitchen, and it's followed by a creak on the stairs as someone climbs to the third floor and treads past our room. A door closes with a quiet click, and all goes silent.

---

I WAKE with a start sometime later, not realizing I even fell asleep. My senses are alert, but my body is frozen. I have no idea what woke me. Judging by the total darkness and Ethelind's still-even breathing, it's the middle of the night.

The stairs creak one after the other as someone descends. That must be the sound that woke me. I'm wide awake, so I roll from the bed, tiptoe across the room, and open the door. It squeaks, and I grimace, but Ethelind doesn't move. I slip from the room and pull the door closed behind me.

Soft light radiates up the stairs, and I follow it all the way to the kitchen, pausing in the doorway when I see Cass seated at the table in front of the wall of windows. He wears navy-blue pajama pants and a gray T-shirt. His hair sticks up in comical spikes all over his head. Half a sandwich sits in front of him alongside a glass of milk and a glowing, propped-up tablet.

Sensing my presence, he looks up. His eyes are dark behind his glasses. "Can't sleep?" He pulls out the chair beside him and pats it.

"Nope." I pad into the kitchen and sink into the chair, curling my toes against the cold floor.

"Here." He slides his plate in front of me and points at the remainder of his sandwich. "Made this earlier, but I'm not that hungry now. You can have it."

I glance at him, and his lips curl in a small smile. I'm startled again by a strange sense of familiarity. "Thanks," I say with an answering smile.

He turns back to his tablet, and I take a bite as I try to decipher the pictures on his screen. What looks like dozens of pieces of cylindrical pasta rotate around one another, growing smaller and then bigger as they move. Some expand faster than others. Some duplicate. Complicated math formulas are attached to some of them.

"What is this?" I ask once I swallow.

Cass leans back with a sigh and crosses his arms. "Project M. Probably better known to you as the purple gas Duncan used to help you escape the Guard."

My eyes widen. "Project M. As in *M* for *Maren*? This is what Omri used in the attack?"

He nods and points to one of the objects as it spins and grows. "This is its molecular breakdown. We were able to restructure the original gas at its base level. Instead of dispersing like you'd expect gas to do, it actually targets specific victims." He pauses and stares unblinking at the screen. Then, with a quick shake of his head, he taps the screen, and the objects disappear. They're replaced by a diagram of the human body.

"Once the gas locates its victim, it enters through the nose." He taps the head, then drags his finger down and places it on the chest, drawing a purple line on the screen. "Then, it makes its way to the heart, where it causes what's called 'chronic vascular rejection.'"

"And that means what?" I set the remaining bit of sandwich on my plate, no longer hungry. I remember with renewed terror watching the gas split into strands and weave toward each guard and Duncan.

"It means, once it's inside the body, it mutates the heart's cells to make the body think the heart is a foreign object. When that happens, the immune system attacks the heart and eventually causes heart failure. Depending on how healthy the person is, death can occur within a few minutes to a few months."

I sit up and turn to face him. "A few months?"

He nods, but his expression is wary. "I know what you're thinking, Nyssa. There's no guarantee your family is still alive.

We have no way to know how healthy they were when they were attacked."

He's right. Still, I can't help but hope. "You worked on this?"

"Someone had to know what Omri's been up to." He shifts in his seat so that we're face to face. "Working on this monster also means I worked on the antidote, you know, and that's even more important."

"So, you were a mole?"

"Something like that." He turns back to the tablet and taps the screen. The body disappears, and the screen turns blue.

"How will you make the antidote?"

"That's the easy part." Cass pushes his glasses up his nose. "All I have to do is draw Duncan's blood and extract the antibodies."

He makes it sound simple, even though I'm sure it's more complicated than that. I lean back in my chair and turn my head to stare out at the black sky. The only sound is the crash of waves on rocks.

"Do you remember Maren?" I ask after a while. I sit forward, press my finger into the bread of the uneaten sandwich, and watch an indentation form.

"A little." He turns off the tablet and slides it to the side. "I left Maren with my grandfather before Omri attacked. I was only four. But I'd already been labeled a prodigy, and my parents thought it was best if I continued to study under him. His voice grows bitter. "I assume they died after the attack. I haven't heard from them since it happened."

I grab his hand without thinking. He lays his free hand over mine. His skin is warm, and something in the way he folds his fingers over mine makes me relax. "Try to go back to sleep, Nyssa." He squeezes my hand, then lets go.

I nod, stand without another word, and tiptoe back upstairs.

## 28

I wake when Ethelind's bed creaks, and I peek through my
eyelashes as she sits up with the quilt pulled tight against
her chest. Sunlight streams through the windows, and
she squints in the brightness.

"Morning," I say, curling my knees to my chest and
burrowing deeper beneath my quilt.

She ignores me, slides out of bed, and pads to the door. "Are
you coming or what?" she asks over her shoulder before
turning the knob.

I uncurl myself from the bed. "Right behind you."

She steps into the hall. "I'm still mad at you, you know."

"I deserve it." I smile and follow her out. She's thawing.
Soon, we'll be back to normal. I'm sure of it.

We find Duncan, Cass, and Asaph in the kitchen. The
aroma of coffee and bacon lingers though their plates are clean
and their cups are empty. My stomach growls, loud and angry,
and I press my hand against it.

Cass stands when we enter. "I'll make more coffee. Bacon
and eggs are in there." He nods toward a sealed platter on the
counter.

Ethelind and I are halfway through our plates when Cass sets coffee in front of us. "Just have black. Sorry."

Asaph stares into space between Ethelind's and my shoulders. "When you're finished, Cass will show you the lab. He's already been explaining to Duncan what has to be done to create a new antidote."

Duncan sits across from me, arms propped on the table, his head turned so he can stare out at the ocean, which rolls and swells beneath a line of low gray clouds. His forehead is furrowed, and his mouth is a thin line.

"Where will we go after the antidote is ready?" I ask, turning to Asaph.

Asaph tilts his head in my direction. "You'll go to my brother Zeb in the valley. He operates the largest dairy in the Western Region as well as a transport to Fortune's Fall." He pushes his chair back and stands. "Now, I believe you have work to do, so I'll leave you to it." He shuffles from the kitchen, the *tap*, *tap*, *tap* of his cane fading as he disappears down the hall.

Cass clears the table, and Ethelind and I help him clean and dry the dishes. Duncan ignores all of us, his head still turned toward the ocean, his fingers wrapped around his coffee cup.

Scrub. Rinse. Dry. Repeat. The chore is mindless, and I'm grateful. We're so close to Fortune's Fall, so close to getting the antidote created. If anything were to happen now—I shake away the thought and snatch another plate from Cass. Scrub. Rinse. Dry. Repeat.

When the last plate is put away, I hang the towel on a hook.

"Ready to go to the lab?" Cass raises an eyebrow at me before turning toward Duncan.

Duncan sighs and stands. "Let's get this over with."

Cass gestures toward the pantry, which is about the size of

my small walk-in closet at the presidential compound. "This way."

I stare for a moment at the pantry lined with food-filled shelves, then turn to Cass, my eyebrows raised.

He chuckles. "Come on. I'll show you."

He steps into the pantry, and the three of us huddle behind him. He pulls a box of cereal from the shelf to reveal a red button on the wall. When he presses it, the whole wall rumbles and then slides to the right, revealing a staircase that winds down and to the left.

We follow Cass over the threshold, and he presses a similar red button to close it. The temperature difference between this strange tunnel and the kitchen is startling. It's cold and damp, and I can hear the waves somewhere below us.

The stairs lead down to a small landing that abuts a rock wall, which has an oval-shaped metal door that curves toward us like a bubble. Cass presses his finger into an indentation in the door's center, and it pops inward and slides to the side.

We follow him into an oblong structure. It's filled with light from a wall of ocean-view windows.

"Whoa." Ethelind walks to the windows and peers down.

"Welcome to the lab." Cass makes a sweeping gesture around the room.

A rectangular table is welded to the center of the floor, and on it sits a case filled with test tubes, glass beakers in all sizes, safety goggles, and a small computer that looks older than Asaph. A small flask hangs above a camping stove, and a lab coat is tossed in a heap at the end.

Cass turns to a set of shelves screwed to the wall beside the door, pulls out a long white cord, and sets it on the table. "Whenever we conducted a new experiment in Ward C, I was able to get a sample to my grandfather, and he could study it here." He glances at me; then, his gaze shifts over my shoulder.

"We're attached to the cliff with steel cables," he says in a louder voice. "We won't fall into the water."

I turn and see Ethelind leaning against the window. She's pale and presses her lips together, like she's trying to keep herself from throwing up. She gives a hesitating nod, crosses the lab, and collapses in a chair at the end of the table.

"Sit here, Duncan." Cass points to a chair on the opposite end from Ethelind. "I promise your part in this only takes a second."

Duncan slides onto the chair with a scowl, and I hide a smile behind my hand at his obvious discomfort. How can someone who takes so many risks be queasy about having his blood drawn?

"Knock it off, Nyssa," he says. "I can see you smiling."

I turn away, fighting the urge to laugh.

"Hold still," Cass says.

I peek over my shoulder. Cass tightens the white cord around Duncan's upper arm, then inserts a needle into Duncan's vein.

"Ouch!" Duncan says at the same moment his arm sprays blood.

"Sorry," Cass says. "This isn't normally in my job description." He rummages with his free hand through the various things scattered across the table.

"What do you need?" I ask him.

"First aid kit." He freezes. "It's in the kitchen. Had to refill it and forgot to bring it back. Can you get it?"

I dash into the stairwell, careful to leave the door open so I can get back inside. At the pantry door, I bounce from foot to foot as I wait for the door to slide open. The yellow first aid kit is easy to spot on the kitchen counter, and I've grabbed it and turned back toward the pantry when someone knocks on the front door. Something about the sound, the firm rap of knuckles twice, then twice more, makes me pause. I tiptoe to the kitchen door and peer down the hallway.

Asaph exits the library and unlocks the door to reveal two guards. I suck in a breath, my feet frozen to the floor. They're tall and broad chested, intimidating in their black uniforms and steel-toed boots.

I force myself to tiptoe backward until I'm hidden in the pantry and have just turned to press the red button when I hear the thud of boots in the hall.

"You're not permitted in private residences without a warrant!" Asaph says.

The footsteps stop with a suddenness that fills me with dread. A quick *swoosh* is followed by something clattering to the floor. Then a soft thud. Despite the risk, I race back across the kitchen and peek into the hallway.

The guards stare at a still form sprawled in the space between their feet.

Asaph. He's face up, eyes wide open, mouth parted. Motionless. I don't have to get closer to know he's dead.

"No!" I throw my hand over my mouth, but it's too late.

The guards pivot toward me. With a gasp, I dart back into the kitchen, the first aid kit clutched to my chest. Into the pantry. The stairwell. I press the button to close the door and bound down the stairs. Shouts come from behind me. Boots clunk against stone. The guards made it onto the stairs before the door closed.

Panic buzzes in my ears. I leap through the lab door and close it. When I turn, Cass, Duncan, and Ethelind are staring at me.

"Asaph's dead," I gasp. "The Guard is right behind me."

Cass doesn't move. One hand stays frozen on Duncan's arm, the other grips the edge of the table. The door shudders. I lunge to the left, certain the guards are seconds away from breaking it down.

Cass motions me forward. "Wrap his arm." He nods toward Duncan.

I hurry to the table. My fingers shake so hard it takes me a second to get the box open and find the bandages. Blood drips from Duncan's arm onto the floor. He squeezes his eyes shut. I wrap his arm as tightly as possible, then turn to find Cass. He's at a keyboard mounted below three rectangular screens that curve with the lab's oval shape. The middle screen flickers to life, and a big circle appears. A dot blinks in its middle and grows into a line that stretches toward the top of the screen.

The door shudders again.

"Cass!" I can't keep the panic from my voice.

"Sit down and hold on!" Cass says.

The entire lab shakes. I kneel beside Duncan's chair and grab hold of the table leg. Duncan and Ethelind fall to the floor and do the same.

"Open up!" One of the guards pounds on the door.

"Here we go!" Cass says.

The whole lab plummets into the sea.

## 29

When we hit the water, white foam splashes across the windows. Something rolls off the table and shatters against the floor. Ethelind shrieks. The chairs topple and slide toward Cass, who has somehow managed to keep his balance and stands with his hands still on the keyboard. The waves push against us, and I'm sure we're going to crash into the cliff.

After a few seconds, a low hum comes from somewhere beneath our feet, and lights flicker on above my head. When I peek out the windows, my fingers tighten around the table leg. The sky is a mere sliver, and water laps higher against the windows. "We're sinking!"

"Not sinking," Cass says. "I know what I'm doing."

I can't tear my gaze away from the windows as we sink lower. After what seems like forever, we skim the bottom of the sea, weaving between hills of sand that shape-shift against the current of murky blue water. We motor toward a school of fish, and they dart out of our way, their silver scales like a beacon in the dark. It's eerie and otherworldly but also kind of fascinating.

I stand on shaky legs and inspect the damage. Everything that was on the table is now on the floor. Ethelind is curled in a ball in the center of a ring of broken glass with her eyes squeezed shut. Her hands are wrapped around her ankle, and blood trickles from between her fingers.

"Ethelind!" I kneel beside her and try to pry away her fingers.

Her eyes fly open, and she wrenches away from me. "Leave me alone!"

My mouth falls open at her reaction. "I'm getting the first aid kit."

"I said, 'Leave me alone.'"

I throw my hands in the air. "Fine." I grab the kit from where it fell beside the table and slide it to her. "Here you go."

I catch Duncan's gaze. He's pulled himself back into a chair and slouches with his legs stretched out. He shrugs as if to say, *Leave her alone.* I shake my head. Ethelind can be moody, but this reaction is weird, even for her.

I join Cass at the keyboard. His fingers lie motionless across them. "Cass?" I touch his arm.

He flinches but doesn't speak until a few seconds later. "Grandfather thought this might happen." He glances at me, then turns back to face the center screen. The line ticks back and forth across the circle. "When he built the lab, he made sure it could be used to escape." He laughs once. "This is an old submarine. Who knows how he managed to find it. Or rig it to the side of the cliff." He smiles, but it's sad. "He was brilliant, you know."

"I'm so sorry." I squeeze his arm, then let my hand fall to my side.

He turns so we're face to face. "You're sure he's dead?"

I see Asaph again, lying motionless in the hall, blood seeping into the hardwood around his head, empty eyes staring at the ceiling. "Yes." I bow my head.

A few seconds tick by. "He was always prepared for the worst," Cass says. "I laughed at him, but he was right." He presses his fingers into the corners of his eyes. After a moment, he clears his throat and turns back to the keyboard to type. "We'll head north for about a hundred miles, then hike inland from there. We'll have to backtrack a bit to get to Zeb, but it's our best option."

"Can't the Guard track us?"

Cass gives me a quick smile. "Did anyone ever tell you Fortune's Fall was unplottable?"

I nod. "Pallas told me. Is that important?"

"Grandfather was the one who developed the technology for that. He installed it in the lab, too."

"So, we're invisible?"

"Yep."

The tension eases from my shoulders but only for a second. "What about the antidote? Can you still make it?" I roll forward onto the balls of my feet and wrap my arms around my chest.

"It shouldn't be a problem. I have everything I need in here with us. I just have to grow the antibodies now." He taps something on the keyboard, and the circle blinks three times. "There. The autopilot is set."

"Get away from me!" Ethelind's voice rises in anger.

Cass and I turn toward her at the same moment she aims a kick at Duncan. He leaps out of the way but lunges forward a second later and tries to grab her injured ankle, which has an unraveling bandage wrapped around it. Blood oozes through the fabric.

"There's a chunk of glass popping out of your ankle!" Duncan says. "It'll get infected if you don't get it out."

Ethelind scoots out of his reach. "I said I'm fine." She tries to kick him again, but this time, he grabs her leg and pins it to the ground with one hand while unwrapping the bandage on her injured leg with his free hand.

"Let me go!" Ethelind tries to wriggle free, her eyes wide.

"Hold still," Duncan says. "What's your problem, anyway?"

Duncan pulls her bandage off, and I recoil at the swollen, bloody mess. Something sticks out of a deep gash above her anklebone, and before anyone can blink, Duncan pulls it out.

Ethelind screams and wrenches backward, scooting like a crab until she's pressed against the wall. She wraps her hand around her still-bleeding ankle and glares at us with tear-filled eyes.

I grab the kit and hurry to her. "Here. We have to stop the bleeding."

She doesn't respond, but she doesn't pull away, either, so I clean the wound and wrap her ankle with the one remaining clean bandage. When I'm done, I stand and turn to find Duncan and Cass squatting behind me, peering at the bloodied object Duncan pulled from Ethelind's ankle. I kneel beside Cass and study it, too. It's black. Small. A perfect square.

"That's not a piece of glass," I say.

Duncan holds it close to his eye. His face is grim. "No, it isn't." He glances at Ethelind, then sets the object back in his palm. "It's a tracer. Somebody's been tracking us the whole time."

## 30

"What do you mean, someone's been tracking us?" I shoot a look at Ethelind, but her gaze is trained on the floor.

Duncan doesn't reply. Instead, he stands, yanks Ethelind up by her elbow, and throws her into the only chair that managed to stay upright when we fell. I wince at her cry of pain, but Duncan ignores it.

"Who implanted that tracer?" He kneels in front of her, his hands clamped so tight over her wrists a vein pops along his good arm.

She doesn't respond.

Duncan pulls her to her feet, and she cries out again as she stumbles on her injured ankle.

"Duncan! You're hurting her!" I wriggle into the space between their bodies and press my hand against his chest. "Stop!"

Duncan clenches his jaw and steps back, releasing her. "You'd better talk." He leans around me and jabs a finger at her.

Ethelind collapses into the chair and hides her face in her

hands. Her shoulders shake with silent sobs. I kneel beside her, torn between confusion and fear.

"Leave her alone," I say when Cass moves toward her.

"She's faking," Duncan says. "And we need answers."

I glare up at him and put a protective hand on Ethelind's shoulder. "You can't just shake her around and expect her to talk."

"Let me try." Cass blinks at me from behind his glasses. "Trust me."

I hesitate, doubting whether his tactics will be any different from Duncan's. Maybe Ethelind's faking, but what if she's not? She deserves a little sympathy, at least until we know the truth.

"Nyssa?"

I don't move.

"Duncan's right," he says. "We need answers, and we need them now."

I can't argue against that. Sighing, I squeeze Ethelind's shoulder, stand, and step away.

Cass kneels in front of her. "Ethelind, you have to tell us about the tracer." His voice is soft but commanding. "We have to know who implanted it. And why. Please tell us."

Ethelind stares straight ahead. "I have nothing to say."

Cass sighs and stands. "In that case, I'm afraid it's time for you to go." He walks to the keyboard, and the keys click as he types. The hum beneath our feet grows louder, and the sub begins to rise.

Ethelind's eyes grow wide. "What do you mean? Go where?" Her gaze darts toward the windows.

Cass turns and crosses his arms. "Either tell us about the tracer, or you and it are both getting tossed out there the moment this thing surfaces." He jerks his head toward the window.

"Cass!" I stare at him, my mouth agape. "You can't do that."

Cass raises one eyebrow at me, then turns back to Ethelind.

"Did that tracer have anything to do with my grandfather's death?"

I clamp my mouth shut. I get it now. There's no way I can talk Cass out of what he wants to do if Ethelind is the reason the Guard showed up at Asaph's, if she's the reason he's dead. I release a breath and turn to Ethelind.

Her eyes have grown even wider. Her chin wobbles. But she presses her lips together and stares at Cass in silent defiance.

"If you think I won't throw you out there, think again." Cass's voice shakes. "My grandfather deserved better than what happened to him."

The sub surfaces in a swarm of bubbles, and light flickers through the window. Cass strides to the table and climbs on top, then presses a code into a keypad on a circular hatch in the ceiling. It opens with a suctioning sound, and sunlight pours inside.

"Get her up here," he says to Duncan.

"With pleasure." Duncan pulls an ashen-faced Ethelind from the chair. She kicks his shin, and he grunts but doesn't release her.

"You can't do this!" Her gaze darts to me. "Stop them!"

I open and close my mouth. Ethelind's eyes bulge. Her nostrils flare. Duncan sits on the edge of the table and wriggles backward with her on his lap. She fights him like a caged animal, but his grip is strong. Cass helps Duncan stand with Ethelind still in his arms.

"Nyssa, help me!" Ethelind says.

I step toward the table, my hand outstretched.

"Don't even think about it," Duncan says through gritted teeth.

"You have to trust me, Nyssa," Cass says before turning to Duncan. "I'll climb through the hatch, and we can pull her through."

Duncan jerks his head in a nod, and Cass clambers through

the hole, reaches back through it, and grips Ethelind beneath her arms.

"Lift her up," he says to Duncan.

My pulse is racing. Cass told me to trust him, but does that mean I have to stand by and do nothing while they throw her into the ocean? They begin to yank Ethelind up and out. I open my mouth again, ready to say something—anything—to make them stop.

"Wait!" Ethelind sobs. "I'll tell you! Put me down!"

My shoulders sag in relief. Cass lowers her back through the hatch, and Duncan grips her arms as he waits for Cass to slide back inside and close the hatch. Once inside, Cass jumps to the floor, and Duncan passes Ethelind to him before leaping off the table, too. Together, they take her back to her chair and push her into it. Duncan hovers in front of her, arms crossed, while Cass hurries to the keyboard.

A few seconds later, we sink back into the depths, and the humming beneath our feet fades to a muted roar. Cass rights the fallen chairs and sets them in a line in front of Ethelind, then plops down on the left. Duncan takes the middle, and I sit on Duncan's other side.

"Now talk, or you're going through that hatch." Duncan leans forward, his eyes narrowed, his hands balled on his knees.

Ethelind licks her lips and nods. Her gaze darts to me, to the ceiling, and back to me before settling on a spot somewhere to the left of Cass. "When you didn't come back to our room the night Pallas was arrested, the Guard did come looking for you. That part's true." She turns to me. "They took me to Omri. When I couldn't tell him where you were, he ordered one of the guards to hit me." She closes her eyes, and a tear slips from beneath her lashes. "Then he told them to get out."

"Who?" I ask.

"The guards." She opens her eyes and takes a deep breath. "After they were gone, Omri told me what I had to do."

"Which was?" Duncan stands and paces behind Cass and me, tossing menacing glances at Ethelind every few steps.

"He said I had to come with you, Duncan." Ethelind's answer is so quiet I have to lean forward to hear. "He'd just learned you'd escaped, and he wanted to know exactly where it was you were going. I don't think he knew yet that Nyssa was with you." She pauses and licks her lips again. "He inserted that tracer in my leg and then ordered the Guard to take me to the Central Hub." She exhales a shaky breath.

"That doesn't make any sense." Duncan rakes his hand through his hair. "How did he know we'd be there?"

"You said Gideon told you we'd be at the Central Hub," I say to Ethelind. A tight ball of fear curls in my stomach.

Ethelind shakes her head. "Omri told me to tell you Gideon sent me to you."

A weight settles in my chest. "Omri knows Gideon is helping people leave the Central Capital?"

"Yes," she says.

I brace my elbows on my knees and cover my face with my hands. Has Gideon been arrested now, too? Or worse, is he dead? I take a shuddering breath and force myself to sit up and face Ethelind. "What about the exile key?" I ask, remembering the necklace she said Pallas gave her. "How did you get that?"

"It was Pallas's," she whispers. "Omri told me to show it to you. He wasn't sure what it was for, but he suspected it was important."

I exhale an incredulous sigh at Ethelind's deceit. At Omri's brazen orders to sort through and steal Pallas's things.

"What happened to her?" I ask in a shaky voice. "Did he tell you what he planned to do to Pallas?"

She shakes her head again. "Why would he tell me that? But everyone knows how much Omri hates disloyalty."

I inhale through my nose. My head knows it's likely Pallas has already been executed, but my heart refuses to accept it.

"How did Omri know we'd be at the Central Hub?" Duncan asks again. "There's no way Gideon would give us away."

"From the people executed in the arena," Cass says in a quiet voice. He stares at Ethelind. "I'm right, aren't I? The two scientists I escaped with—they were supposed to go with me to Fortune's Fall. We got separated, and they were arrested, but I managed to get away. That's when I decided to go to Cardiff instead." He pulls his glasses off and presses his fingers against the inside corners of his eyes. "They could've told Omri about Fortune's Fall and the safehouses, hoping it'd keep them from the arena." He returns his glasses to his face. "But there's no way they told him exactly where the safehouses are located— or Fortune's Fall for that matter. The only specific thing we knew was that we had to be at the Central Hub for the midnight train. It's how all the exiles who want to get to Fortune's Fall leave the Central Capital."

Ethelind doesn't respond.

My eyes widen as understanding dawns. "I've thought this whole time that the Guard was tracking us to take us back to the Central Capital. But I was wrong, wasn't I?" I study Ethelind with a frown. "It's Omri who's tracking us. He wants us to lead him to Fortune's Fall. And he's killing off everyone who helps us along the way." I lick suddenly dry lips. "Am I right?"

Ethelind glances at me, then looks at the floor. But it's enough. I saw in her eyes that it's true. I press my hands against my cheeks. Nausea roils my stomach. "That's why the guard shot Greer but didn't come after us, isn't it? Even though Omri knew we were at the Central Hub, too. It's why they didn't arrest us after we escaped with Sander. Why Sam wasn't arrested at the checkpoint even though the Guard must've known we were hiding in the truck. Omri figured he might as well go ahead and get rid of everyone extra. But not us. We're the only ones who could get him to Fortune's Fall."

I stand and pace with Duncan, but my gaze is trained on Ethelind. "You weren't randomly selected by the Guard at the security gate in Cardiff, were you? What happened? Did you need to report back to Omri? Give him an update on what we were doing?"

"He promised, if I did what he asked, he'd let me stay in the Central Region!" Ethelind meets my gaze. Her eyes beg for understanding. "You know how much my family means to me!"

I stop and stare at her, mouth ajar. "We vouched for you! When Sam didn't want to let you into the warehouse, we told him you were okay! You were willing to let people die so you could stay in the Central Capital?"

"I tried to leave you," she says. "In Cardiff, I talked the guards into taking me back to the Central Capital. And Omri was considering it, or so I was told. But then Asaph showed up, and they changed their minds."

I shake my head. "You think just because you wanted to leave, it makes everything okay? Greer is gone because of you. Sander. Asaph." I turn to Duncan and Cass. "We've played right into Omri's hands."

Silence descends.

"We might still have a chance," Duncan finally says to Cass. "Where are you on the antidote?"

Cass clears his throat. "The blood sample should be clotted by now. I have to separate the serum and eliminate the proteins before it's ready."

Duncan stares at him. "Just tell me how long until it's ready."

"An hour, maybe a little longer."

Duncan nods. "Perfect. Here's what we do. Once it's done, we ditch the sub with her in it." He curls his lip at Ethelind. "If we leave the tracer in here, Omri will never know we've jumped ship."

Cass nods. "I can pause the autopilot long enough for us to get off and reset it to keep heading north once we're gone." He studies Duncan. "You really think we should leave her?"

I listen to them with growing dread. They want to leave Ethelind? I get it—she's responsible for everything that's gone wrong. But this seems extreme. Can't we leave the tracer behind and take her with us?

"Please," Ethelind says. "Please don't leave me. I didn't have a choice."

"You always have a choice." Cass's voice is hard. "We can't trust you now. How do we know you don't have another way to contact Omri?" He shakes his head. "Duncan's right. This is what we have to do."

They're right, as much as I don't want to admit it. We can't trust her. But isn't leaving her behind a little too cruel? I chew on my thumbnail. Even if I defend her, I'll be outvoted. Too many people have died. Safehouses have been discovered. I don't doubt she'll betray us again to protect herself.

"I promise there's nothing else!" she says. "I don't have any way to communicate with Omri. Please, just get rid of the tracer!" Ethelind turns to me, hands clasped in a plea. "Nyssa?"

I bow my head. "I'm sorry."

## 31

Against my objections, Duncan ties Ethelind to a chair he's dragged to the corner. He drops the tracer into a jar and slips it into a cabinet.

"Was that really necessary?" I ask him when he joins Cass and me at the table. I'm watching a small machine Cass called a centrifuge. According to him, it's separating the plasma from Duncan's blood.

"Definitely necessary." Duncan plops into a chair and rests his elbows on the table.

I peek at Ethelind. She's turned away from us, her forehead resting on the window. With a sigh, I turn back to Cass and Duncan.

"This isn't enough for all the people who need it," Duncan says to Cass. "I've been wondering about that ever since I stole the original. I'm guessing it's going to be duplicated somehow?"

Cass nods, then opens the centrifuge, pulls out a vial, and brings it close to his face to study it. "They wouldn't have sent you into the presidential compound to steal it if they didn't have a plan for how to replicate it." He nods with satisfaction and places the vial in a small holder. "Now to separate the proteins from the antibodies." He picks up a small bottle, holds it over the vial, and squeezes three drops of liquid into it. He sets the bottle down and turns to us with a frown. "There's only one problem."

I raise one eyebrow. "Of course there is."

He gives me a tiny smile that quickly disappears. "I'll pack it with ice when we go. But once that ice melts, we won't have much time before it spoils."

"It has to stay at the same temperature," I say, remembering the freezer-like compartment that was strapped to Duncan. "How much time do you think we'll have?"

"A few hours at most."

I gulp. "Can we get to Zeb in a few hours?"

Cass shakes his head. "We're going to pull in farther south than I'd like, so no, I don't think so. But the good news is that Grandfather kept a coded list of all the safehouses on the lab's central database and mapped the ones closest to Cardiff." His eyes droop with sadness. "He really did prepare for something like this to happen. He even created a messaging system so we can contact them. Actually, all the safehouses use it."

I remember the phone Duncan used to contact Sam and to alert the Cord about Sander's body. Asaph created that system along with the security for Fortune's Fall. He was part of so much, and now, he's gone.

"Anyway"—Cass points at the center screen over the keyboard—"I found a safehouse we can aim for once we're on land, and I've already sent them a message to expect us." He looks toward Ethelind, and I follow his gaze. "And then I wiped it clean," he says in a raised voice. "So, there's zero trace of any safehouses now. I destroyed the sub's ability to use the messaging system, too."

Ethelind gives no indication she's listening.

"Okay." I return my focus to Cass. "So, we can get to that

safehouse before the antidote goes bad. What about between there and Zeb's house? And Zeb and Fortune's Fall?"

Cass hesitates. "That's the problem. Taking it in and out of a steady temperature so many times is risky, and I'm not sure how far this safehouse is from Zeb or how far he is from Fortune's Fall." He turns to Duncan. "Do you know?"

Duncan shakes his head. "Sorry, I don't. I've never been this route before. But it sounds like it's our only option, right?"

Cass nods.

Duncan flashes a grin at me. "Looks like we're going to have to be sure of what we hope for and certain of what we don't see."

"Would you knock it off?" I roll my eyes. "What's that from, anyway?"

"The Bible," Cass says.

I whirl toward Cass. "The Bible?"

Cass raises an eyebrow. "Haven't you ever heard of it?"

I search my brain. "It was one of the religious books the government destroyed after the terrorist attack, right? The Christians used it." I shake my head, but the memory stays fuzzy. "So, you're like Duncan, then? You believe in God?"

"Yes, of course. And the Bible, in case you're interested, tells us all about God. How He's protected us for thousands of years, how He sent Jesus to die for us." He pauses, his gaze searching mine. "You don't believe in God?"

"Nope," Duncan says.

I scowl at him.

"Huh," Cass says.

"Huh?" I say. "What does that mean?"

"Let me ask you something," Cass says. "Can Omri explain why he has dreams?"

I bite my lip, not sure where this is going. "Well, that's why Pallas and I were there, wasn't it? To explain them to him."

Cass shakes his head. "That's not what I asked. Yes, you can interpret them. But do you know *why* they occur?"

"Do you?"

"Because of God," Cass says, as though it's obvious. "God warned us through dreams about what was going to happen to Maren fifteen years ago, and he gave Pallas the ability to interpret them so we could prepare. Our faith in God has kept us safe. It helped us trust that the dreams were sent by God as a warning."

He stops and scratches his nose. "I know my grandfather had a theory about why Omri has dreams. Don't know if I agree with him. Don't know if it even matters. But what I do know is that I don't have to have all the answers to believe God's in control." His gaze drifts to the windows, then back to me. "God gave you the ability to interpret those dreams, too. Don't you think you should at least consider the possibility He's real?" He smiles. "We have to trust that He's with us now, even if we can't see Him. And that He'll help us get where we need to go."

The center screen over the keyboard emits a series of beeps. Cass squeezes my shoulder, then hurries away. The floor vibrates, and a few minutes later, he returns to the table. "It's time to go. Once I change the autopilot coordinates, we'll have about forty-five seconds to jump." He picks up the vial. "It's ready. I'll pack it."

"Jump?" My mouth goes dry, and my gaze darts from Cass to Duncan.

Nobody responds. Duncan is fiddling with his bandage. Cass puts the antidote in a small container, then tucks it inside a book bag I don't recognize. The book bag Talos gave us is long forgotten somewhere at Asaph's house.

Duncan and Cass pull their shoes off and use the laces to tie them around their necks like capes.

"I'd do it, too, if I were you," Duncan says when he catches my gaze.

I turn toward the windows and watch the water dip beneath them. The sky appears. Ethelind has shifted to watch us, and I meet her gaze, then turn away when I see the panic in her eyes. Cass pivots back to the keyboard and presses a button, then climbs onto the table and opens the hatch. He peers out, then ducks back inside.

"It's a little bit of a swim." He gestures to me. "Come on. I'll help you up."

Stifling an urge to argue, I bend, pull my shoes off, and tie them around my neck with shaking hands. Then, with a deep breath, I climb onto the table, my shoes bouncing against my back. Cass grabs my hands, Duncan heaves me up from below, and I clamber onto the top of the sub. I stumble forward, and Cass catches me. Our gazes meet. His cheeks burn red as mine grow warm.

"You good?" he asks.

I nod. He hesitates for a split second, then drops his arms and clears his throat. I blink fast, then turn toward the hatch to await Duncan.

He joins us, and the three of us stand side by side, gazing toward the shore. I squint against the glare that bounces off the sub's metal exterior.

The water is as smooth as the fields around the Central Capital after they've been mowed short for winter, though I can see waves crest and break against the beach, which is closer than I expected but smaller, too. It's a narrow strip of sand that abuts rugged hills dotted with trees, the same scene we've hiked for as long as we've been in the Western Region. My feet ache in protest of climbing more mountains.

"You'll be fine," Cass says as though he's read my mind. He nudges me with his elbow.

I glance back at the open hatch. "Are you sure we have to leave her?"

"Don't think about it anymore. Just go." Duncan gives me a

gentle shove, and I take a step forward. My shoes press against my back. I tighten my ponytail.

"I'll never forgive you for this!" Ethelind's voice rips through the air.

I close my eyes, take a deep breath, and jump.

Icy water rushes over me. When my head breaks the surface, an unexpected wave pushes me back under, and my clothes weigh me down. When I manage to surface again, gasping for air, Cass and Duncan are ahead of me, their stroke stronger than mine. I focus on them and force my already-numb arms to propel me forward.

As we get closer to the beach, the waves grow violent, and I'm knocked under more than once. But each time I resurface, the mountains are closer, and somehow, I make it to shore, dragging my waterlogged body onto the sand to collapse next to Cass and Duncan.

Goose bumps prick my entire body, and I start to shiver. I pull my legs against my chest and wrap my arms around them, but it doesn't help. My teeth chatter so hard my jaw hurts. Cass opens his book bag and pulls out three small squares that shimmer like tinfoil.

"Take your clothes off, and wrap these around you," he says. I stare at him. Is he serious? There's no way I'm taking my clothes off in front of them.

"Do what I said, or you'll get sick." Cass tosses his shirt onto the sand, stands, and begins to shimmy out of his pants. Duncan does the same.

Heat creeps up my neck and onto my cheeks. I stand and spin around, tilting my head to the sky so all I see is blue. I hear the crinkling of something, like someone's balling up paper, then something hits my back.

"Take it," Cass says, and I whirl, keeping my gaze trained on the sand. One of the small metallic squares sits at my feet. The sun's reflection bounces off it and makes my eyes burn.

"We'll turn around," Duncan says, and I look up. Both guys are wrapped in thin blankets the same color as the small object sitting in front of me. They stand with their backs to me.

I peel off my wet clothes with numb, shaking fingers, and toss them to the side. But not before I remember to pull the broken necklace from my pants pocket. With it gripped in my teeth, I unfold the blanket and wrap it around me.

"All done." My teeth still chatter, but warmth seeps into my skin. The necklace is secure in my fist.

The boys pivot.

"Feel better?" Cass asks.

I nod, then turn back toward the sea. The sub is gone, headed north beneath the waves. I don't want to think about Ethelind all alone inside it. I don't want to think about what might happen to her. All I can do is hope that someone finds her before it's too late.

"I've got dry clothes," Cass says, and I turn back to him.

He pulls a vacuum-sealed bag from his pack and tosses it into the sand in front of me. "Ladies first."

I kneel and open it. "Which is mine?" I eye T-shirts and three pairs of sweatpants. Everything is at least two sizes too big for me.

"Whichever you want." Cass shrugs. "It's all mine, so it'll probably be big on you. Sorry."

I gaze longingly at my wet clothes that sit in a soggy, sandy pile beside me. My bra and underwear, which I kept on, are damp but drying fast beneath the blanket. "Turn around again, please."

They obey without comment, and I duck into a plain blue T-shirt and a pair of blue running pants that, even though they have an elastic waist, still have to be rolled a few times to keep them from falling. I pull on my wet shoes over dry socks, which isn't at all comfortable, but there's nothing I can do about it.

"Done." I toss the bag to Cass when he turns, then spin

around before he and Duncan drop their blankets to pull on dry clothes, too. If we weren't on a life-or-death mission, I'd laugh at how ridiculous this situation is.

The minutes tick by, but I'm not given the all clear to turn back around. All's quiet. "Guys? Are you dressed?" I'm met with silence, so I turn.

They're dressed, but Duncan sits in the sand with his head cradled in his hands. Cass kneels beside him, frowning.

I squat beside them. "Any idea why he keeps getting these headaches?" I ask Cass.

He shakes his head. "If the gas were the cause, I would've expected the antidote to have cured them by now."

"It started before the gas," I say, causing Cass to look up sharply. "They started after he escaped Ward B."

"I'm not sure I want to know what they did to him to cause this." Cass sighs and looks at Duncan. "Can you walk?"

Duncan nods and gets to his feet. "It's better. At least there's that, right? They always go away."

Cass and I share an uneasy frown.

"The safehouse is to the east." Cass glances at Duncan once more, then turns toward the mountains that tower above us. "Countdown's on. Let's go."

We walk in silence, our feet making squelching noises with each step. On and on, we hike. Up. Down. Sometimes, we walk through trees so thick the sky disappears, only to be surprised an hour later when we pop into stretches of thick green grass and sunshine.

Just as I've decided my feet ache too much to keep going, we make it to the top of yet another hill, and when I look down from the precipice, I gasp. The mountains have given way to rolling countryside divided by row after row of shoulder-high wooden fences covered by vines. A two-story house sits straight ahead, beyond the last stretch of fence.

"Please tell me this is it," I say to Cass.

He smiles. "Should be. Lady's name is Madeleine, and she runs our next safehouse. This must be her vineyard."

With renewed energy, we scurry down and onto a path carved between the rows of grapes. Puffs of dust explode into the air with each step, and I glance at the clusters of small green fruit that hang from the stems on either side of us. A yellow-speckled butterfly flits across the path, and I stop to watch it dance among the twisting green vines.

"Nyssa, come on!" Cass says. He and Duncan are almost to the end of the row, and he gestures for me to hurry.

Just before I reach them, a woman steps into the path between us from the vines to our left. I stumble to a stop. She's dressed in a tank top tucked into cargo pants. Hiking boots are laced almost to her knees. She crosses her arms like one of the Guard.

"May He be with you." She flicks a thick auburn ponytail over her shoulder and pushes her sunglasses onto the top of her head.

"And with you," I say.

I see Cass's and Duncan's surprised expressions from the corner of my eye, and heat creeps across my face. Why didn't I let one of them say it?

The woman holds out her hand, her gaze never leaving mine. "Key?"

I pull it from my pocket and hand it to her, then hold my hand still so she can scan my thumb. She returns my necklace, then turns and strides to the boys to go through the same process.

"Are you Madeleine?" Cass asks once she's done.

The woman returns their necklaces with a brief nod. "I got your message." She slides her sunglasses over her eyes. "Follow me."

## 32

As we leave the vineyard behind and cross a small yard toward the house, a little girl with braided brown pigtails dashes down the front porch steps.

"Aunt Mad!" She jumps into the woman's outstretched arms. "Mama says I'm good today and we can make cupcakes!"

Madeleine's stern demeanor changes. She chuckles and wraps the girl's legs around her waist. "Did your mama tell you I have pink sprinkles I've been saving for exactly that reason?" She stomps up the steps onto the porch and pauses to smile at the girl.

The girl's mouth forms a perfect O. "Are they 'trawberry? And yellow cupcakes! That will be delicious!" She claps her hands, then peeks at us with big brown eyes from around Madeleine's shoulder.

I smile at her and wave, then peer up at the two-story blue stucco. White shutters frame windows open to a breeze that tempers the hot sun. A strange ivy-like plant with hot-pink blossoms climbs a trellis beside the front steps. I chew on the inside of my cheek and fidget from foot to foot. This is unlike any safehouse I've experienced. There's a family here. Are we putting them in danger?

"Nyssa?"

"Yeah?" I blink twice and see Cass standing on the steps in front of me. Duncan stands behind him, staring down at me with eyebrows raised. Madeleine and the little girl have disappeared.

Cass gives me a quizzical frown. "You coming?"

"Sorry." I hurry to join them, and we step into a square foyer. To the right is a staircase, and straight ahead are a living room and kitchen. Madeleine stands at the kitchen island, and the little girl sits in front of her on the counter. Another woman stands beside them, frowning at an empty mixing bowl. She has the same thick red-brown hair, but hers is cut in a wavy bob that brushes her shoulders.

"Where's the flour, Madeleine?" She looks up, sees us, and smiles. "You found them."

Madeleine gives us a brief look, then turns, reaches into a cabinet, and pulls out a box. "Here."

I nudge Cass. "The antidote has to go in the fridge."

Madeleine tilts her head toward us. "What was that?"

"I need to put something in your fridge," Cass says, pointing to his pack.

She raises one eyebrow. "Of course." She nods toward it. "All yours."

Cass hurries over, pulls out the container with the antidote, and places it inside. "Thanks." He steps back and closes the door.

"No problem," Madeleine says with one brow still raised.

"Charis, no! You can't eat that yet!" The other woman yanks a spoon out of the little girl's hand and puts it in the sink. "Wait until it's cooked, monkey."

"Monkey! I'm a monkey, Aunt Mad!" Charis grins at her aunt, her cheeks covered in batter.

Madeleine taps the little girl's nose. "Why don't you sit with me while we talk to our guests, little monkey?" She wipes the batter from Charis's face, pulls her from the counter, and walks to a small table centered between two windows that overlook the vineyard. "Make yourselves comfortable."

She gestures to the empty chairs, sits, and waits for us to join her. Once we're settled, Charis wiggles down and stands in front of me, arms hanging at her sides, eyes big and curious. "Can I sit on your lap?"

I laugh and pat my knees. "Come on up."

She grins and climbs onto my lap. I lean back in my chair and wrap my arms around her waist, then peer around her at Madeleine, who gives me a small smile.

"Which one of you is Cass?" Madeleine asks.

Cass raises two fingers.

Madeleine tilts her head. "I was sorry to get your message about Asaph. I remember him from when I was a little girl in Maren. He was always kind to me."

Cass bows his head.

"And what are your names?" she asks Duncan and me.

"I'm Nyssa," I say with a promptness learned from years of on-the-spot questions in my classes at the presidential compound.

"Duncan." He jerks his head in a nod of introduction.

"You're probably about my size," Madeleine says to me. "I'll get you a few things to try on in a bit."

"Thank you," I say with a surprised smile.

"I'm Leah!" says the woman from the kitchen. She scoops batter into a muffin tin and glances up to meet my gaze. "I'm Madeleine's little sister. And that's my daughter, Charis."

"I'm three!" Charis turns and holds four fingers in my face, grinning with pride.

I giggle but quickly sober. "Thank you for taking us in under such short notice."

Madeleine leans back in her chair and shrugs. "It's what we do, isn't it?" She tilts her head again. "You're heading to Fortune's Fall?"

I hesitate and shoot a glance at Cass. He notices and clears his throat. "Actually," he says, "we're hoping you can get us to my Uncle Zeb's house first."

Madeleine's eyes widen for a split second. "*Uncle* Zeb? You don't mean dairyman Zeb?"

Cass nods. "That's the one."

She's silent for a moment, her finger curled against her chin. "So, Asaph was your grandfather. You didn't say." She clears her throat. "I heard Zeb got everyone out of Maren after it was attacked a few weeks ago."

Cass leans forward. "We're carrying an antidote to Fortune's Fall because of that. But it's temperature dependent. It won't make it there from your house, so we're hoping to stop over with my uncle."

"That's what's in the fridge?" Madeleine purses her lips. "How quickly do you need to get there?"

"As soon as possible," I say. "We don't know how much longer the survivors will make it without the antidote." I pause and tuck a still-damp strand of hair behind my ear. "Or even if there are any survivors left now..." My gaze drifts to the floor.

"Hear that, Leah?" Madeleine asks her sister. "Another chance for you to go to Fortune's Fall."

"I heard."

I look up. Leah is bent over the open oven. She backs away and closes the oven but not before a sweet lemony smell wafts toward me. My mouth waters. I can't remember the last time I had something other than stale bread.

"I've been trying to talk her into taking Charis to Fortune's Fall for weeks now, but she refuses to go," Madeleine says, lowering her voice. "Her husband was arrested four months ago, and we haven't heard a thing from him since. She needs to make sure Charis is safe, and that's not a guarantee at my house."

"Are we putting you at risk being here?" I bite my lip and tighten my grip around Charis. "We don't want to put you in any danger."

Madeleine dismisses me with a wave. "I operate a safe-house; I know the risk." She smacks her hands against her thighs and stands. "We stay vigilant at all times. It's the best we can do." She gives me a reassuring smile. "Sleep here tonight. Rest. Shower. I'll take you to Zeb in the morning."

---

I LIE on a cot in Leah and Charis's room later that night, nestled in the glow of the nightlight beside their bed. It reflects golden highlights in Charis's hair, outlines her hands tucked beneath her cheek and the blanket tight against her chin. Her eyes are closed, and her nose whistles with each breath.

Leah lies beside her. I can't see her from my cot, but I know she's still awake. Every so often, her feet rustle against the sheets, and she sighs.

I roll to my side. I've showered. Washed my hair. And now, I'm tucked under a warm blanket, wearing clean clothes that fit. I know I should sleep, but I can't. I'm restless. Anxious. When we're forced to run, forced to figure out where to go next and how to get there, it's easy to forget how scared I am. Or how much we've lost along the way. But in silent moments like this, my brain forces me to think about everything I'm usually able to avoid.

Asaph. Ethelind. Sander. Pallas and Greer.

I squeeze my eyes shut and flip to my back. But I can't make their faces disappear.

Asaph. Blood pooling beneath his head.

Pallas. Asking me to take her place in Fortune's Fall.

Greer. Motionless on the train platform.

Tears leak from the corners of my eyes and slide onto my pillow. I press my palms against my lids and take deep breaths, but I can't make the images stop.

Duncan's face. His voice.

*Being sure of what we hope for and certain of what we don't see.*

Cass.

*I don't have to have all the answers to believe God's in control.*

How can someone like Cass believe that? He spends his life solving scientific questions, finding solutions to problems that need evidence. But he believes in God? How can a scientist trust in something that has no proof?

"Are you afraid?" Leah's voice drifts across the room. Quiet but curious.

I draw a ragged breath. "Yes."

Silence.

"After Maren was destroyed, my parents somehow made it to the Eastern Region," she says. "They didn't trust in Fortune's Fall. Didn't think it could be created. Madeleine eventually made her way back here, to the Western Region, but I met Eli —my husband—and stayed." She pauses, then sighs. "He broke the Regional Movement Policy. I know Madeleine told you he was arrested, but she didn't tell you the whole story. It was an accident, you know, him breaking the policy. He's a cargo pilot for the government, and his plane nearly crashed on the way to the Western Region. It's a miracle he survived, but he couldn't get back to the Eastern Region when he was supposed to." Her voice catches. "You'd think they'd be understanding, wouldn't you? But they arrested him anyway. Now I don't even know if he's still alive."

I'm not sure how to respond, so I remain quiet.

"We'd planned to go to Fortune's Fall," she says. "Sometimes, I wonder if they found out and that's why they arrested him." Her sheets rustle, and the blanket shifts. "I'll tell

Madeleine in the morning I'm going with you. She's right. We can't stay here anymore, wondering if the Guard will come for us, too. I have to keep Charis safe, even if it means—" Her voice catches again. "Even if it means I won't see my husband again."

"You don't know that," I say, my voice sharper than I intended. "What I mean is—what if he escapes? Duncan did. And maybe he'll be able to get to Fortune's Fall later."

A longer silence.

"Are you a believer, Nyssa?"

A laugh escapes my mouth before I can stop it. "In God, you mean?" I shrug, even though I know she can't see it. "No. I mean, I don't think I am." I shake my head and roll to my side again. But my pillow's wet from my tears. I sit up, flip it over, lie down, and stare at the ceiling again. "How do you believe in something you can't prove exists?" I ask at last.

Leah's sheets rustle again as she changes position.

"Well," she says after a moment, "it's kind of like believing in Fortune's Fall, isn't it? I've never seen it. You've never seen it. But we know people who have, and they've told us about it. They've even created a way for us to get there."

"That's true," I say.

"Believing in God is the same. Maybe we can't see Him yet, but He sent Someone to tell us about Him and show us the way to Him."

"What?" Now, I'm confused.

"Jesus Christ," she says.

"Oh. Jesus." I can't keep the disappointment from my voice. "Cass mentioned Him, too. The Christians worshipped Him, right?" I shake my head against my pillow, trying to remember the little bit we learned in school. "He was just a crazy guy who claimed to be God. But it's not true."

"What if it is true?" Leah's voice is soft. "Every time you show your exile key to someone, what do they see? A lamb. Know what that represents? Christ."

Omri's dream flashes across my mind, and my breath catches. He dreamed of a lamb. Is it possible that the lamb represents—I shake my head again. No.

*Can Omri explain why he has dreams?* Cass's voice whispers through my mind. *Don't you think you should at least consider the possibility He's real?*

"That image of a lamb binds together those of us who still believe. It's a symbol that we're not alone," Leah says. "It reminds us that Christ came as a lamb, that He died as a sacrifice for us so that we could come into the presence of God and then rose again as proof He *is* God."

I blink, and Omri's dream disappears. "But there isn't any proof any of that actually happened. Why should I believe that?"

"Lots of people saw it when it happened. And they told other people, and then, it got written down. Maybe we weren't there to witness it, but we can read about it. There are still Bibles, you know. Not everyone gave theirs up when the government ordered them to do it." She coughs quietly. "It's kind of like one of your history exams. You didn't actually *see* what happened a hundred years ago, but you read about it. You study it. And you accept that it's true."

"Faith." I sit up and squint toward the shadow I know is Leah. "You're talking about faith, aren't you?"

"Faith," she repeats, and I can hear the smile in her voice. "Why can't you apply the same faith you have in history to God?"

I've just decided she's fallen asleep when she speaks again. "Faith is what I hold tightest to. I trust that God's in control, even though I don't always understand why things happen. Faith gives me hope. Without it, where would I be?"

I curl onto my side and tuck my hands beneath my pillow. Charis smacks her lips and whimpers, and Leah soothes her back to sleep.

"Good night, Nyssa," Leah whispers.

I close my eyes without replying. *Being sure of what we hope for and certain of what we don't see.* I don't have all the answers, but something has flickered to life inside me, whispering that Leah might be right. That Duncan and Cass and Sander and Talos and everyone else I've met on this journey might know what they're talking about.

Omri's dream plays on repeat in my mind as I drift to sleep.

## 33

It's still dark the next morning when Madeleine wakes us, and I sit, bleary eyed and silent, at the table with the others, a steaming coffee mug warming my hands. Charis munches on a strip of bacon, the only one who seems undaunted by the day.

"We'll leave in fifteen minutes." Madeleine's announcement breaks the silence, and it takes a moment for it to register.

"Zeb will be happy to see you," Leah says with a wink that's met with a scowl from Madeleine.

I catch Leah's gaze.

"Oh, Madeleine and Zeb used to be engaged," she says with a mischievous smile.

"Leah." Madeleine's voice is a low warning.

Leah shrugs, her eyes wide and innocent. "You're the one who broke it off. He'd take you back in a hot minute."

Madeleine glares at her, and I glance from one to the other. But no more is said, and it's clear Madeleine won't welcome any questions from me.

I watch Cass from beneath my lashes as he leaves the table.

"Fog's pretty thick," he says as he leans against the sink and peers out the window.

Frowning, I shove my chair back and join him at the window, coffee mug in hand. Fog—thick, white, and eerie— hovers above the ground, stretching in every direction.

"We can't drive in that," I say to Madeleine.

She shrugs. "Definitely unusual for this time of year, but it won't be the first time I've driven in it. It should lift soon."

When I follow the others outside, it's like stepping into a cloud. Icy fingers press against my skin. I can't see anything beyond Madeleine's beat-up truck, which is parked in front of the house. Everything is quiet, but there's expectation in the air, like the world is waiting for something to happen.

Madeleine, undeterred by the weather, strides to the hood of the truck and pats it twice. "You'd never know this baby's older than me." She slides into the driver's seat once the rest of us are inside.

"I guessed it as soon as I saw the missing hubcaps," Duncan mutters from his seat next to me. We sit with Madeleine in the front. Cass is in the rear with Leah and Charis, who has finished her bacon and now holds a pancake with both hands, nibbling at it like a rabbit.

"You're in a good mood," I say to Duncan.

He hunches in his seat and crosses his arms. "Somebody decided to snore all night."

"Sleep deprivation and stress affect my cognitive function," Cass says from the back, "which leads to a soft palate relax—"

"Shut up," Duncan says. "Nobody understands any of that." He leans his head against the window and closes his eyes.

I giggle, and something releases inside me. We're nearly there. Excitement wells up and pumps through my veins. Could this be what it's like to have faith? To trust that God will get us to where we're meant to go? We're so close I can almost taste it.

*No more fear*, I tell myself. We're going to make it to Fortune's Fall—I know it. A lump forms in my throat. Could I see my parents tomorrow? Maybe even today?

"Ready?" Madeleine presses a button to start the engine, then grabs a small circular device from the dashboard, sticks it in her ear, and twists a dial beside the steering wheel. "Warns me if we're heading toward any checkpoints," she says to me. "It'll give us time to take a detour." She sits ramrod straight, gripping the steering wheel like it's a lifeboat as we roll down the driveway, gravel crunching beneath the tires, and onto the empty, nearly invisible two-lane road that winds east toward Zeb.

"Are there many checkpoints on this road?" I ask.

"Seems like they're happening more and more. But they pop up and go away fairly quickly. Shouldn't be a problem."

I glance into the back. Cass and Leah stare unblinking out the windows. But Charis meets my gaze.

"We're on a a'venture," she says with a grin, revealing a mouth full of half-chewed food. Her now-empty hands are clasped in her lap. Her ankles are crossed. She wears a dress and pink tennis shoes.

Leah turns and kisses the top of her head. "That's right, monkey," she says. "An adventure." She pushes her own hair away from her face and gives me a small smile, her eyes reflecting her memory of last night's conversation.

I blink and give a fleeting answering smile before turning toward the front. The coffee I brought along is lukewarm now, and I set it between my legs with a grimace. "How long will it take us to get to Zeb?" I ask Madeleine.

"About two hours." She frowns and presses her finger against the device in her ear.

"What's wrong?" I search the road around us, but the truck lights are weak, and it's impossible to see more than a few feet ahead. I imagine the Guard appearing out of the mist, blocking the road and forcing us to stop. I shiver. What do we do if that happens?

Madeleine places her hand back on the steering wheel. "Checkpoint right before we get to the valley." She narrows her eyes as a vehicle approaches us from the opposite direction, then relaxes after it passes. "I'll make a decision soon."

The sky lightens. As we wind higher into the mountains, we rise above the fog and are able to see the pink-streaked dawn and forests of shadowed green. Eventually, the mountains slope into rolling hills, but when we reach a stretch of flat road, we hit pockets of thick fog again and are forced to slow down. Knee-high grass stretches on either side of us, peeking out from beneath the ghostly cloak.

"Is this the valley?" I squint toward the gray shadows of more mountains smeared against the brightening sky. "Guess we avoided the checkpoint then, huh?"

"This isn't the big valley," Madeleine says. "You'll know that one when you see it—trust me. The real thing's beyond those mountains up ahead." She narrows her eyes and presses her finger against her earpiece again, then smiles. "Checkpoint's gone. We'll be there soon."

---

"Oh no."

Madeleine's voice startles me from the daze I've fallen into. I have no idea how much time has passed, but we're deep into the next stretch of mountains, following a road that twists and turns alongside a lazy river running in the opposite direction. The fog has lifted, and the river sparkles in patches of sunlight that blink through the trees.

"What is it?" I ask. There are too many bends in the road to see far, but I sit forward and stare through the windshield anyway, my hands clenched against my legs.

"It wasn't supposed to be there anymore," Madeleine mutters to herself. "I got the all clear."

I twist toward her. "The checkpoint's still there? Where?"

"Halfway through the pass into the valley," Madeleine says, "and too close for us to get around now."

"What?" My mouth goes dry. "What will we do?" I peek over my shoulder. Cass snores quietly, his head propped against the window. Charis is asleep against Leah, whose head is tilted back, her mouth slightly open as she, too, sleeps.

Duncan stirs and rubs his eyes. "What's up?"

"Checkpoint ahead," I whisper to him, not wanting to wake the others. "And it's too late to go around it."

He sits forward, alert and wary. "Turn off the road."

"And go where?" Madeleine asks. "Into the river? There's nowhere to go except straight." She slams her hands against the steering wheel. "I don't understand. Why'd I get the all clear?"

"What's going on?" Leah yawns from the backseat.

"We can't go through a checkpoint!" Duncan's voice is louder this time, and I shrink away from him.

"A checkpoint?" Leah asks. The panic in her voice makes me turn.

"I broke the Regional Movement Policy, too," she says, her eyes full of fear. "After Eli was arrested, I came to Madeleine without getting permission first." She stifles a sob.

"We're a truck full of wanted fugitives." Duncan grips his knees with whitened knuckles.

"If we're lucky, the fog hasn't lifted from the valley," Madeleine says through gritted teeth. "We can outrun them."

"Duncan's right," I say. "We need to—"

But there it is. A checkpoint manned by two guards. One stands in the center of the road and motions for us to stop as we approach. The other lounges, bored, against the vehicle parked on the shoulder.

"What will you do?" I wipe my sweaty palms against my jeans.

"Turn your face away as best you can without being obvious," Madeleine says. "You, too, Duncan. You two have been all over the news."

I tilt my head down so my ponytail drapes across my shoulder and brushes my cheek. Duncan turns his head to the right.

Madeleine slows to a stop and rolls down her window. "Morning," she says to the guard. "Glad the fog's gone. Can't imagine it's fun to stand in that for too long."

"I'll need to check your ID, ma'am," the guard says. "All your passengers, too."

"Sure. No problem."

As Madeleine speaks, her foot lifts from the brake and moves toward the accelerator.

"Stare straight into the scanner, please," the guard says to her.

The truck lurches forward, tires squealing. Charis screams. The other guard on the side of the road shouts and breaks into a run in our wake.

"Pray the fog's still there!" Madeleine says over the roar of the wind through her still-open window. "We'll need it."

## 34

We careen down the road, around hairpin curves that make every muscle in my body tense. Charis cries out again from the back.

"Sorry about that. No way they were going to let us through though." Madeleine's face is white. Her eyes are narrowed and focused. She maneuvers the truck with skill, but it doesn't ease my fear, especially when we curve up and onto a ridge. A sheer rock wall stretches up to our left, and a cliff drops on our right, straight into the river.

I squeeze my eyes shut and don't open them again until the ground flattens. We've reached the valley. Madeleine was right: I know it when I see it. It stretches in every direction as far as I can see. She was also right about the fog. It lingers here like a threadbare blanket. Patches of farmland and houses and trees poke through the mist, but the entire eastern horizon is covered with a thick bank of clouds. It's desolate and unwelcoming.

"Zeb lives northeast about ten miles away," Madeleine says loud enough for Duncan and me to hear. She rolls up her window and glances in her rearview mirror. "Everyone okay back there?"

"Fine," Cass says.

Madeleine nods and presses a finger against her earpiece. "The Guard's alerted its valley station that we jumped the checkpoint. We have to get off the main road. Hold on!"

She wrenches the truck to the right. I grip the edge of the seat and clench my jaw. We bump onto a dirt path that divides row on row of trees rising out of a lake of clinging fog.

"Pistachio orchard," Madeleine says to me. "There are a million of them in the valley. The Guard will be on the main road, so we have a better chance of getting to Zeb if we stay in the orchards." She jerks her head toward a small compartment on the dashboard in front of me. "There's a phone in there. Give it to Duncan."

I find it and hand it over.

He presses a button, and the screen turns blue. "Zeb?" he asks Madeleine.

She nods. "Do you know the emergency code?"

Duncan nods.

"Use it. Tell him we're ten minutes away."

Duncan nods again, and a small box blinks onto the screen, then disappears. A few seconds later, an answering box appears.

"He says, 'Here and ready,'" Duncan says.

"Good," Madeleine says.

We reach the edge of the orchard, and she stops the truck just short of a narrow dirt road that separates it from the next section of trees. She rolls down her window, and a dull *bleep, bleep* echoes through the stillness.

"I was afraid of that," she says on a sigh. "They've activated the alarm. If anyone sees us—Guard or otherwise—we're done."

She presses the accelerator, and we shoot across the road and back into the shadows. We do this three times through three sections of trees. Each time we arrive at the dissecting road, Madeleine stops, and we listen for the alarm. It remains a steady warning, tolling a reminder of the danger we're in.

Finally, we come to the edge of an orchard that gives way to a vast, grassy field. The fog has begun to disappear with the rising of the sun. It's thinner now, and it offers zero concealment.

"Zeb's place is just past this," Madeleine says, pointing at the field.

She rolls down her window, and I hear a new sound alongside the alarm, but I can't figure out what it is.

"Cows!" Charis says. She wrinkles her nose as a breeze wafts through the truck. "They stink."

Madeleine chuckles. "That's the smell of safety, little monkey." She inches the truck forward. "Everybody hold on. Gotta get across this field."

We shoot out of the orchard and bump through the field. I spot Zeb's house straight ahead, beyond a long stretch of paddocks in which black-and-white-spotted cows cluster. To our right are rows of grapevines, and past them is a road.

My heart slams against my rib cage. "Madeleine." I tap her arm and point toward the caravan of vehicles that glide along the pavement in a straight line. Black and sleek. Windows tinted and hubcaps gleaming. The Guard. There's no way they haven't spotted us. Madeleine's truck is like a fleck of gold in a dirty pail.

"Nearly there." She jerks the wheel to the left, and I peer over my shoulder to see the caravan turn off the main road. It heads down Zeb's long, twisting driveway.

"We're trapped," I whisper. My hands begin to sweat.

"Where's your faith?" Madeleine careens across the driveway and whips the truck around the house toward a tall, square building that glints silver in the sunlight. "Get ready to run."

The back of the building slides open, and a man runs out.

He's tall and rugged, with the same wavy hair as Pallas, though his is golden where hers was white. The tips of his boots peek from beneath jeans, and when he reaches the truck, I see his face is crinkled and tanned by the sun rather than by age. If this is Zeb, he's nothing like I'd imagined.

Madeleine screeches to a stop, and the man wrenches the door open. "Zeb!" She jumps out. "The Guard's coming up the drive."

"Everyone to the hangar!" he says.

Leah slides out with Charis gripped in her arms and races toward the building. The rest of us follow, leaving the truck doors wide open like the hollowed sockets of a skull.

We clamber onto the wing of a small plane parked inside. It's dirty, and the door is so rusted Cass has to yank on it three times before it opens. I duck and follow him into a tiny cabin. It's a tight fit, and I'm wedged between Cass and Duncan on a pair of seats meant for two people. They're old leather, and the stuffing puffs out of a ripped seam between my legs.

Leah sits on a single seat facing us with Charis on her lap. Zeb and Madeleine are in the front. The doors are barely shut, our belts just secured, when we roll out the open door.

"Hold on," Zeb says. "Gonna be bumpy."

I bite my lip. I've never been in a plane, and I don't like heights. We lurch as the plane bumps over a rudimentary runway that stretches between two fields dotted with cows. The fog is nothing more than a strand of white that wanders east.

When we lift into the air, my stomach drops, and I think I might be sick. I swallow hard against the saliva that fills my mouth, lean back, and glance out the window. Fear makes my whole body clinch into a tight, terrified mass.

"They're going to shoot!" I say.

The caravan is parked below us, and the Guard has spilled out. They stand in a line, weapons aimed at the sky.

"I see 'em!" Zeb says.

The plane jerks to the right and climbs so fast I fall into Duncan. "I don't like this," I moan. The turbulence is terrifying, like we're caught in an ocean wave that yanks us in every direction.

Cass grips my sweaty hand. "We got past them," he says in my ear. "It's going to be alright. Look."

The plane steadies, and I peek out the window. The valley lies below us, perfect green squares of farmland and orchards and vineyards that stretch in every direction.

My gaze roves toward the eastern horizon, and I gasp. The clouds are gone, and snow-capped mountains—majestic and imposing—stretch across the blue sky like a charcoal drawing, almost too well etched to be real. The scene pricks something in my subconscious, and goose bumps chase one another down my arms. I meet Cass's gaze. His eyes twinkle.

"It's like the dreams," I say.

He squeezes my hand. "I wondered if you'd recognize it." He points toward the mountains. "I think Fortune's Fall is somewhere in there."

I gaze out at the mountains, then down at the valley, half expecting to see a hawk fly below us or a tree spring up in its center. My gaze sweeps back to the mountains. Pallas and I never talked much about a dream's setting, just the moving parts within it that needed interpretation. I never considered the idea that the place in a dream might actually exist.

As I gaze out at this almost-surreal scene, it's like I've flown into Omri's or Asaph's dream, and suddenly, I understand.

"I think I get it," I say to Cass. "At least, I *want* to get it. Having faith, I mean." I hesitate as I try to form my thoughts into words. "I believe those dreams didn't happen by accident. But I never questioned *where* they came from or who might have sent them, because I didn't need to." I glance again at Cass, and heat spreads across my face when he smiles. I turn back toward the window. "But looking out over this"—I gesture toward the scene—"it's impossible not to believe those dreams really were sent by..." I hesitate over the unfamiliarity of the name.

"By God," Cass says.

"By God," I say.

"I knew you'd get there," Duncan says in my other ear, nudging me with his elbow.

I turn to him, eyebrows raised.

He mimics my expression. "What? Couldn't help but over-hear, mainly because I was trying to listen."

The plane lurches, and the moment is gone. I squeeze my eyes shut, breathing through my nose until we steady.

"Drop-off point for Fortune's Fall is straight ahead," Zeb says from the front. "But I'll swing around from the back. Make sure we're not being followed."

Cass wraps his hand tighter around mine, and I open my eyes to find him watching me, his eyes dancing. "We're going to make it."

black pinprick appears on the western horizon, hovering like a dragonfly in the distance.

"Zeb," Cass warns.

"I see it," Zeb says. "Only thing we can do is try to outrun it. We're almost there."

"Helicopter," Cass says to me when he sees my questioning glance.

We descend into the mountains, and the sun is replaced by shadow. I'm lifted from my seat and slammed back down more than once, my stomach diving over and over again. I stare at my hands clenched in my lap rather than at the treetops that seem to brush our bottom, forcing ragged breaths through my clenched teeth to try to keep from throwing up.

We land smoother than I expected and roll into a field of wildflowers that dance in thick waist-high grass. Zeb steers the plane to a stop, kicks open the door, and slides out onto the wing before jumping to the ground.

"No time to waste." He holds out his arms so Leah can hand him Charis from the wing.

"How's it going, little monkey?" he says to Charis once she's secure in his arms. "I've missed you."

Charis pinches his nose. His brows arch in pleased surprise. "Shall I carry you the rest of the way?"

She nods. "Bye, Mama!" She waves at Leah, who's jumped from the wing to the ground.

"Entrance to Fortune's Fall is due north," Zeb says over his shoulder as he jogs across the meadow toward the tree line. "This way!"

We run behind him, our shoes silent in the thick grass. Sunlight dazzles against the myriad of colors that explode around us, and a particular bunch of black-eyed Susans has just caught my eye when Duncan lets out a cry like an animal that's been shot. I stumble to a stop, his scream still ringing in my ears, and see him collapse to the ground. He curls into a ball and grips his head with both hands.

Cass and I drop to our knees beside him. When I see the blood that oozes from Duncan's nose, I look at Cass with a worried frown.

"This isn't good," Cass says. "We need to get him to Fortune's Fall fast."

Together, we pull him to his feet and balance his weight between us.

"Can you walk at all?" Cass asks him.

"Everything's spinning." Duncan grimaces. "Keep hold of me and I'll try."

We've made it a few steps when a low hum breaks the silence. We freeze. Zeb and the women are a few yards ahead of us, and they stop and turn.

"Run!" Zeb gestures with one hand while his other stays wrapped around Charis. "They're coming!" He doesn't wait to see whether we obey. He and Leah disappear into the shadows of the trees.

But Madeleine sprints back to us.

"I can help!" She shoves me closer to Duncan so that we can balance his weight together.

Gritting my teeth, I force my legs to move faster. Cass and Madeleine do the same. But I stumble over a basketball-sized rock hidden in the grass, and the four of us come crashing down. Pain ricochets through my ankle, and I cry out.

"What is it?" Cass crawls around Duncan and squats beside me.

"My ankle." I wince and wrap my hand around it.

The roar of whatever's approaching grows louder.

"You have to go," I say. "Help Madeleine get Duncan to the trees."

"No way," he says. "I'm not leaving you."

"She's right." Madeleine stands, helps Duncan to his feet, and wraps his arm around her shoulder.

"I'm not leaving you," Cass repeats.

"Go!" I say. "You have the antidote! I'll be right behind you."

He hesitates for a split second, then nods and pulls Duncan's other arm around his shoulder. I struggle to my feet and watch them jog away.

I don't follow.

Just as they disappear into the trees, a helicopter explodes into view above the forest on the opposite side of the meadow, an eerie black orb that hovers in the air, turning in a wide arc, like a spotlight searching for a shipwreck.

With one last glance at the trees, I turn and run as fast as I can on my swollen ankle back toward Zeb's plane in the middle of the meadow. The helicopter will see me. I'll distract the Guard and give the others time to get to Fortune's Fall.

"Nyssa!"

Cass yells my name, but I ignore him. The others won't let him come after me because he's too important. A wave of fear and disappointment threatens to overwhelm me. I probably won't ever see my family again.

But I've made my decision, and I'm not turning back.

## 36

The helicopter doesn't move from its vigil in the sky, and though I can't see its occupants, there's no way they didn't see me. I squat beneath the wing of Zeb's plane to catch my breath, hidden from view at least for a moment, and wipe the sweat from my face.

I stand, ready to hobble toward the opposite side of the meadow, at the same moment two more helicopters appear above the treetops in front of me.

Their noses tip down, and a blue light beams from one of them, shining a small, perfect circle above my head. A dull, whirring vibrates the air, and my gut tells me I need to move *fast*. I stumble to my feet and stagger past the plane's tail toward the trees at my left, swallowing the fear that I could be shot at any moment.

An explosion rips through the air.

I'm lifted from my feet and propelled forward. I slam into the ground just short of the trees, and my face smashes into the dirt. The world goes silent except for a ringing in my ears. I sit up slowly. Orange flames flicker against the charred frame of Zeb's plane. The helicopters haven't moved, as though they're waiting to see what I'll do next. I tell myself that's what I want—if they're here with me, the others can still make it to Fortune's Fall.

I push to my feet, lurch into the trees, and shove my way through brambles. The shadows are thick, and my eyes refuse to adjust to the darkness. A creek trickles past me, and when I hear the tinkle of the water rushing over rock, I'm relieved. The sound is muted, like it's farther away than it is, but at least I can hear it.

I stumble down into the water, and it slops over my shoes. I slip and slide to the other side, collapsing onto all fours to crawl across the bank and onto dry ground. My ponytail sticks to the back of my neck. Sweat beads along my lip. My breath comes in gulps brought on by fear and adrenaline.

Because I'm on hands and knees, I don't see the vehicle until I'm almost upon it.

Boots emerge from it and stride toward me. An arm reaches down and yanks me up.

I lift my chin and stare in defiance at the guard. He's built like a machine. His hat rests on a bald head, and the gloomy light can't hide the smirk on his lips.

"Where are the others?" A fleck of spit lands on my cheek.

I don't reply.

"Where are they?" he repeats, shaking me.

Still, I'm silent.

He drags me toward the vehicle. "Doesn't matter. I know they're not far." He snaps his finger, and at least a dozen more guards emerge from the trees, camouflaged to near invisibility.

"Spread out," says the guard who holds me. "I suspect this one's a decoy." He jerks my arm again, then leans down until his mouth is inches from my ear. "Omri will be happy to see you."

I kick his leg, and he gives a roar of outrage. He sees my

satisfied smirk and twists my arm. A howl of pain escapes my lips.

"Don't test me again," he says. He throws me into the back of the vehicle, slams the door, and slides into the driver's seat.

My ankle and now my arm, too, throb with dull pain. I press my face against the window, searching for any hint of movement as we move through the forest. But all is still. The guards have disappeared into the shadows. Have I given my friends enough time to get to safety?

No more than a few minutes have passed when the guard's murmur interrupts my thoughts. I drag my gaze forward, narrowing my eyes when he presses his finger to his ear. He nods and says something before jerking the vehicle to the left. We pick up speed, and the sun bursts through the treetops. The creek appears again. Wider. Deeper. I frown. Something's not right. I glance at the guard to make sure he doesn't see, then slide my necklace from my pocket to check the compass.

We're going north. Back toward Fortune's Fall.

"Where are you taking me?" I ask, trying to hide my fear.

The guard doesn't respond. He swerves around a fallen tree, and there, beyond a scraggly pine, I see light.

The edge of the forest.

A shiver of fear darts down my spine. Have the others been spotted? Are we on our way right now to arrest them, too? My gaze roves to the door. Back to the guard. To the door. Is it possible?

I lunge for the door and press the button to open it. To my surprise, it opens. I throw myself out of the car and land hard on my side. The guard slams on his brakes. I struggle to my feet, grit my teeth, and half run, half hop toward a meadow that sparkles beyond the trees.

It's different from the one we landed in earlier. It's almost as big as the arena in the Central Capital. The grass is more yellow than green, but it's tall and thick, too, and I hurry toward the concealment it will provide. Beyond it, I glimpse the sheer rock side of a mountain that looms into the sky. A waterfall cascades over the edge and down into a pool that feeds a river, likely the same one we crossed in Madeleine's truck.

The guard shouts, and I know without turning he's chasing me. I half expect him to shoot me, and my shoulder blades prickle as I stumble into the meadow.

I collide with a warm body.

We fall together into the grass, and I roll to the side, my chest heaving. "Duncan!"

He lies on his back, his eyes squeezed shut. "I couldn't leave you." He groans. "Just didn't expect finding you to hurt so much." He opens his eyes, rolls to his stomach, and lifts his head high enough to peer above the grass. "Get up when I say. All we have to do is make it to the waterfall. The entrance is in the rock behind it." He looks over at me with a twinkle in his eye. "Stay low and go, remember?"

I lift my head, too. The guard stands at the edge of the forest, his finger pressed to his earpiece as he scans the meadow. I twist toward Duncan, scowling. "We'll lead them straight to Fortune's Fall. Omri will know where it is!" I punch his shoulder. "Why did you come back for me? You should be in there!" I jerk my thumb toward the waterfall.

Duncan shakes his head. "There's no time to explain, but I promise, everyone will be safe. Fortune's Fall will still be secure."

I want to ask so many questions, but there isn't time. All I can do is nod. "Okay."

We grab hands, hunch low, and run.

## 37

I stumble more than once, but Duncan holds tight to my hand, and somehow, we manage to keep going. I can hear the roar of water rushing over rock, see the swirling eddies in the pool beneath the waterfall.

"We're going to make it!" Duncan says, his voice triumphant.

A roar erupts behind us, and the three helicopters appear out of nowhere, racing above us so low in the sky that we duck even lower beneath their shadows. When they turn to face us, hovering like angels of death, I expect a blue light to appear on my chest. Is this the moment I'll die?

But no blue light appears. Instead, the helicopters descend until they sit on the ground. One in front of us. The others on our left and right.

"No!" I say.

We're so close, but our way is blocked. My ankle pulses with pain. I'd collapse in defeat if Duncan didn't keep his hand wrapped around mine.

The door of the helicopter in front of us opens. Omri steps out. And behind him, Ethelind.

My eyes widen in shock that's overwhelmed by anger so strong nothing else matters. "Traitor!" I jerk free of Duncan's hand and stumble toward her, my chest heaving. "And to think I felt bad leaving you behind!"

"You left me to die!" Ethelind stands beside Omri, her hands clenched at her sides, her eyes shining with hatred.

"Enough." Omri puts a hand on Ethelind's shoulder, and she blinks, as though coming out of a trance. "Enough," he repeats.

Ethelind dips her head and steps behind Omri.

"Bring him here," Omri says, motioning with one finger toward someone on my left without taking his gaze from me.

I turn as two guards march forward, grab Duncan, and shove him toward me so that we're once again standing side by side.

"You think Ethelind's the traitor?" Omri clucks his tongue. "Here's your traitor, Nyssa." He presses his thumb against something in his hand.

Duncan clutches his head and falls to the ground, groaning. Before I can react, Omri jerks his head in a nod, and one of the guards yanks Duncan up and pinions his arms behind his back. Another guard steps forward with a knife.

"Stop!" I say.

But nobody listens.

In one quick motion, the guard jerks Duncan's head to the side and slices into his scalp above his ear. He scoops something from the deep gash, and blood spills down the side of Duncan's face. His mouth forms a perfect O of surprise and pain.

The guard tosses the object at my feet. It's black. Small. A perfect square.

My mouth falls open.

Duncan had a tracer, too?

Duncan's eyes roll so that all I see is white before his head lolls forward. He hangs between the guards; his blood seeps into the ground.

I lean to the side and vomit, then wipe my mouth. My legs won't stop shaking, and a cold sweat breaks out across my skin. "A tracer," I whisper.

My gaze moves between Omri and Ethelind, who still lurks behind Omri. Everything makes sense now. The headaches. The appearance of the Guard where we didn't expect them, even after Ethelind was gone.

"A tracer," Omri says with a small, unpleasant smile. "Did you think I'd rely on only Ethelind?" He shakes his head. "I'm disappointed in you, Nyssa. You should always have a backup plan, especially when it involves this place." He gestures toward the waterfall, and his eyes bulge with a terrifying mixture of triumph and rage. "I've been looking for Fortune's Fall for over a year, you know. But those Maren exiles are a tight-lipped group. Until the scientists, that is." He shakes his head again. "Shame I had to execute them, but the law's the law."

He blinks, and his gaze travels to Duncan. "I assumed he'd try to escape, so I made it easy for him in hopes he'd lead me here." Omri holds out a small rectangular object. A smile flickers across his face. "After he was arrested, I decided he'd be a good candidate for a new, experimental tracer. So, while he was still unconscious, I had him sent to Ward C, where my excellent and loyal scientists implanted it. He woke up in a prison cell in Ward B and never knew what happened."

He closes his fist around the object. "Not only was I able to follow you, but I could also stall you whenever I needed you to stay somewhere a little bit longer." He smiles at me. "My scientists were very clever, really. This button sent a tiny electrical pulse directly into Duncan's brain whenever we wanted. It caused quite the headache."

Omri's face hardens. He nods at the guards who hold Duncan, and they release him. He falls to the ground, arms twisted at his sides and eyes closed. Drool seeps from his mouth.

I kneel beside him and lift his head onto my lap so he can breathe. His face is covered in blood that oozes from the gash in a thick, steady stream.

"I have to say, Nyssa," Omri says, "it surprised me when I discovered you left the compound with him, but it worked in my favor in the end, didn't it? I learned you couldn't be trusted, either." He sighs. "So many people who aren't trustworthy. I'm particularly disappointed about Zeb. He was the finest dairyman in the country."

I glare up at Omri. "I'd leave everything behind all over again now that I know who you really are."

Omri stares down at me, and the silence grows thick and tense. At last, he blinks and shifts his gaze to somewhere behind me. "Call the others back from the search. I need them here."

I glance over my shoulder and see the guards step to the side, their hands pressed to their ears as they mutter instructions.

Omri watches them through narrowed eyes.

"Nyssa."

My name is a whisper that drifts up from the ground. It's Duncan. Relief washes over me. I bend toward his face and grab his hand.

"Use your exile key." He opens his eyes and tries to focus on me. "Press it into the rock behind the waterfall. Your thumb, too."

I glance at Omri. Ethelind. The guards. No one pays attention to us.

"That'll let Omri right in!" I whisper. "Besides, I won't leave you."

"Don't be the hero," Duncan mutters. "If you stay, you're dead."

"If I leave, you're dead."

"I think it might be too late for that." He squeezes my hand. "One key, one person. I promise they can't get into Fortune's Fall. Only you can." He blinks three times, as though he's forcing himself to stay awake, then fixes his eyes on me. "What's the point of choosing faith if you forget about it the moment you really need it? You have to try to get there, Nyssa. Don't worry about me." His breathing comes faster, then stops. His eyes drift out of focus, and his head lolls to the side.

"Duncan!" I lean closer to his face and shake him. "Stay awake!" But it's too late. He's gone.

I take a deep breath, release his hand, and place it at his side. Panic, thick and suffocating, threatens to engulf me. I glance up at Omri. He's still distracted. The guards face away from me, toward the forest.

*Faith.*

It's almost as though someone's spoken the word aloud. I wipe my eyes. *We have to trust that He's with us now, even if we can't see Him.* Cass's voice arcs through my mind. *And that He'll help us get where we need to go.*

When I chose to have faith, I had no idea it'd mean choosing it over and over again every day. I study Duncan's face. Is it possible? Can I still make it to Fortune's Fall? I have to try. For him. For Greer. For everyone else who wanted to make it and didn't.

"Thank you," I whisper.

I stand and balance my weight on my uninjured leg. I take one step toward Omri. Two. Three.

"You want into Fortune's Fall?" I ask.

He turns toward me, his face expressionless.

"You'll have to catch me."

## 38

I dart to the left and race across the meadow. My brain screams that this is pointless. I can't outrun the Guard. My ankle rolls, and I stumble. For a moment, I believe my brain's warning. But my heart says something different. *Keep going*, it whispers.

The sun shines on me, bathing me in warmth. Peace. The wind blows through my hair—and with it come uninvited images from Omri's dream, flashing through my mind in rapid succession.

The pinecones and the lamb. The oak tree snapped by the two pine trees. And the hawk as it flies across the valley toward the mountains. With sudden, sharp clarity, I know what the hawk represents.

Me.

The image disappears as fast as it appeared, and I smile despite my circumstances. When I reach the pool, spray from the waterfall tickles my skin. I skirt to the right, where a ledge wraps behind it, my jaw set. I *was* meant to come to Fortune's Fall.

I'm going to get there.

An arm wraps around my waist and jerks me backward. My feet fly out from under me, and I fall hard, the breath knocked from my lungs. When I lift my head, Omri stands over me, his shadow blocking the sun.

"You ought to have that ankle looked at," he says, his tone pleasant.

I'm hauled to my feet by two guards, and more circle behind me. They drag me behind the waterfall. Omri follows. We splash through icy puddles, following the ledge along the pool until the waterfall is a roaring curtain behind us.

Omri steps close to me and leans down. "Thank you, Nyssa, for leading me here. I've waited a long time for this." He steps back. "Now, show us how to get inside."

Something sharp presses into my back and pushes me forward. "Try to run again, and I'll stab this into your spine," a guard says in my ear.

I take two shaky steps forward and stop, my gaze roving the wall for any indication of a door. I don't see anything.

*Faith*, Duncan's voice whispers through my mind. *One key, one person.*

I nod, pull the key on its broken chain from my pocket, and —with a deep breath—press it against the rock. I do the same with my thumb.

The key sticks like a magnet. When the compass, which faces out, begins to glow, I pull my thumb away and cross my arms. The key is sucked through the rock and disappears. My mouth falls open.

A crack appears along the rock's base, and my guard and I step back as it grows. It stretches left and right, then up so far that I strain my neck to watch it cross above our heads to form a perfect square. Then, it slides inward before sliding up, slow and silent. Within seconds, we stand in front of a gaping square hole that stretches at least twenty feet above us. It's covered by a shimmering silver screen from which a low hum emanates.

The guard pushes me forward, and boots shuffle behind me as the others prepare to march inside.

"Wait." Omri steps beside me and peers at the screen, his head tilted as he listens to its hum. "Nyssa will go alone. Let's see what this thing is first."

"After you." The guard shoves me forward so fast I stumble through before I can argue. My breath catches as a strange magnetic force latches onto my body and pulls me forward.

Suddenly, I'm through. I turn toward those standing on the ledge. Omri steps forward, a murky shadow on the other side of the screen. The Guard is a gray silhouette behind him.

*One key, one person.* If Duncan's wrong... I shake my head. I can't think about that.

Omri steps closer, reaches forward, and touches the strange curtain.

The humming grows louder, and Omri is lifted off his feet. I watch in horrified fascination as he hangs suspended above the ground, his hand still pressed to the vibrating shield.

The edges of the screen light up. It's so bright I step back and shield my eyes. As I watch through my fingers, the light stretches toward the center, like a thousand smaller stars fusing into a giant one. The middle flares into a blinding ball and, with a mighty *whoosh*, erupts out toward Omri, tossing him backward into the Guard and toppling everyone into the water before it explodes into brilliant orange fireworks.

The rock wall slides down.

Absolute darkness.

Absolute silence.

I collapse onto the cold, damp ground, my forehead pressed against the wall, my ankle screaming with pain that leaps up and down my leg. Something niggles at the back of my brain, but I can't catch hold of it. I'm too overwhelmed by what just happened.

"Hey there, young lady," says a familiar voice from somewhere behind me. "I think this belongs to you."

I struggle to my feet and turn on one leg to find a shadowy figure outlined by a small shaft of light far behind him. He reaches forward and presses something into my hand. My exile key, I realize, as I feel it with my thumb.

"Sam?" I ask, my voice awash with relief and amazement. After he left us at the edge of Cardiff, I hadn't dared hope he'd make it to Fortune's Fall.

"Ya made it," he says, and I can hear the smile in his voice.

"So did you," I whisper.

He scoops me into his arms before I can protest and heads toward the light.

## 39

S am strides with purposeful steps through the tunnel, though it seems more like a cavern on closer observation. It's cold and damp. Water droplets cling to the rock, and the darkness stretches up toward a ceiling I can't see. The waterfall's roar is muted, as though it rushes above and beside us on the other side of the rock.

"You were waiting for me," I say to Sam.

"Security system," he says. "Get an alert when anyone's near the waterfall. Happened to be me on duty today."

"Duncan saved me," I whisper. "And now he's dead." It's so unfair, after everything we went through, that I'm here and he isn't. That so many others who should be here aren't. Who am I that I deserve to be safe? To be reunited with my family?

"Reckon he was one of the Cord's finest," Sam says after a moment. He shifts my weight in his arms. "Don't you go feeling guilty now, ya hear? Nobody would want that, least of all Duncan."

I wipe the tears that slide down my cheeks and don't reply. Guilt isn't something I can seal in a box and store away. "Did the others make it?"

"Yes, ma'am. Cass—that's his name, right?—he went straightaway to the clinic. Reckon that antidote'll be ready soon."

My body sags in relief. My friends made it here. "So, there are still survivors from the attack?"

Sam nods. "We lost one, but the others ought to make it." He pauses. A silence to remember those lost. "Your folks are alive, Nyssa," he says at last. "I've seen 'em myself."

My breath catches, and I squeeze my eyes shut against a flood of emotion. The faces of everyone I've lost flicker through my mind uninvited. Will I ever *not* be caught off guard?

And then, I remember what I couldn't quite sort out.

"Sam!" I sit up straight in his arms.

He stops and peers down at me with a frown. "What's the matter?"

"Ethelind has an exile key!" *One key, one person.* "Can Omri get inside if she gives it to him?" I lean back and peer around Sam into the darkness. Is someone stalking us even now? Hiding in the shadows and following us inside?

"Didn't ya tell me it wasn't her key?" Sam studies me, his frown deeper.

"That's right. It was stolen from someone else."

Sam's frown disappears. "Nothin' to worry about then." He begins to walk again. "Since our keys are programmed specific to our identities, only the person it belongs to can use it to get into Fortune's Fall."

"You're sure?" I clasp my hands tighter around his neck.

"Course I am. We're okay—I promise."

The sound of rushing water grows louder as we step out of the darkness and onto a small ledge a few feet above the ground. My mouth falls open. A waterfall, which is close enough to mist my face, roars down beside us into a huge valley encircled by sheer rocky peaks that rise a thousand feet into the air. The sky is blue but shimmers strangely. It reminds me of the screen that protects the entrance, and I wonder whether it, too, is covered by a shield that makes this place impenetrable and invisible.

"This is our namesake." Sam nods toward the waterfall. "It's the other half of the waterfall that covers the entrance. The survivors scoured the mountains for a place to come after Omri destroyed Maren all those years ago, and this was the only spot where they could divert the water to keep everyone alive." He points at the enormous turquoise pool into which the water tumbles. "We named our new home Fortune's Fall in honor of our good fortune."

Beyond the pool are small, identical houses. There are at least a hundred, maybe more, in expanding squares around a large courtyard. In the middle of the courtyard is a two-story building with people coming in and out.

I try to take in everything. Pastures beyond the houses that are full of cows. Orchards and fields. I smile. I can't wait to learn about this place. Something is growing stronger inside me, a certainty that this is where I belong.

Sam maneuvers down three stone steps, and someone emerges from the shadow of a shack attached to the rock on our left. When I see who it is, I don't try to stop the tears that well up and flood down my face.

"Hey there, Nyssa," Cass says with a weary smile.

Sam lowers me to the ground, and I hobble to Cass, who embraces me in a tight hug.

"Wasn't sure I'd see you again." His voice is muffled in my hair.

I lean back and press my hands against his chest. His arms loosen, but he doesn't let me go.

"Duncan?" Cass's voice is quiet.

I open my mouth to explain, but the words won't come. Instead, my tears fall faster, and all I can do is shrug. He doesn't say anything else, just pulls me to him again so that I rest my head on his chest.

We stand like that until Sam clears his throat. Embarrassed, I step back from Cass and turn to Sam as I wipe my face.

"Gotta get back to my post," Sam says. "Cass'll take it from here." He taps the end of my nose. "Reckon I'll see you again soon, young lady."

"Thank you, Sam," I say.

He gives a quick salute before he turns and makes his way to the shack.

I turn back to Cass and find him studying me with that now-familiar intensity.

"I sure am glad to see you," he says, almost shyly.

"Same," I whisper.

Cass pulls my arm around his shoulders and wraps his arm around my waist. "Think you can make it to that building?" He jerks his chin toward the two-story structure in the courtyard.

"I think so." I take a step forward. "What's in there?"

His eyes sparkle. "Your family."

## 40

Cass leads me down a long hall through the clinic, which spans the back of the building's first floor. He pauses in front of a closed door with his hand on the knob, glances at me, and opens his mouth.

"What is it?" I ask.

"It's your brother." He falters and clears his throat. "He's pretty bad. I want you to be prepared."

"Okay." I hear what he says, but I'm so anxious and exhausted that I have a hard time understanding.

"Ready?" he asks.

I nod, and Cass opens the door.

Everything comes into focus in slow motion. Two beds placed beneath two windows. A table squatting between them. There's a boy on one bed. Jek. His eyes are closed, and tubes extend from his nose and the top of his hand.

A man lies in the other bed. My dad. Our gazes meet, and his eyes widen with recognition. With shock. Sadness and joy. Fifteen years of pent-up emotions play in a slideshow across his face.

"Nyssa?" A woman's voice.

I turn and find myself gazing into my own eyes—only, they're older, with pencil-thin lines stretching from their corners. A single streak of white darts through otherwise dark hair that's curly and unruly. She wears a flowing blue dress that reaches her toes.

My mom.

We stare at each other. I'm paralyzed. Numb.

"Nyssa." Her eyes well with tears. And then, as if some unseen barrier has shattered, she rushes to me and wraps me in her arms.

I close my eyes and breathe her in. She smells like the purple verbena that dances in the fields of the presidential compound. Lemon and grass and instantly familiar. I melt into her arms and clasp my hands against her back.

After a few moments, she steps back and rests her hands on my arms. "We've prayed for you every day for fifteen years." She presses her lips together and blinks several times. "And now look at you. So grown up. So beautiful." She tilts her head, and her lips turn up in a small smile.

"Stop hogging her," says a voice from behind us. My dad.

My mom dabs at the corners of her eyes before linking her arm through mine and guiding me to his bed.

"You're hurt!" she says when she sees I'm limping. "Sit." She presses me onto the edge of the bed, and I smile gratefully at her, this woman who is and isn't a stranger.

"I'm heading back to the lab," Cass says from the doorway. I'd forgotten he was here. Our gazes meet, and a smile plays on his lips, but then, his attention shifts to my parents, and the smile disappears. "We should have that antidote done soon, Mr. and Mrs. Ardelone." He shoots me one last glance before he leaves.

"Nice boy, that Cass," my dad says.

He eyes me with such obvious curiosity that a laugh bubbles from my mouth. Delight and relief and surprise rolled into one. A cough racks his body, and the moment sobers. He twists his head to the side and covers his mouth with his hand. When he turns back to us, the pale purple circles that frame his eyes seem darker. But the hand with which he grabs mine is strong.

"Nyssa." His voice shakes with emotion. "We weren't sure we'd ever see you again."

"Oh, hush," my mom says before she, too, doubles over from a hacking cough.

I watch her with growing alarm.

"I swear it's contagious," she says once she's got her breath. "He coughs; I cough. And so on, and so on." She pats my hand. "Just some lingering aftereffects from the gas—nothing more." Her gaze drifts to Jek. "I'm one of the lucky ones."

I turn toward my brother. He has dark hair like my mom and dad and me, but his eyelashes are a black contrast to his sallow skin. The thin blanket that covers him barely moves as he breathes.

"We have faith that the antidote will cure us all," my mom says.

There's that word again. *Faith*.

Not just a word, I remind myself. A choice. A deliberate decision to trust in something—Someone—I can't see. To trust in God.

I study my parents. They both stare at me. I should be uncomfortable, but there's something so deeply familiar about them—about the way they've already embraced me without being overly emotional, as though we've been separated for only a few days rather than fifteen years—that puts me at ease.

I find myself pouring out to them everything that's happened since Pallas was arrested. My mom sits beside me and clasps my hand as I speak. I want them to know why I left the Central Capital. To understand how important everyone is who made the journey with me. Especially the ones who died along the way. I want them to appreciate and love me for what I know now about faith and family and betrayal and trust. And God.

I tell them about my life in the Central Capital. About Pallas and Omri and watching dreams that foretold the future. I talk of Duncan. Greer. Talos and Madeleine and Leah and Sander. Of the lonely stained-glass church in the middle of the mountains and Luna the mountain lion.

When I'm done, I'm exhausted. Silence falls over us, and my gaze shifts to the bumps my dad's toes make against the blanket.

"I knew it," my dad says after a few moments.

I blink at him and wait for the wisdom I'm certain he's about to impart.

"I knew I saw a mountain lion in the orchard!" he says. "What was she like?" He winks at me, and I'm pulled into his teasing like an embrace. I smile.

"You are the absolute worst." My mom smacks my dad's leg through the blanket, but she's smiling as she turns to me. "I apologize for your father."

"Oh, come on. It made her smile, didn't it?" He pats my hand.

My mom shakes her head, stands, and pulls me to my feet. "What a time you've had, Nyssa." She studies me with a sad smile. "How I wish I could've seen you grow up." She turns to my dad. "I'm taking her to get some rest."

She helps me stand, but before we've taken more than a few steps toward the door, it opens. Cass peers inside. "The antidote's ready."

# 41

When my mom and I arrive at my parents' house, I shower and dress in her clothes and then let her slather a "special blend of oils and herbs" on my ankle before she wraps it. She tucks me beneath a downy white blanket in a room painted blue, like the sky before the sun rises. The bed I lie on is the only furniture other than a small table beside it and a rocking chair tucked in the corner. A window on the opposite wall overlooks an orchard, which is swathed in increasing shadows as the sun sinks behind the mountains.

"Sleep, my Nyssa." My mom pushes my hair away from my forehead. "We have all the time in the world now to get to know one another." It should be weird, this treatment of me like I'm a child, but it's not. She radiates warmth that covers me like a blanket, and my eyes grow heavy under her gaze. I'm home now. I'm safe.

I sleep through the whole night, and when I wake, the sun shines bright through my window. I pull the blanket away and study my toes peeking from beneath the bandage. My entire leg throbs with a dull ache, but the shooting pain from yesterday is gone.

My stomach growls, and as if it set off a silent alarm, the door opens. My mom floats into the room, carrying a tray full of food. She wears the same dress, and her hair is pulled into a messy bun on top of her head.

"You slept well." She waits for me to sit up, then sets the tray on my lap.

"Thank you." My stomach growls again, and I pick up the bowl of broth and sip. It's like nothing I've ever tasted. Sweet and sour and citrusy and delicious. When I'm finished, I set it down and shift toward my mom. She sits in the rocking chair, her hands clasped in her lap. A small smile plays on her lips. She seems different somehow, more alive.

"The antidote." I return the orange I was about to eat to the tray. "Did it work?"

Her smile grows. "Jek's awake and talking. Others are up and walking around, your father included. And I haven't coughed in several hours." She shakes her head in awe. "Miracle medicine."

"Can I see them?"

Her smile disappears, and her eyes become serious. "Not yet. You've been summoned to the Council meeting." She glides to the bed and brushes her hand against my forehead. "I was instructed to escort you there once you woke."

I lean against the headboard and close my eyes. I don't want to leave this room. I'm warm and full for the first time in days. "Can't they wait?"

She chuckles, and the bed squeaks when she perches on its edge. "I'm afraid not."

I open my eyes to find her giving me a rueful smile. "They've been waiting for your arrival—"

"You mean Pallas's arrival." I lower my gaze to the blanket and trace the flower pattern with my finger.

"Well, yes, but they know she wouldn't have sent you in her place if she didn't trust you."

I freeze, my finger hovering above the blanket. "So, they know why I'm here?"

"We received word." She pats my leg. "We could hardly believe it when we heard we would see you again."

My eyes well with tears, and I turn toward the window. "What is the Council?" I wipe an errant tear from my face before I turn back to her.

"The Council is made up of the twelve people who run our government," my mom says. "Most of them helped get us here —to Fortune's Fall—after Maren was destroyed. They built our homes, designed our farms, and installed the security that keeps us invisible to outsiders. You might have noticed it when you passed through the entrance. It surrounds us."

I nod, remembering the strange magnetic screen I passed through beneath the waterfall and the way the sky seemed to shimmer behind an invisible curtain.

"Your father and I created the system for cloning seeds," she says, "and he sits on the Council as the Agriculture Head. He'll be there, so there will be at least one familiar face."

"Will they show me the dream?" I ask. "The one Pallas was supposed to interpret for them?"

"Yes. Thaddeus has been having it for almost a year now, and—"

"Thaddeus?" I ask. "Pallas's brother?"

She smiles. "Yes. He's one of her three brothers. They're who had the original dreams that warned us Maren would be destroyed. That's why his new dream has been taken so seriously."

"I know. Pallas told me about it." A lump forms in my throat. "I wish she could've seen her brothers again." I squeeze my eyes shut. I don't want to forget anyone I've met—and lost— but will their memory ever stop hurting so much?

My mom reaches down and grabs my hand. "Interpreting that dream is your responsibility now. Time to go."

## 42

I use rudimentary crutches to walk with my mom from our house to the building that sits in the center of the courtyard.

"Headquarters," she explains on the way. "It's where we do all our business."

Before we reach the entrance, someone calls my name. I turn toward the voice. "Leah!"

She jogs to us—Charis bouncing in her arms—and crushes me in a hug with Charis squished between us. "We made it, Nyssa," she says. "We're all safe because of you."

I squeeze my eyes closed for a moment. "Not Duncan. He didn't make it."

She steps back, and her eyes are glassy with unshed tears. "I know. I'm so sorry."

I can't reply. It hurts too much to think about what happened.

"Why you using those?" Charis points at my crutches.

I give her a shaky smile. "I hurt my leg, little monkey. I can't walk very well right now."

Leah kisses Charis's cheek, and the little girl wriggles out of her arms. Leah watches her dash away to play with a few other kids, then turns back to me, her face glowing with joy. "Eli's alive, Nyssa. Madeleine has a contact here, and he knew about my husband." She swallows hard. "He's in prison, but at least he's alive."

My mouth falls open. "I'm so glad!"

Leah nods, then turns and introduces herself to my mom. "We'll be off then," she says a few minutes later. She squeezes my shoulder. "I'm so thankful you're here."

"Me, too. See you around, little monkey!" I call to Charis, who twirls around and around with two other girls in the courtyard.

She runs back to us and gives my leg a hug. "Aunt Mad's making me pancakes! And she gives Zeb kisses!"

I turn to Leah, one eyebrow raised.

"Only a matter of time before Madeleine came to her senses," Leah says with a grin.

"I'd better get a wedding invite," I reply with a laugh. Lightness spreads through my chest as I watch them walk away.

---

I FOLLOW my mom to a set of stairs inside headquarters. She helps me maneuver to the second floor and to an open door at the end of the hall. A man appears in the doorway, and I lurch to a stop. It's my dad. He's different, too, now that he's out of bed. The purple hue has disappeared from beneath his eyes, and he's taller than I expected, lanky and thin. And smiling.

"I'll take her from here," he says to my mom. He kisses her cheek and guides me inside. Eleven people turn toward me from where they sit around a rectangular table.

"Nyssa," says a man from the far end. "Welcome."

My gaze meets his, and I know it's Thaddeus. Pallas's blue eyes look back at me from deeply lined skin. He isn't tall or rugged like Zeb, nor is he stooped and frail like Asaph. He's somewhere in the middle. Shorter. Rounder. But he exudes the same authority as Pallas and his brothers.

He gestures to two empty seats beside him, and my dad and I sit. I glance around at the strangers. What if I let them down? What if I can't do what they expect of me?

"You've grown up since I last saw you," Thaddeus says.

I blink. He's right. I have grown up, in more ways than he means.

"It's imperative we learn what this dream means as quickly as possible." He tilts his head to study me, a gesture so similar to Pallas that my chest aches. "Are you ready?"

I nod and sit a little straighter. God gave me the skill to interpret dreams, and now, I choose to have faith I can do what Pallas sent me here to do.

---

THANKS FOR READING *Fortune's Fall*! Please consider leaving a review wherever you purchased or on Goodreads.

---

KEEP READING for a sneak peek of *The Exiles*, Book 2 of The Exiled Trilogy.

# THE EXILES

BOOK 2: THE EXILED TRILOGY

# 1

The air hangs thick with expectation. Nobody moves. No one speaks. The only sound is from my own heart, which thrums a nervous rhythm, a frantic pacing that ricochets against my rib cage and echoes through my ears. My brain is so muddled with questions that I don't know whether I can complete the task I came here to do. How do I explain to the twelve Fortune's Fall Council members seated at this table what I'm just beginning to understand myself?

The chair in which I sit presses against my tailbone. Its ridged back curves into my spine. But the physical ache is nothing compared to the pounding in my skull, a discomfort brought about as I try to focus my thoughts on the images from Thaddeus's dream that flashed on the dream screen seconds ago.

All I have to do is interpret that dream, to explain the prophecy it contains. That's the sole reason I sit in this room surrounded by strangers who depend on me for answers no one else can give. It's what brought me here, away from my life in the Central Capital to Fortune's Fall. But my thoughts won't cooperate with the task I'm meant to complete, and I can't find the words necessary for a clear explanation.

Instead, in my mind, Thaddeus's dream collides with all the dreams I've seen before. Their edges adhere to one another until they become a single, abstract painting. A blurred conglomeration of color that defies a simple interpretation. I know what Thaddeus's dream means beneath its complexities. And I know why its symbols are identical to those in the dreams that preceded it. But his dream also adds something new to all the previous dreams—it contains the next scene in the prophesied story.

How do I explain all of this in a way that makes sense to the people seated around me? I'll have to be careful. I don't want to stir up too much hope, not when so much more has to happen before our ultimate triumph.

"Well, Nyssa, can you tell us what my dream means?" Thaddeus asks from his seat at the head of the table.

I sense his gaze on me, but I'm not quite ready to look away from the now-black dream screen that hangs behind where he sits. I need to focus my thoughts, to figure out a way to explain the truth embedded in his dream, while also acknowledging that I've seen these symbols before. Doing that is a delicate balance between creating too much excitement and too much fear.

I close my eyes, curl my hands into fists on the tabletop, and use all my energy to force Thaddeus's dream to the forefront of my mind. The other dreams fade into a murky backdrop, and the symbols from Thaddeus's sharpen. I see the rushing river and the birds trapped on boulders anchored along the water's midpoint. The birds take flight and burst from the gorge into a valley surrounded by mountains and—

"Nyssa?"

My dad's voice slices through my concentration; his hand

covers mine. My eyes pop open, and I turn to him, searching his face for some sign of sympathy or glimmer of awareness at my predicament.

But why should I expect that? He can't read my mind. A few hours together won't create a connection after fifteen years of separation. Despite our instant camaraderie when we were reunited yesterday, he's still a stranger. A stranger whose expression can't mask the excitement—the anticipation—of what this dream might mean to the people in Fortune's Fall.

I scan the faces of the other eleven Council members seated around the table, and my gaze locks with Thaddeus's piercing blue eyes. He looks so much like his sister—like my old mentor, Pallas—that my throat constricts. He gives me a small smile, as though he realizes the train of my thoughts, and his face folds into deep wrinkles.

I nod, a subtle gesture that I'm ready to get on with it. To tell the Council what Thaddeus's dream means. I'll try to be brief and to the point. When the questions come—and they will— I'll take them one at a time. Maybe by then, my internal storm will have settled.

I pull my hand free of my dad's and straighten my shoulders. "This dream prophesies our return to Maren."

My announcement—as I expected—has an immediate effect, like everyone has been released from invisible chains that bound them to their chairs. Thaddeus sits forward, a smile playing on his lips. Others glance at each other, their faces relaxed and excited.

We're going to return to Maren. The home President Omri attacked fifteen years ago. He forced everyone at the prestigious university there to march to the Central Capital, but he left everyone else behind to die, including my parents and brother. I was one of those taken, though I was only two years old at the time and don't remember it. Those left behind managed to find their way here, to Fortune's Fall, where they've created a life while they await their moment to return to their true home.

Voices swell across the room in a rising tide of jubilation. No one other than me seems to notice the man seated across from my dad. He stares down at the table with a frown, the antithesis of everyone's delight. I study him with a growing sense of familiarity. Thick arms and broad shoulders. Black hair with an equally dark beard trimmed along a square jaw. Have I met him before?

"When will we return?" asks the woman seated beside him. She sits forward in her chair, her fingers pinched around the edge of the table, her brown eyes focused on me. Her hair is parted in the center and pulled into a tight ponytail at the nape of her neck.

I inhale a sharp breath through my nose. This is the question I most expected. Still, my stomach fills with dread at knowing I'll disappoint her and everyone else in this room with my answer.

"I don't know." I tuck a stray hair behind my ear, then slide my hands into my lap. "Dreams don't work like that. I can read the symbols and explain what they mean. But there's no way for me to know when this will take place." My gaze shifts to the window behind her through which sunbeams shine like spotlights. Thaddeus's dream dances in my head, and I wish I could watch it again—alone this time—without such a captive audience, to analyze and mull over each symbol, separate the pieces and put them back together in a logical, perfectly fitted puzzle.

"Is there anything else, Nyssa?"

I snap to attention and turn back to Thaddeus. He stares at me, his face inscrutable. My throat has gone dry; my lips are chapped. I press them together and take a deep breath. "I've seen a version of this dream before."

A hush falls across the room. I keep my attention on Thaddeus, aware of the surprise that my announcement has created, that everyone waits for me to explain what I mean.

Understanding dawns in Thaddeus's eyes. "So, the anomalos has happened." He rests his elbows on the chair's arms and steeples his fingers so he can prop his chin on them.

I nod.

"The anomalos?" My dad's gaze darts between me and Thaddeus. "I know we've discussed this before, but can someone remind me what it is?"

"Why don't you do it, Nyssa," Thaddeus says to me.

I turn so that my dad and I are face to face. "Do you remember Asaph?"

"Of course," he says. "One of Thaddeus's brothers. Brilliant man."

"Right. Well, Asaph had this theory that a prophetic dream is about to come true if more than one person has the same dream. He called it the theory of anomalos."

My dad raises a brow. "Someone other than Thaddeus has already had this dream?"

"Sort of. President Omri had a dream similar to this one last year. Pallas interpreted it as a warning people would try to flee the Central Capital." I resist the urge to press my fingers against my still-throbbing temples and instead shoot a cautious glance around the table, my gaze landing once again on Thaddeus. "Your dream is the same as his, Thaddeus. But yours adds an extra scene, a scene that tells of our return to Maren. It's classic anomalos theory, according to Asaph. He believed that prophetic dreams are pieces of a story, and each dream adds a new part to that story."

"Didn't Omri have a dream prophesying his own downfall, too?" the woman across from me asks.

"Yes," I say. "Omri had another, different dream a few weeks ago that prophesied his downfall. That's another example of anomalos because his dream is similar to one that Asaph had years ago. So, when Omri had it, too, it became evident that his downfall could happen soon."

An unexpected wave of exhaustion washes over me, and I sit back in my chair, though I'd rather rest my forehead on the table, to close my eyes and pretend that I'm still asleep in the cozy bed at my parents' house. I'm not used to interpreting a dream the moment after I've watched it, not by myself at least. Pallas and I used to analyze them together, to parse them apart until we were certain about all the symbols and their meanings. But Pallas isn't here. I'm on my own in a meeting that's much more complicated than I anticipated.

Someone pounds on the table, and I jump, look up. The familiar, bearded man across the table stares at me. "Let me get this straight," he says. "The anomalos has happened for two dreams now: the one that prophesies Omri's downfall, and this new one"—he jerks his thumb toward the dream screen—"with a prophecy we'll return to Maren." His eyes narrow. "Am I right?"

I nod, resisting the urge to shrink down in my seat. Animosity radiates off him, and I get the feeling it's directed at me. But why?

"Wouldn't it make sense that if we get rid of Omri, we can return to Maren?" he asks. "Voila. Both dreams come true."

I shake my head. "It's not that simple." My voice is quiet, too quiet, and I clear my throat. "We can't run out of here and attack the Central Capital." My words are louder now, stronger, and it gives me more confidence in the face of his unexpected anger. "Yes, Thaddeus's dream indicates we'll return to Maren, and since the anomalos has happened, it could be soon. And yes, Omri is standing in the way of our return. But the dream prophesying his downfall also prophesies that two people will command the fight against him, and we don't know who those two people are yet."

I push my chair back in a burst of inspiration and limp to the dream screen on my still-throbbing ankle, a physical reminder of the nightmare of the last few days. "Can you fast forward to the end of the dream?" I ask Thaddeus.

He presses a button on a controller that sits on the table in front of him and the first bit of the dream streaks across the screen: the river that rushes through the gorge. Birds swoop down from crevices in the cliffs to land on the boulders that line the center of the water. A moment later, they burst into flight and shoot out of the ravine into a valley framed by mountains.

"Stop," I say.

The screen freezes on the birds mid-flight. Their path forward is blocked by a giant oak that stands in the center of the valley, and they hover in front of it, wings flapping to keep them aloft. "That oak represents Omri." I tap the screen. "And the birds represent the exiles. Actually, they represent everyone here, too, in Fortune's Fall. Omri's preventing all of us from getting to where we want to go." I look to Thaddeus. "You can play it."

He presses the button.

"Stop." I point at the two pine trees that have risen up on either side of the oak. The pines press into the oak, forcing it down into the earth. "Those pine trees represent the two people who will lead whatever happens to overthrow Omri. They appear in Omri's dream, too. The one that prophesies his downfall. Whoever those two people are, they play a huge part in all of this." I nod at Thaddeus. "Play it through to the end."

The oak disappears. The birds shoot through the space left in its wake and vanish in a brilliant flash of stars.

I turn to the Council. "Once Omri's gone, we'll have safe passage back to Maren, but like I said already, until we know for sure who the two prophesied leaders are—and I really believe that'll be made clear—I don't think we should do anything to antagonize him. I think we should wait."

I limp to my seat, slide into it, and look up to find that the bearded man is once again glaring at me. I stifle a sigh. "I know it's hard to wait when you've already waited fifteen years. But it's the right thing to do. It's the safest way to ensure we ultimately return to Maren."

"Says the teenager." The bearded man leans back in his seat and crosses his arms against his chest.

I stare at him, mouth ajar and brows pulled together. I'm too stunned to reply.

"That's not necessary, Fitz," Thaddeus says with a frown.

So, that's his name. Fitz. I search my memories for anything that might explain why I feel like I know him. I come up empty.

"She doesn't know anything about us, and she's suddenly in charge of the most important decision for our future?" Fitz scoffs, his eyes still fixed on mine. "She's just a girl."

I laugh once, a shocked reaction to what he's said. "A girl who managed to break someone out of prison, escape the Central Capital, and get to Fortune's Fall alive." Anger makes my breath shallow, and I clench my jaw to keep my chin from quivering. "You have no idea what it took for me to get here."

"I know more than you think." The contempt in Fitz's scowl makes me want to flee the room. "How many people had to die for you to do that?"

My skin grows cold. What does he know that he's not telling me?

"That's enough." Thaddeus smacks his palm on the table. He glances from person to person until he has everyone's attention, mine included, though I wish I could crawl under the table.

"I know the news Nyssa's given us is what we've hoped to hear these past fifteen years, but it doesn't mean we throw caution off the cliff," Thaddeus says. "Of course, we all want to return to Maren, but she's right. Moving too soon against Omri could be disastrous. We have to tread carefully." He pauses, but his gaze continues to rove around the table. "Furthermore, there are only a handful of people outside of this room who know about this new dream, and none of them knows what it means. Nyssa's interpretation remains classified until I say otherwise. Is that clear?"

His question is answered by a collective murmur of assent, except for Fitz, who stands and leans forward, his fists pressed against the table. The woman beside him touches his arm, a tentative plea to calm him. He jerks away from her.

"We had a plan, Thaddeus," Fitz says. "Everyone here agreed it was the best way to move against Omri. You included. But this girl showed up and now you're telling us that plan is off the table? All because she claims we can't get back what's rightfully ours until two strangers appear out of nowhere to destroy Omri?" He gives a derisive snort. "It's ridiculous! Waiting to act against Omri is a huge mistake. He knows where Fortune's Fall is now, or have you forgotten that? We have to act before he does." He slams his fist against the table. "I've already lost my son to that monster. I don't want to lose my wife, too."

Fitz's son? My ears buzz, and I shake my head, an involuntary denial of what I've just realized. I know now why Fitz seems so familiar.

"Who's your son?" I hold my breath, my fingernails pinching into my palms.

Fitz swivels toward me, and a flash of grief flickers across his face before his expression hardens. "Oh, you knew my son very well. He's the reason you're here safe and sound." He pauses, and his Adam's apple bobs as he swallows hard. "And you're the reason he's dead."

I exhale a gush of air, and my body goes numb. "You're Duncan's dad." My voice isn't much louder than a whisper, but Fitz hears me, and he's silent. It's all the confirmation I need.

I close my eyes. Duncan came to the Central Capital to steal an antidote needed for the victims of a gas attack brought about by Omri's orders a few weeks ago. He left with the antidote and an unexpected addition: me.

Duncan saved me. He was my friend. My last moments with him flit through my brain like a movie on fast-forward, and there's nothing I can do to stop them. I'm forced to re-live our race across the country and our final sprint through the meadow, toward the waterfall that hides the entrance to Fortune's Fall. Duncan's hand gripped mine so I wouldn't fall, and even now—knowing that he's dead—my heart swells with remembered hope.

"We're going to make it!" he'd shouted.

But Omri and his retinue showed up. A guard sliced Duncan's scalp open, and I see again the tracer that fell to the ground, implanted beneath Duncan's skin without his knowledge so that Omri could find Fortune's Fall. I see Duncan collapse. Hear him whisper that I can still make it on my own before his hand went limp in mine.

I force my eyes open and blink to make my too-vivid memories disappear. But I can't look at Fitz. I can't look at anyone. Too much has happened in such a small amount of time. Thaddeus's dream. Fitz's rage and the blame he's set on my shoulders for Duncan's death.

The room closes in on me, and my vision goes blurry. I push back from the table, grab my crutches, and stagger from the room without a backward glance, my tenuous grip on happiness slipping farther away with each step that I take.

In the hall, I throw the crutches away from me. They clatter against the wall. I limp down the stairs and burst through the door into mid-morning sunlight. It's so blinding that I have to duck my head as I hobble down the path that splits the multi-layered rows of houses that surround Headquarters, or HQ, as I've been told it's called. The waterfall roars against the mountainside beyond the path's end, sparkling cheerfully as though all is right with the world.

I choke back a sob. This morning I was excited to be here. I was ready to interpret Thaddeus's dream, relieved to have something to focus on other than the nightmare of the last few weeks. Now, I wonder if I ever should have come.

# 2

I cut away from the roar of the waterfall and follow the well-worn track that frames housing. My gaze is focused on the almond orchard straight ahead, a lush green landmark that parallels the eastern mountain wall. All I want is to get to my room without running into anyone. To close the door and pull my knees to my chest and retreat from everything that's happened.

When I reach the trees, laughter floats out from somewhere within, and my shoulder blades squeeze together. I veer left to continue down the path, stepping from sunlight into shade created by the orchard's thick foliage.

My parents' house comes into view. It's identical to all the others. White clapboard. Front door with a small, covered stoop and framed on either side by a single window. Some houses are plain with nothing to show of their inhabitants except for an occasional pair of boots set beside the door. But many—like my parents'—are bordered by flowers. White and hot pink and yellow with green vines that trail in the dirt and snake up the walls.

My mom plucks weeds near the door, her lips pursed in

concentration. I slow my stride—my ankle's weak from my hasty retreat—and tighten my ponytail as I cross my parents' small yard. My mom looks up and smiles.

"Hi there." She stands and wipes her forehead with the back of her arm, leaving a streak of dirt along her brow. Her hair is wrapped in a scarf, and she's traded her long skirt from yesterday for a pair of gray linen pants. She brushes her hands against her thighs. "You're back sooner than I expected."

I take another limping step forward. There's a ringing in my ears, and my stomach hurts. I'm scared that if I speak, I'll start to sob, and I can't do that with my mom. Not now, maybe not ever. She's still too much of a stranger, like my dad.

"Everything okay?" A crease appears on her forehead, and she squeezes my arm.

I jerk away without thinking, eyes stinging, and catch a glimpse of her wide-eyed surprise before I duck my head.

"Nyssa?" There's a hesitancy in her voice that makes me want to kick myself. All she wants is to be kind, to attempt to begin making up for the years lost between us. But what's the point of embracing her or anything about life here if I'm also going to be surrounded by people who hate me?

"Sorry." I shuffle backward, away from her concern, and press my palm against one cheek to stop an errant tear. "I'm just going to go to my room for a while."

Before she can respond, I lurch past her and hurry inside, through the small living room, past the kitchen, and down the hall. But I stop short of my door and turn to study my brother Jek's still-empty room. Jek, my parents, and several others were attacked a few weeks ago in Maren. The group had gone to see whether the city was inhabitable, but President Omri somehow discovered their plans. The antidote Duncan stole from the Central Capital helped save everyone's lives—Jek's included—but he's taken longer than the others to recover.

I rest the side of my head against the doorway and let my

gaze wander from bed to closet to window. Yesterday, when I arrived, Jek was still unconscious in the clinic. Pale and thin and covered in tubes. I heard earlier this morning that he was awake and talking, but I have no idea when he'll be home.

With a sigh, I turn from his room and go into my own, close the door, and slide to the floor. My ankle radiates pain, and I stretch my leg in front of me to rotate it. It pops, and I gasp on a pain-filled breath as my eyes well with tears.

How have things gone so wrong here? Fitz's angry words sting me like wasps, and I replay in my mind everything about the Council meeting. I walked into that room brimming with too much confidence, oblivious to the possibility that things might not go the way I expected.

I bend my uninjured leg and wrap my arms around it, a weak effort to distract myself from the surge of despair welling inside me. But it doesn't help. The Council meeting disappears from my mind's eye, and in its place is Duncan's face again. I inhale and hold my breath, trying to quench the panic inflating like a balloon in my chest. I don't want to relive his death, or anyone else's for that matter. Everything is too recent, too raw and horrifying.

I force myself to exhale, breathing in and out until his face fades away. But my relief is short lived. Pallas's face flares into existence next, like it's part of a cruel slideshow conjured by my overstressed brain, and I relive my final moments with her in her prison cell after she was arrested for lying to Omri about what his dream meant.

Her voice springs to life, an echo of its true self, but gut-wrenching nonetheless, and I remember her whispered explanations to me about my past—the confession that my parents were still alive, though I'd believed them killed in the attack on Maren fifteen years ago.

Pallas was meant to come to Fortune's Fall to interpret Thaddeus's dream, not me. I had a future already set. A good one, too, as Omri's dream interpreter, the most prestigious job in the country. But I ran away from it to reunite with my family and to interpret Thaddeus's dream, my final promise to Pallas. Has she been executed yet? Probably. Omri isn't the merciful type.

Pallas's face disappears, and I lean forward to rest my forehead on my knee. But the slideshow isn't finished, and I press my fingers against my temples, desperate now to erase the new image that's forming in my mind. It's no use, though, and Greer's face shimmers to life, sharper than any other memory of someone I've lost.

My nose begins to burn, and hot tears slide down my cheeks. I've tried not to think about my best friend—or about losing him. It hurts too much. But in this moment, there's nothing I can do to keep him from my thoughts, no task to distract me from the gaping hole his death has created in me. He was meant to come to Fortune's Fall, too, but he never made it out of the Central Capital. A guard shot him on the train platform, and there was nothing I could do to save him.

My tears fall faster. I should be grateful to be here, to have found my family after so many years of having believed they were dead. And I am thankful. But I don't know them. They don't know me. All I want is for Greer to be here, his presence the balm to my misery. I slide down onto my side, and give in to my despair.

After a while, my tears begin to slow, but I don't move. The sunlight has shifted across my room. The shadows stretch longer. But why should I get up? What's the point? I have nowhere to be. Nothing to do.

"Nyssa?" My mom's voice is followed by a light tap on my door. "It's almost time for dinner. Do you want to help me set the table?"

I don't respond, and she taps again. "Sweetie, if you don't let me in, I'll come in all by myself. I need to know that you're all right."

My hip aches from lying on the hard floor for so long. My eyes are puffy and sore. I sit up and use the bottom of my shirt to pat my cheeks dry, force myself to stand, and open the door.

An herb-rich tang wafts into my room, and my mouth waters. But my attention is on my mom, whose eyes have widened at my appearance. She gives me a thin smile, and she holds out a basket overflowing with bandages and various bottles. "Thought we could change the bandage on your ankle before dinner."

I step back, conscious of how I must look to her, and smooth my hair as she floats inside to perch on the edge of my bed.

She pats the mattress. "Put your foot in my lap. I found some eucalyptus oil. You'll be better in no time." She holds up a small, amber-colored bottle.

I trudge to the bed, sit, and turn so that I can put my ankle in her lap. She peeks at me as she unwraps my old bandage, but she doesn't speak, and the silence stretches, interrupted only by my occasional sniffle.

When the bandage is off, she unscrews the amber-colored bottle and waves it beneath her nose. "I love this smell."

The pungent, minty scent reaches my nose, and I wrinkle it. "That's intense."

My mom chuckles. "It's a miracle salve." She rubs the oil across the inner part of my ankle, and it's like ice-cold fingers press into my skin. "Stay off it for the next twelve hours or so, and I promise it'll be as good as new." She wraps a clean bandage around it. "All done."

I give her a small smile. "Thanks."

She answers with an identical smile, but it disappears fast, replaced with a concerned frown. "I'm a pretty good listener, you know," she says after a moment.

I blink away from her and stare out at the orchard until the leaves merge into a green blur, and my eyes get dry and itchy. "I met Fitz," I say after a while without turning away from the view. "He said it was my fault Duncan died." I let my gaze slide back to my mom's.

"Oh, dear." My mom's eyes widen. "I guess that explains things." She sighs, and her shoulders sag. "I didn't even think to mention he was on the Council."

"He's right." I shrug, as though the truth is no big deal, that Fitz's accusations haven't burrowed deep into my bones. "If Duncan hadn't come back for me, he'd be here, too." I gulp in a great breath of air, half expecting to start crying again. But my eyes are desert-dry. My body is limp like a rag doll. All of my grief has soaked into the floor, and my mind is blank, erased and spotless, like every thought has been placed into separate locked boxes. I'm thankful for the respite, but how long will it last?

"No one's death was your fault," my mom says in a firm voice.

I pick at a thread on the blanket and watch it pop loose from its seams. I want to believe what my mom says is true, but I can't. "So many people died..." I pat the thread flat against the blanket and look up at her. "I miss Greer the most. More than Pallas. And Duncan." I inhale and exhale through my nose, my lips pursed to keep my chin from wobbling. "Does that make me an awful person?"

"Oh, sweetie." My mom presses her hand over mine until I'm forced to look up at her again. "No, of course it doesn't." She watches me for a moment, her pupils steady. "You're never going to stop missing anyone, especially Greer. He was your best friend. But things will get easier, I promise."

Greer was so much more than my best friend, at least in the end. But I don't say that out loud to my mom. I'm not ready to share with her the time when his fingers laced through mine or when he let me cry on his shoulder after life stopped making sense. I can't explain the rush of warmth that exploded through me when he told me he was coming with me to Fortune's Fall. Or how the world stopped spinning when the guard shot him.

"Nothing's better here," I say instead. "I interpreted Thaddeus's dream, and all that happened was that Fitz yelled at me." I laugh. Bitter. Disbelieving. "You should've seen him. He was so angry. He made it clear I wasn't welcome here."

"Your dad and I would disagree with that." My mom releases my hand and sits back with a thoughtful frown. "Fitz has always been a complicated man. After Elise was taken—"

"Is that his wife?"

She nods. "She'd gone to the university to visit a friend the day Omri attacked Maren. And as you know, anyone who was there when Omri attacked was forced to march to the Central Capital. So, she left Fitz and Duncan behind."

"Why didn't she ever try to come to Fortune's Fall?"

My mom shrugs. "I didn't know her very well, so I can't answer that with any certainty. But I suppose it came down to being a risk she wasn't willing to make. I know she saw Duncan sometimes when he was on Cord missions. Maybe that was enough for her."

The Cord is a clandestine group that scouts out safehouses —places for food and shelter—for exiles who want to flee life in America and come to the safety of Fortune's Fall. My brother, Jek, is in the Cord. Duncan was, too. He was tasked with infiltrating the presidential compound to steal the antidote to the gas that Omri used to attack everyone at Maren a few weeks ago.

"Try not to let Fitz bother you too much," my mom says.

I snort. "That's not going to happen. Sorry."

My mom pats my knee and stands with the basket of bandages clasped against her hip. "I don't want to preach to you, Nyssa, so I'll say this one thing and leave it at that. You told me yourself you had faith God got you to Fortune's Fall. Remember that, and don't give up on Him or the peace that He can provide. Even if you have to live in close proximity to Fitz." Her lips quirk with her last words. "Fitz is one of a handful who sees Fortune's Fall as a prison. I choose to see it as an oasis. You should try that, too."

I sigh and twirl my ponytail around my finger, ignoring her attempt to make me laugh, my thoughts focused on everything I learned about God on the way to Fortune's Fall. About His existence, how He wants me to believe in, and trust in Him. Growing up, I never learned about any of those things because religion has been banned in America since before I was born.

In the Presidential Education Program—the elite school I attended in the Central Capital—we were taught that religion wasn't real. But on my journey here, I began to see that the prophetic dreams and my ability to interpret them came from God, and I decided to have faith in Him.

What if I'm wrong, though? What if everything I've chosen to believe isn't real?

"I thought I got it, you know. The faith thing. The God thing." I shake my head. "But I didn't expect everything to be so..." I search for the right word.

"Complicated?" my mom asks.

"Yeah." I shrug and flip my ponytail over my shoulder.

"Things will sort themselves out. They always do." She turns to the door. "Ready to help me set the table? Your dad will be home any minute."

I stand and follow her down the hall, half annoyed at her cool confidence that everything will be fine. How can she be so sure? Nothing is like I thought it would be here. If Fitz's reaction to my arrival is any indication of others' sentiments, Fortune's Fall has some serious problems. What's the point of being here if nobody is going to take me seriously? And is God really the reason I'm here if nobody cares what I have to say?

"Plates are in that cabinet beside the sink," my mom says. "Silverware's next to the stove."

I cross the kitchen, pull out three plates in mechanical obedience, and set them on the table. Forks and knives are next, placed on either side of each plate like I was taught in my etiquette class at school. When I'm done, I stand beside the table and stare out at the orchard. Long shadows stretch between the trees, which are enclosed in the warm amber halo of twilight. Everything looks so peaceful, but something is off about this place, and I have a feeling I've only begun to scratch at its surface.

The front door closes with a decisive click, and a few seconds later, my dad steps into the kitchen. "Something sure smells good." He hones in on the food cooling on the counter and rubs his hands together with obvious delight. But when his gaze shifts to meet mine, his arms fall to his sides. "I'm so sorry about what happened," he says to me. "Don't pay Fitz any mind. He's an angry man."

"Okay." I resist the urge to roll my eyes. Why does everyone think I can do that so easily? I sit at the table and scoop roasted chicken and potatoes onto my plate. My parents pull out chairs on either end of the table and do the same.

"Shall we pray?" my mom asks.

My dad nods and bows his head. "Bless this food, Father, and thank You for Your continued provision. For bringing Nyssa back to us and for healing our family. We ask that You watch over those of us in Fortune's Fall and everyone outside its walls. Amen."

"Amen," my mom says.

I don't say anything. Instead, I pick up my fork and eat.

"You doing okay?" my dad asks me after a while, and this time, I do roll my eyes.

"I'm great," I say. "I won't worry about Fitz—just like you said—and everything's fine." I pretend not to see the look he shares with my mom, and I do a decent job ignoring the little voice that whispers I'm acting like a jerk.

Silence stretches in the wake of my response, hurtling toward an awkwardness that makes my cheeks begin to burn. I should apologize for being rude, but I can't even bring myself to look up from the chicken that I push around my plate.

At last, my dad clears his throat, and I peek through my lashes to find his focus is on my mom. "Jek should be well enough to come home at the end of the week," he says. "I ran over to the clinic and saw him after the meeting. He tried to climb out of bed and come home with me, but he has to stay a few more days." He sits back with a smile. "Almost back to normal though."

My mom presses her hands against her chest. "That's great news!" She turns to me, eyes gleaming. "Do you remember your brother?"

I bite my bottom lip. "No, sorry." I don't have any memories of my family from before I was marched with the exiles to the Central Capital. But they can't expect me to remember, right? I was only two years old.

My mom's smile falters. "It was silly to hope you might." She forces her smile back into place. "We'll have to have some sort of welcome home dinner. For Jek *and* for Nyssa."

"Oh, I don't really want—" I say.

"That's a wonderful idea." My dad cuts me off with a low-browed look.

I set my fork down. The idea of a welcome dinner after my decidedly *un*welcome from Fitz makes me queasy. "May I be excused, please? Dinner was delicious, but I'm tired." I'm suddenly weary of this entire day.

My mom nods. "Of course. We'll see you in the morning."

I slip from the kitchen without another word and hurry down the hall to my room. When the door is closed behind me, I shuffle to the dresser and pull out the old pair of sweats and T-shirt my mom found for me from Jek's room, change into them, and drag myself to the bed to curl beneath the blanket.

The window is open, and the cool air brushes against my face. I snuggle deeper beneath the blanket. I want to be happy. To embrace this life in Fortune's Fall that I've been offered. But I'm clueless how to do that. How do I live alongside Fitz knowing that I'm alive because his son is dead? And if Fitz is able to convince enough people that we should move against Omri now, what's the point of settling in here? If we go after Omri, peace won't last very long.

I roll to my back and stare at the ceiling. "If you're there, God, it'd be really great to know it. Why did You bring me here? What happens next?"

Silence is my only answer.

---

*THE EXILES* RELEASES OCTOBER 21, 2025. Pre-order now!

*Follow the QR code to order your copy of* The Exiles.

# ABOUT THE AUTHOR

Katherine Barger is an award-winning author of clean young adult science fiction and fantasy. When she's not busy wrangling kids, she's writing, editing, eating Mexican food, or snuggling with one of her family's three rescue pets: Elsa, Jasmine, or Nala. Katherine and her forever-forbearing husband live in Texas with their three children.

Subscribe to her newsletter at katherinebarger.com to stay up-to-date on new releases and learn more about her books.

## ALSO BY KATHERINE BARGER

**The Exiled Trilogy**

*City of Secrets, The Exiled Trilogy prequel*

(Available exclusively to newsletter subscribers)